DOUBLE DATE

It would be an enchanting evening, Linda thought, if only she were with Gordon Kenyon instead of sweet, unexciting Peter.

But Babs had calmly appropriated Gordon for her own, and was clinging to his arm as they walked along. Linda's heart filled with resentment toward this beautiful, spoiled girl who just reached out and took what she wanted. How could she blame Gordon for not seeing beneath the glamorous surface?

All the way home, only half listening to Peter's banter, Linda's thoughts were on Gordon. She had never known a boy who appealed to her as much, but Gordon Kenyon was the moon, and reaching for the moon could bring hurt and heartache. Was she ready to take the risk?

D1527737

Other SIGNET Titles You Will Enjoy

LINDA'S HOMECOMING

By
Phyllis A. Whitney

A SIGNET BOOK from
NEW AMERICAN LIBRARY
TIMES MIRROR

SIGNET TRADEMARK REG. U.S. PAT. OFF. AND FOREIGN COUNTRIES
REGISTERED TRADEMARK—MARCA REGISTRADA
HECHO EN CHICAGO, U.S.A.

SIGNET, SIGNET CLASSICS, SIGNETTE, MENTOR AND PLUME BOOKS
are published by The New American Library, Inc.,
1301 Avenue of the Americas, New York, New York 10019

FIRST PRINTING, OCTOBER, 1971

PRINTED IN THE UNITED STATES OF AMERICA

Contents

LINDA'S
HOMECOMING

1 Homecoming

Linda Hollis laughed and held the excited little dog off with one foot, while she juggled suitcase, handbag and key. The Roughneck had been an apartment house dog since puppyhood, so he knew better than to bark in the corridor as he waited for his mistress to open the door and let them in. But they'd been visiting friends uptown for two weeks during Mrs. Hollis's absence and his excitement ran over in wriggles and waggles and snorts, though he was reasonably quiet about it.

"Don't be so impatient, Roughy," Linda told him. "I know it's good to get home, but we needn't break the door down. Now if you only had a couple of hands so you could hold things for me!"

The key clicked in the lock and the door swung open. August in New York City could be pretty torrid and Linda gasped at the heat of the closed apartment. But the Roughneck didn't mind. He rushed in ecstatically and tore about the living room, searching out his favorite nooks and corners, making sure no enemy lay hidden in ambush.

Linda set her things down and hurried to fling up windows and let the breathless heat escape in the cooler air of late afternoon outside. A welcome breeze stirred her boyishly cropped brown hair and she lifted her face to it gratefully.

There was no china doll prettiness about Linda, no fragility. The tilt of her chin and the straight look of her brown eyes hinted at independence. Not a chip-on-the-shoulder, don't-step-on-my toes kind of independence, but the sort that let you be the way you wanted to be, if you'd let Linda be as she wanted to be.

As she flung open another window she thought what fun it had been to stay with Liz Johnson and her family while her mother was away. But it was even better to get home to the familiar pattern. They could just as well have met Mother's train this afternoon, she and the Roughneck, if they'd known when it was coming in. It was odd that her mother had not let her know.

She turned from the window to regard the scampering little dog thoughtfully. The Roughneck was not any one particular kind of dog. There was a touch of cocker, but he was mostly what Linda's father had called "assorted pooch." Noting her attention, he bounced joyously over with a rediscovered rubber bone in his mouth.

"Why," she asked him, "do you suppose Mother was so mysterious about her train? Do you think she's up to something, Roughy?"

Roughy laid his treasure generously at her feet, but he apparently had no opinion about the train or Mrs. Hollis's behavior. Linda gave him a thank-you scratch behind the ears and magnanimously returned the bone. Then she hurried into the other rooms, pulling up shades and opening windows.

When warm, live air stirred through the apartment to replace the hot stuffiness, she went into her own room and sat down on the bed. Liz was fun and awfully good company, but there was something satisfying about being by yourself in a room that was your own.

On her dressing table her father's face looked out at her from the silver frame. There was a flyaway quirk to his eyebrows, like Linda's own, and a fun-loving lift to the corners of his mouth.

"Hi, Butch," Linda said to the picture and she could almost imagine that the pictured mouth returned the greeting in the old way—'Hi there, Toots!"

The old hurt throbbed again. It wasn't the sharp, sick longing it had been at first, but even after two years since her father's death the aching need was there. She knew her loss could never be made up, and that the soreness would never quite heal. It had seemed to her at the Johnsons that Liz's father was just a father. She'd kept comparing him with Bob Hollis, who had been dearest friend, counsellor, comforter, booster, and companion-in-scrapes. She'd never known anybody who was more fun, or kinder, or had more courage.

On the wall above her bed hung a picture Bob Hollis had taken of lower Manhattan from the Staten Island ferry, and her eyes sought it now. She'd been with him on that trip. New York, she was sure, had never had a better news photographer than Bob, and that was one of the best shots he'd ever taken. He'd loved New York, just as she loved it, and he'd told people about it with his camera the way O. Henry had told them about it with his pen. If he hadn't been forever poking around in odd corners, searching out new facets of life in the city—perhaps he'd be here now.

She winced again as she thought of the complete needlessness of what had happened. That particular time she had not been with him when he'd gone down to the waterfront to get pictures of life around the docks. The drunken derelict who had tumbled into the water might just as well have drowned, for he'd never have been missed. There was no one waiting for him, no one who cared about him, and he'd never done the world much good. But Bob Hollis had dived into the icy March water and brought him out. The derelict had recovered and gone his bum's way, while his rescuer fought a losing battle with pneumonia in the hospital.

It had been senseless, meaningless. And yet it had been typical of her father's warm-hearted compassion toward humanity in general. He'd never been willing to grant that the good-for-nothings were wholly bad. Wherever he looked he found men better than they were. That was why everyone had loved him, why he'd had so many friends.

Mr. Roughneck put his forelegs on the bed and laid his head on Linda's knee, regarding her wistfully. Roughy was a derelict, too, when her father had found him. A kicked-out pup with an infected foot, but Bob Hollis had seen spirit and loyalty and downright dog-goodness in him. So he had become one of the family.

In the beginning he'd looked like a toughy—hence his name. Afterwards it had been fun to go on calling him a roughneck, though he was far from being one.

Linda picked him up and put her cheek against his neck. Roughy was wonderful to weep a secret tear on now and then. He missed Bob Hollis too. He hadn't forgotten a friend. Then she put the dog down resolutely and stood up.

"Come along, my lad. I've got to do a bit of straightening before Mother gets home. Want to supervise?"

She liked to work to music, but today she was in no mood for haphazard radio programs. Her fingers flicked across the record albums in the case and hesitated on one. This afternoon she was in the mood for something gay in the popular vein, but it had been a long time since she'd played the tunes from *Oklahoma!* The Hollises had gone to that show together and since her father's death whenever she heard a snatch of tune from the *Oklahoma!* score something twisted inside her even before she recognized the music. But today, perhaps *today*, it would only remind her pleasantly of happy times.

She slipped the records into place and began to hum the melodies of the overture as she set to work tidying the apartment. The familiar twinge of melancholy was there, but it had softened a little. She could bear it now. Here was something she had shared with her father which still went on. He was still a part of the music and that was a comforting thought.

The brief sadness slipped away as she dusted and set things in order. There was so much in her life that was good. So much to be satisfied with and look forward to. Living here in New York in the city her father had loved, romping with the Roughneck in Central Park just around the corner, looking toward her senior year in high school—all these were good. After that college here in town probably, since she had no desire to go away. And then, surely, New York would open to her in some wonderful, fascinating way she hadn't figured out yet. Liz Johnson was lucky. She had a talent for designing and her life was mapped out. Linda Hollis was still directionless, but there was no hurry. Things would work out somehow. She'd like to get a good job later on, so that her mother could stay home from the store.

Not that Joyce Hollis wasn't happy in her work of advising other women how to beautify and improve their homes, but to Linda's eyes there was something a little ironic in the fact that a woman who was a natural homemaker herself should have to spend more time on other people's homes than she did on her own. Someday Linda herself would change all that.

A quick, triple ring of the bell made Linda drop her dust cloth and rush to wash her hands. There was her mother now, giving their special signal from downstairs before she took the self-service elevator to the tenth floor.

"Smile pretty now—we're the welcoming committee," she told the excited Roughy, who knew as well as she the meaning of that bell.

This vacation trip her mother had taken back to the Midwestern town where she'd grown up should have done her a lot of good. Somehow Joyce Hollis had never fitted the New York pattern the way her husband and daughter did. She could not understand their joy in tall buildings with the play of sunlight and shadow upon them in the daytime, and the magical lighting of them at night. Not even Central Park held any charm for her. She was a hick, she admitted happily. She liked quiet streets, and old trees, and houses that held only one family at a time. Not that she did any yearning. She loved her exuberant husband too much for that, even though she didn't always understand his jokes quite as well as Linda did.

On the phonograph Ado Annie swung into *I Cain't Say No,* and Linda pulled the door open to scoop her mother into her arms. It still surprised her to find that she was tall enough to do the scooping now and that she could even catch her mother about her slightly plump waist and swing her around the room if she chose.

Mrs. Hollis returned the hug, laughing a little breathlessly over its vigor. Then she held her daughter away for a good searching look that seemed to check color,

weight, and general spirits and add them up to a satisfactory total.

Linda did a bit of checking herself. "You look wonderful, Mums. Pretty as peaches. You've got a new
hair-do and a new hat and I like them both. Looks like
the Midwest has done you up proud."

Mrs. Hollis tipped the small gray hat at a smarter
angle over the upswept wave that was still nearly as
dark as Linda's own.

"Of course," she said gaily. "I like the hairdressers in
Cedarhill much better than those in New York. And I
think the hats are better, too. Hello, Mr. Roughneck,
how's the boy?"

Her words came in a little rush and while Roughy
explained with his usual wriggles just how he felt and
how glad he was to have the rest of the family home,
Linda regarded her mother more seriously. There was
still the mysterious matter of not being asked to meet
her train. And there was something about her manner, a
sort of glowing happiness that Linda had not seen in a
long time.

Linda caught her hand and drew her over to the
sofa. "Sit down and catch your breath," she directed.
"No, Roughy. Down! Be good! And now, Mrs. Hollis,
you may tell your only offspring what you've been up
to. Why the mystery?"

"Mystery?" her mother began. Then she laughed
softly and settled back against the pillows. "You're as
bad as your father, Linda. Nobody could keep anything from him for two minutes. He always saw right
through you and wangled it out in no time at all."

Linda nodded solemnly. "You might as well come
clean. If it's three new hats instead of one, all right. I
think you should be frivolous when they become you
like that. But if it's a fur coat—the budget won't stand
it. You'll have to take it back. I'll buy it for you later
when I—"

Mrs. Hollis touched Linda's arm gently. "It's a lot
nicer than a fur coat. Oh, honey, I do want you to
understand, but I—I don't know quite how to tell
you."

For some reason a twinge of dread ran through

Linda. Without knowing the cause she was suddenly disturbed and afraid. "Mother, what is it?"

"It's nothing terrible," her mother said. "Don't look like that. It—it's really very nice. I met an old friend back home. Someone I knew in high school when I was a girl. Oh, of course I've seen him other times I've been home, but sort of from a distance. After all, I was married, and for a while he was, too. But his wife died about eight years ago and—"

"Mother," Linda said quietly, "you'd better tell me whatever it is right away."

There was a brief, tense silence, and it seemed to Linda that she could hear her heart thumping as she waited. Then her mother rushed into words.

"It's Martin—Martin Stevens. He wants me to marry him. And, Linda, I think I'm going to."

Linda sat very still looking at her mother. She had heard the words, but somehow they were without meaning. Her mother was going to marry someone named Martin Stevens. Her mother. Bob Hollis's wife. It didn't make sense. It wasn't possible. You didn't love a man like Bob Hollis and get over it in two years' time.

Her mother's hand was small and plump on her own—a hand Bob Hollis had thought was pretty. "Linda dear, I know I'm being clumsy in the telling. I should have managed this some other way. But there was no time. He's waiting for us now. He wants to meet you and take us out to dinner. He has to catch a train back to Cedarhill tomorrow afternoon. That's why I didn't let you know when I was coming in. I wanted to see you alone first and tell you about him. He had to make this trip on business, and it was such a wonderful opportunity."

She stopped because she was listening to the song of that gay little surrey with the fringe on top. They were both remembering. Quietly Linda went to the phonograph and lifted the needle from the record. She stood there with her back to her mother, trying to rouse herself. She had seen the concern in her mother's eyes, but somehow she could do nothing about it.

"I suppose I'd better wear a hat," she said. "And gloves."

"Linda, wait!" There was distress in her mother's voice, and hurt for Linda's hurt. "Martin isn't someone who could ever take your father's place. Not in my heart or in yours. But he was dear to me before I ever met Bob. Of course I was a young girl and it didn't come to anything. I married someone else. And after a while he did too. Now we've come together again and we're very happy. You're young, Linda, you don't know what it's like to be lonely."

Linda went quickly to the door and into her own bedroom. *She* didn't know what it was like to be lonely? The pictured face on her dressing table looked back at her and the eyebrows seemed to quirk more quizzically than ever. She'd been lonelier than her mother had ever been. She'd been hurt more. And she hadn't got over it. She never would. But even as she insisted to herself, she knew her words weren't true. Joyce had loved Bob Hollis too. But then how—how—?

From a box in the closet she took her navy blue straw and pulled it indifferently over her cropped hair. She hated hats, but this one went with the blue and white seersucker she was wearing. Out of a drawer she took crocheted white gloves and picked up her handbag from the bed where she'd dropped it when she came in. She moved automatically, rubbing a powder puff over her nose. Lipstick she had no use for, though Liz Johnson was always after her to use it.

"I like to be me," Linda would say in defense. "Frills and fuss aren't Linda Hollis."

She could hear Liz protesting comically, "If you'd just fall in love and get some sense! It's not that you don't like boys—you just like 'em all, as buddies. Wait'll you meet one and go getting stars in your eyes!"

Linda smiled wryly, remembering the words, even while part of her was surprised that she could think of such frivolous matters at a time like this. She was still numb, probably. She had heard her mother's words, but they hadn't got through to her feelings yet. When they did—

She went back to the living room and spoke to Mr.

Roughneck. "We're going out, ducks. Be a good boy and no chewing up my slippers while we're gone."

Roughy understood those dread words "going out" and knew they excluded him, so he sat on his haunches and looked offended. "Chewing slippers!" he seemed to be saying. "As if I were a callow pup!"

"Where are we going?" Linda asked her mother.

Mrs. Hollis regarded her with troubled eyes. Then she came over to slip a hand through her daughter's arm. "Martin's waiting for us at his hotel downtown. We'll catch a cab and I'll tell you more about him on the way. Linda dear, I do know how you feel. I wish there were some way to make this easier for you. It will be easier after a while when you've got used to the idea."

Easier? Linda wondered. No, it wasn't going to be easy ever. Each step she took was going to become harder and harder. She let her arm stay unresponsive to her mother's touch, instead of giving her hand a quick squeeze against her side in the old way.

2 Dinner with Martin Stevens

The cab had turned over to Madison and was following the path of traffic streaming downtown. Both Linda and her mother were silent. Not till the first stoplight brought the cab to a halt did Mrs. Hollis attempt conversation again.

"Martin isn't at all like Bob," she explained gently. "He's older, for one thing. And he's quite different in appearance and manner."

That was good, Linda thought. She couldn't bear it if this Martin Stevens was to prove a second best imitation of Bob Hollis.

"He holds a very interesting position in Cedarhill," her mother went on. "The Cedarhill Museum is remarkable, considering that it belongs to a small town. Even people from big cities come to visit it and it has a fine reputation for the work done there. Martin is general curator. Since it's such a small museum, that means he's in complete charge."

A museum in a small town! That sounded stodgy enough. Certainly this Martin Stevens wouldn't be a romantic, exciting person like Bob Hollis had been. Which made her mother's interest in him all the more strange. The entire thing was more and more beyond Linda's comprehension.

"Not that his work pays him any large income," Mrs. Hollis said. "There isn't too much money. And he has a family. A boy and a girl."

Linda turned her head quickly. "How old are they?"

"Babs is about your age. The little boy, Roddy, is ten. He's sweet. A little surprising sometimes, but sweet. I remember Babs from when she was a small girl and she was lovely then. But I didn't meet her on this trip because she was away visiting an aunt. It will be nice for you to have a sister close to your own age. Remember how you used to wish for a sister to play with when you were little?"

Linda nodded, remembering.

"Martin's house is pleasant," her mother said, "but it needs someone to love it and turn it into a home. He's had a succession of housekeepers for years and I don't think they've done very well."

There was a warm glow of anticipation in her eyes that Linda steeled herself to resist. Her mother had always wanted a house instead of an apartment. She had always wanted someone who needed her, and over whom she could fuss as she had never been able to over independent Bob Hollis.

"What about me?" Linda asked abruptly. "I've a year to go in school here and I wouldn't want to change."

Out of the corner of her eye she caught the quick movement of her mother's hand in a gesture that meant she was worried. "Cedarhill has a very fine high school. I know you'll like it if you give it a chance. You've never lived in a small town—you don't know how much more fun it can be than in a big city."

Her words rushed out as if she were trying to reassure herself as well as Linda, and then stopped abruptly. When she went on there was a catch in her voice.

"Linda honey, I know how bad this will be for you for a while. But I don't know any other way."

Linda made no attempt to help her. She gazed steadily out the cab window at gray stone buildings moving by; at gay shop windows lighted for early evening, and the familiar throngs on the sidewalk. The dismay that had filled her at the first breaking of this news was deepening now into something frightening. In a little while she would really begin to feel. And then how could she bear what was happening?

"Mother," she said quietly, "you have to arrange your life in the way that's best for you. But I don't want to leave New York. This is where I belong. All my friends are here. My senior year's ahead of me. That's important. I couldn't change. I couldn't give everything up!"

Somehow she had to make her mother understand that she couldn't, wouldn't be uprooted from everything she cared about, everything that was important to her.

But the cab turned a corner just then and came to a stop before the canopied entrance of a hotel. There was no time to continue. Her mother paid the driver and Linda followed her out of the car and up the steps to a big lobby, softly lighted, and filled with the sort of human bustle that was part of the flavor of New York. It was a bustle which still made Joyce Hollis uneasy. She looked hesitantly about until her daughter touched her elbow.

"The house phones are over there," Linda said. "Do you want to call his room and let him know we're here?"

"Of course," Mrs. Hollis murmured in relief and Linda led the way to the phones.

When the call had been made and Martin Stevens was on his way down, Linda and her mother found seats in the lobby where they could wait for him comfortably. Mrs. Hollis's cheeks were pink, but the gaze she turned on her daughter was still concerned.

"You'll like him, Linda, if only you'll try. *I* like him and you will too."

Linda said nothing. She sat watching the shifting crowd in the lobby, and particularly the men who came from the direction of the elevators. Would this be Martin Stevens, this portly, red-faced man with the silly smile on his face? Her tenseness didn't relax until he was safely past. Or could he be this imposing older man who walked with such assurance and seemed to command others by his very manner? She wouldn't want him for a stepfather.

Stepfather! She, Linda Hollis, was going to have a *stepfather*. What an unpleasant word. It reminded her of the fairy tales of her childhood. The wicked stepmother. Were stepfathers wicked too? That was silly, of course, but she could feel herself tightening inside at the sight of every man who came into view.

And then he was there, coming toward them. She knew him at once because of the way his eyes lighted when they found her mother. He was tall and lean and gray-haired. He walked with a faint stoop to his shoulders, unlike Bob Hollis who had always carried himself proudly erect.

His features were angular, and though his gray eyes had a steadiness in them, no love of fun bubbled in their depths. He looked as if he found life a serious affair, as if he would never have understood Bob Hollis's nonsense, any more than her mother had truly understood it.

Perhaps more than anything else Linda noted his clothes. His suit was worn, which was forgivable enough. There'd been times when her father's clothes had not been as new as he might have liked, but Bob Hollis had worn them with a dash that made him look well-dressed, despite telltale wear around buttonholes and seams. This man looked a little shabby, as if he might not care what he wore, as if his mind were on other things.

He smiled at Joyce, a grave smile, and then held out his hand to Linda as her mother introduced her. "I hope we'll be friends," he said.

His handclasp was firm, but somehow Linda could not return the pressure of his fingers. She, who hated flabby handshakes, let her own hand lie limp in his. Her greeting was as grave and she could not move her stiff lips into even the imitation of a smile.

"This has been a little sudden for Linda," her mother explained hurriedly. "We'll have to give her time to get used to it."

Martin Stevens looked at Linda again, rather as though she might be some strange specimen out of one of his museum cases, and Linda found herself thinking with a pang of how easily Bob Hollis had made friends with anyone at all. This man would most likely be more at home with a chunk of rock in a mineral collection than with anything alive. What on earth could her mother see in him?

"I'm afraid I don't know New York," he told Joyce.

"Have you any ideas about where we can go for dinner?"

Her mother considered for a moment and then her expression brightened. "I know a place—" she began, only to break off as her eyes met Linda's. They had, Linda suspected, both thought of the little sea food place where the Hollises had gone so often when Bob had been along. Quickly her mother shook her head and Linda was grateful for her understanding. This would not be the time to go to a place Bob Hollis had loved.

"The restaurant I had in mind is in another neighborhood," Mrs. Hollis said. "Let's just go along the street and take what we find."

Martin accepted the suggestion and they left the hotel lobby and turned west. Martin walked on the outside, with Joyce next to him, then Linda. The evening rush-hour crowd was pouring out of the buildings, and sometimes when they could not walk three abreast, Linda dropped deliberately behind. It was as if she must torment herself by emphasizing her loneliness, her left-outness.

She was no more than an extra wheel, she told herself miserably. Those two wouldn't miss her if she turned up the next block and went home alone. Her mother belied her thoughts just then by turning to smile over her shoulder while they waited for Linda to catch up. But Linda felt a perverse desire to be unhappy and to see everything in the darkest possible light. Somehow she could not respond to the pleading she saw in her mother's eyes. Terrible things were being done to her life and these two needn't expect her to accept them gracefully.

She noticed that Martin Stevens seemed uneasy in the rattling traffic when they crossed streets, and obviously he took no pleasure in the crowds that had always so interested Bob Hollis. Probably in a hick town like Cedarhill three cars on the street at one time would constitute a traffic problem.

They had stopped before a restaurant to wait for her when she finally caught up.

"How's this?" her mother asked. "I don't know a

thing about the place. Do you think we ought to gamble?"

Her mother was asking her directly, not consulting Martin first, but Linda stiffened herself against the appeal and shrugged indifferently. What difference did it make where they ate, or what they ate when her whole world was collapsing about her?

A hostess led them back to a quiet booth and Linda found herself occupying a seat on one side alone, while her mother and Martin took the place opposite her. Of course someone had to sit alone when there were three, and she'd never minded with her father, but now she experienced the same left-out feeling she'd had when she'd dropped behind the others on the sidewalk. With a strange contrariness she seemed to want to experience it.

Her mother made an effort to be gay and cheerful, but Martin Stevens apparently had little talent for rising to an occasion. Linda had no desire to chatter to her mother as she might have done had they been alone and she spoke in monosyllables only when spoken to, so that after a while her mother gave up and addressed her conversation solely to Martin. And again Linda took a perverse pleasure in rubbing salt in her wounds.

When the waitress brought their orders Linda stared with distaste at the plate of spaghetti before her and wondered why she'd ordered it. The day was much too warm for a dish that sizzled with heat. But a relentless inner voice reminded her why she had ordered it. Spaghetti had been one of their favorite dishes when she'd dined out with her father and somehow ordering it now had been the adding of another brick to the wall of her defiance.

She began to cut the spaghetti into bits so that she'd need to put no more than a morsel or two into her mouth at once. Winding it about her fork was no fun any more. Bob Hollis had been an expert spoon-and-fork spaghetti winder.

The other two had given her up for the moment and even though she knew it was her own fault, she felt a resentment of their absorption in each other. Martin was talking about some museum project for which he had come to New York and it sounded dull, dull, dull. The rapt expression her mother wore as she listened looked a little silly to Linda. She was practically acting like a teen-ager in love, which, in a mother, was not at all acceptable.

She yawned to show her boredom and glanced across the restaurant at an opposite booth. Then she sat up startled, and looked again. No, the man in the booth across from them didn't really resemble Bob Hollis. Not when he turned his head. She ought to be used to this thing now. It had been happening for two years—a sudden likeness she would catch in some stranger that would remind her so sharply of her father that it was almost like a painful physical blow.

Now, when the man in the other booth turned away again, she could almost imagine that it *was* Bob Hollis sitting there; that if she chose she could leave these two who were so absorbed in each other that they'd forgotten her existence, and go where she could claim the love and attention her father had given her.

"Linda, you're not eating." Her mother's concerned voice cut into her reverie. "Don't you like your spaghetti?"

"It's all right," Linda said listlessly. "I guess I'm just not hungry. It's too hot today for spaghetti." She sipped her tall glass of iced tea, hoping they would go back to their talk and forget her again, even while, unreasonably, she resented the interest that seemed to shut her out.

But now they wouldn't let her go. Martin even made an attempt to draw her into the conversation.

"It will be splendid for my daughter Babs to have a sister," he said. "You two ought to get along fine."

Did he think she was two years old that he had to talk in a way that was like a patronizing pat on the head? She sipped her tea and ignored him. She hadn't the slightest interest in whether she and Babs would get along together or not, because if she could possibly arrange it she would never see Babs except now and then on a visit perhaps. How could they expect her to trade New York for a one-horse town in the Midwest?

"Linda," her mother said. She looked up to meet her

eyes, but the queer obstinacy in her would not let her give in to the pleading she read in them and her mother hurried on. "Linda, Martin has been telling me that both you and Babs will be starting your senior year at Cedarhill High as newcomers. Babs has been away at a private school in Chicago because—well, because it was hard for Martin to make a real home for her with just a housekeeper. Now we'll be able to have both our girls at home together."

"Both our girls." What a phrase!

"Perhaps you'd like to see a picture of my son and daughter," Martin said. He did not wait for an answer, but drew out his wallet and handed her a snapshot.

She took it and looked at the pictured faces without interest. The girl was pretty, but she wasn't the type Linda decided that she would pick for a friend. Girls who looked like that were usually silly and didn't have much in their heads. It wasn't possible to tell about the boy beside her. because, boylike, he had managed to wriggle just at the click of the shutter and wasn't in focus. But his hair needed combing and he had a sassy sort of grin. Certainly she'd never wished for a brother. Liz had one about this boy's age and he was an everlasting pest. She handed the picture back without comment.

After that the other two made no further effort to manufacture conversation that would draw her in. They gave themselves up to plans for the future, but this time Linda found herself listening, because what they were saying concerned her.

They were planning a honeymoon trip to Oregon, where Martin had a brother who owned a fruit ranch. Martin's vacation was falling due and they would take it before school opened so they could be back in Cedarhill for the opening day. Babs would remain with her aunt until shortly before that time, and some arrangement would be made for Linda, perhaps she could stay at the Johnsons again, until a day or two before school opened. Then they'd all meet in Cedarhill and start their new life with the beginning of the fall term.

Linda listened and said nothing, but she thought her own thoughts. It wasn't as if she were a child, to have her life planned out for her like this and be given no say in it at all. Even as a little girl she had always been asked her opinion by her father. Now the plans seemed to be going on over her head. True, she hadn't shown much interest in taking part in them, but they might consult her nevertheless.

It was Martin who tried to draw her in again when dessert was set down before them. "Cedarhill's a pretty town," he said. "Your mother and I are very fond of it. I think you'll like it there."

Linda returned his look coolly. "I like it here in New York. All my friends are here and the school I want to graduate from is here. I don't care for small towns."

The sharp sound of the words astonished her. They didn't sound like the Linda Hollis she knew. But she would not recall them. This stranger who had come to take her mother away had better know at once how she felt. Then there'd be no mistake about it.

She saw the friendliness go out of his eyes. He was looking at her as if he found her disagreeable and unlikable. No one had ever looked at her like that before and she turned away from him quickly, building up defenses in her mind. What did he expect? What could her mother expect? They made her feel extra and unwanted and then blamed her for feeling that way. They wanted her to be uprooted and like it.

She began to hope Martin Stevens would dislike her. That he'd dislike her so much he'd change his mind and go back where he came from. Go away forever and leave Linda Hollis's life as it had been before.

Her favorite biscuit tortoni had a bitter taste tonight. She let it go uneaten as the others finished their dessert. The shocked look on her mother's face hurt her, even while she steeled herself to resist it.

3 Rebellion

When the uncomfortable dinner was over, Martin Stevens took them back to the Hollis apartment. Roughy met them at the door with overjoyed wiggles and snorts, but Linda caught him up and held him so close he gave a yelp of surprise.

She didn't want the Roughneck to offer his ready friendship to Martin Stevens. He was the one unchanged thing that belonged to her old life. Everything else had shifted its values. She herself, Linda felt, was the most changed of all. She wasn't the same girl who had returned to this apartment earlier in the day. That girl was gone forever.

Mrs. Hollis introduced the little dog in Linda's arms. "Martin, this is our friend, the Roughneck."

Martin Stevens bestowed an odd look upon the dog. A look that was not altogether approving. If, on top of everything else, he didn't like dogs—!

But after a second's hesitation he held out his hand and let Roughy sniff it. At least he knew enough not to make too quick an approach.

"This fellow looks like an important member of the family," Martin said, not minding when Roughy put out a wet pink tongue to lick his fingers.

"Oh, he is!" Mrs. Hollis said quickly, "Linda's father—" she broke off and then hurried on. "Your back yard in Cedarhill will be wonderful for Roughy. He's never had a chance to run loose anywhere."

Linda turned away, squeezing Roughy reprovingly. He was like Bob Hollis. He had no discrimination about people. He liked everyone, and she didn't want him to like Martin Stevens.

"Mm," Martin said, "yes. That back yard ought to be fine for him. I was wondering—"

"Wondering?" Joyce repeated.

"Does he like cats by any chance?"

Linda answered quickly. "He likes everything in the world but cats. He hates cats."

"Oh," said Martin. "Babs has a cat." Then he shrugged as if that was a problem he was not prepared to face at the moment. "Well, I have a heavy day tomorrow. I'd better get back to the hotel and put in my beauty sleep. It's been fine taking you both to dinner."

Mrs. Hollis told him how fine she thought it had been, while Linda restrained Roughy and said nothing. It hadn't been fine at all, and all three knew it. She did not put the little dog down until the door had closed behind Martin Stevens. Then her mother drew her hat off wearily and dropped into the big easy chair Bob Hollis had liked best. She no longer looked young and gay and happy as she had earlier when she'd come home to the apartment. A frown of worry quirked her forehead and there was disappointment in the gaze she turned upon her daughter.

"I've never seen you behave like this before," she said quietly. "You didn't even try to be friendly. I've never known you to be bad-tempered and rude, but you were tonight. Oh, honey, I *so* wanted you to like Martin and have him like you."

Linda turned away, pulling off her gloves and hat, not wanting to face the hurt in her mother's eyes.

"I do realize," her mother went on, "that you'll need time to get used to the changes ahead of you. But I still don't understand your behavior tonight."

If she didn't understand, there was no use trying to explain. Apparently her mother and Martin Stevens thought she was a child who could be pushed around to suit them. And what was worse, her mother seemed to have given Bob Hollis not a single thought all evening. What would her father think of that? What would he think of a wife who was so quickly willing to take another husband.

"I so wanted you and Martin to be friends," Mrs Hollis repeated unhappily. "I'd hoped so much that you'd like each other."

"We don't," Linla said, "and I guess there isn't anything to be done about that."

She went abruptly out of the room in order to end a conversation that was growing more and more painful. After all, she had been badly hurt tonight. To be blamed for the evening's failure on top of that was too much.

She did not turn on the light in her room, but curled herself in the small armchair beside the window. Outside the towers of Manhattan glittered brightly against the soft darkness of the sky. How many times she had sat in this very chair, loving the beauty and mystery of those towers, just as her father had loved them. Behind every sequin of light there was another human being; someone like herself who laughed and cried and hoped and dreamed, but whom she would never know. Were some of those strangers as unhappy as she was tonight? There was a melancholy comfort in the thought.

Roughy's damp nose nuzzled her hand. She patted her knee and he jumped into her lap, wagging himself all over with pleasure. So Babs Stevens had a cat? Martin had spoken the words doubtfully and he'd regarded the Roughneck with something like dismay. Well, Babs could keep her precious cat; Linda had never cared for cats. Cats were self-centered, unloving creatures, thinking only of their own pleasures, unlike a dog, who loved with all his heart and suffered when those he loved were unhappy.

She could tell that Roughy was worried about her now and trying in his own way to assure her of his loyalty and affection. Did these Stevens people think she would be willing to give up Roughy too, along with everything else in her life?

She bent above the little dog and whispered fiercely in his ear. "We'll stay here in New York. We'll stay together. Let her go to Cedarhill if she wants to!"

She put her cheek against his rough coat and wept as

she had not wept since the day of her father's funeral. She felt lonely and hurt and afraid and ashamed. All the feelings were mixed up together and more than anything else she wished her mother would come into her room and hold her lovingly and reassuringly, as she used to do when she was a little girl and something had been hurtful and frightening. For all the wonderful friend her father had been, there were times when only her mother's arms about her, and a soft cheek pressed against her own could be really comforting. But this Martin person was not only making her mother forget Bob Hollis; he was making her forget Linda too.

She could hear the radio in the living room and knew her mother had settled down beside it with a book, as she liked to do. Probably she had put her daughter completely out of her mind and had no idea that she was crying here in the next room. Roughy licked her chin anxiously with a pink sandpaper tongue, but not even his caresses comforted her.

After a while she got up and undressed in the darkness, crawled into bed. Roughy settled down on his own bed in the corner and the room was still. Outside the never-ceasing clamor of New York took on its nighttime tones, a lullaby that had been familiar music to Linda all her life.

But though her tears had ceased she did not go to sleep at once. When her mother came to the door and looked in, Linda knew she was there, though she gave no sign. More than anything else she wanted to be held and comforted as if she were a little girl, but the stubborn core inside would not let her reach for what she needed.

"Asleep?" her mother asked softly.

Linda made her breathing deep and even, wanting her to go away and not wanting her to go away. Then abruptly her mother crossed the room and dropped down on the bed.

"Well, if you are asleep," she said, "you'll just have to wake up!"

Her arms slipped under Linda's shoulders and drew her close and suddenly Linda was a very little girl sobbing gustily in her mother's arms. Joyce let her cry and it was good to be stormy for a while.

"I don't want you to marry him!" Linda choked. "I don't want you to go away to that awful Cedarhill place! You're my mother. He can't have you!"

Joyce hushed and soothed and held her close until the sobbing stopped. But even while her arms reassured and comforted, her words did not.

"It's just the first shock of getting used to the change, honey. It seems hard because you've never had to move to a new place and make new friends. But in a year you'll have friends as dear as any you have here. If only you'll believe that it will help you so much."

But Linda did not want to believe, and while she clung to this moment of reunion, determination grew within her. Later, when her mother had gone off to her own bed, Linda lay awake for a long time, thinking, planning.

By morning she no longer felt weakly sorry for herself. She had thrust all hurt, ashamed feelings out of sight. She had no reason to feel ashamed, she assured herself. Any girl had the right to fight for the things she wanted in life, and this particular girl meant to begin her battle the moment breakfast was over and her mother had gone to work.

She was cheerful over coffee and toast and so was her mother. But neither one mentioned Martin Stevens or the future and despite that moment of closeness the night before, it seemed as if a breach had grown between them and they were smiling at each other from opposite shores.

Her mother kissed her good-bye somewhat formally when she went off to work and when the door closed after her, Linda experienced a moment of weakness. For just an instant she wanted to fling that inner stubbornness aside and run after her mother, but she put the impulse from her sternly. She had to get used to this new way of life because if her budding plans went well the parting with her mother would be more or less permanent. And she hoped it would hurt Joyce as much as it hurt her daughter.

It was strange to have a thought like that. She had never wanted to hurt anyone before.

She hurried to clear the breakfast table and swish the dishes through suds and rinsing. When they were put away she picked up the telephone and dialed Liz Johnson's number. Liz answered promptly, but though she asked about Mrs. Hollis's return, Linda gave out no news over the telephone.

"How about the park this morning?" she asked. "Our usual place? I've got to see you, Liz."

Liz, as usual, could be counted on and Linda changed to slacks and a blue gingham blouse and picked up the anxious Roughy's leash. "Come along, Mr. R., we're combining business and pleasure this morning."

The Roughneck was eager to be out, as always, and he submitted willingly enough to the restraint of the leash. After all, to be restrained when outside was part of being a city dog, and Roughy had never known any other kind of life.

It was one of those bright, invigorating mornings with which New York City sometimes surprises her heat-worn residents. No haze hung above the tall, slim towers, and a blue sky reflected itself in every patch of water in Central Park.

A morning like this made you feel courageous and ready for anything, Linda thought, hurrying along paths that wound between woodland greenery. Roughy frisked and bounded and barked at squirrels, but Central Park squirrels were a sophisticated lot who knew humans were bestowers of nuts, and that yapping little dogs would never be allowed to pursue them. They watched from a distance with bright, greedy eyes and refused to go into hiding.

Liz had farther to come, so Linda and Roughy were first at the meeting place. Linda found a bench where she could sit and soak up a bit of sun, while she watched small boys launch their sailboats in the pond.

How many happy associations the park had for her. She'd played here as a little girl and walked with her father. She knew places where it was so quiet and secluded that except for the distant hum you wouldn't know New York was near. But she'd have missed the tall buildings if they hadn't been there, rimming in the park, rising on all sides the minute you stepped into the open to look. Others could have their prairies, or their mountains, she would take this. And she meant to take it, for keeps.

Roughy jumped up with a bark of welcome as Liz came into sight on a path behind them. She was not as tall as Linda and she was stockier, but she had a lively, interested way about her that was more winning than mere prettiness. Today she, who loved feminine fixings, had gone sloppy in dungarees and a plaid shirt, and her hair was caught carelessly back at the nape of her neck with a red hair ribbon.

"Hi!" she called. "Morning, Roughy. Look what I brought you!"

She drew a slightly squashed chunk of waxed paper from her pocket, to reveal two dog biscuits, the Roughneck's favorite brand. Roughy went politely through the foolish but necessary business of sitting up and begging, then gobbled the treat down in delight.

"Now then," Liz said, "tell me what's up. I gathered by your manner of mystery that something's in the wind."

"Mother's getting married again," Linda said quietly.

"Oh?" Liz looked at her and waited.

Linda went on, keeping all emotion out of her voice. "He's an old beau she knew in high school. She met him again on her trip back to Cedarhill and now they're going in for hearts and flowers."

Liz's warm, friendly face brightened. "How nice! For your mother, I mean. She must have been awfully lonely ever since your father—" she broke off, warned, Linda knew, by the look she must have given her friend. "Don't you want her to marry again?"

"I don't know," Linda said. "I guess I never thought much about it. I don't see how she could find another man who'd come up to Dad. I just never expected her to want anyone else."

"How do you know he doesn't come up to your father? Have you met him?"

Linda noddel. "Last night. He was in town for a day. He took us to dinner."

"And you don't like him?" Liz asked gently.

"I don't like him," Linda said and was again disturbed by the sound of her own words.

"Maybe just meeting him one time isn't enough for you to judge," Liz said hopefully. "Maybe if you give him a chance—"

"It doesn't take that long. He doesn't like me either. I could tell. We'd never hit it off in a million years. But that isn't all. He works for Cedarhill's hick town Museum; he looks the type too. Stodgy. And I'm supposed to move out there. Right before my senior year. I'm supposed to drop all my friends, my school, everything and leave New York."

"Oh, no!" Liz breathed. "Oh, Linda, that's terrible! We can't do without you here. You're always the one who thinks up wonderful ideas and keeps things stirring. Linda, I'll die."

Linda smiled at her friend. It was good to be appreciated by one person, at least. "Don't die right away. Because I'm not going."

"You're not going? You mean they'll let you stay here and finish? But where would you—"

"That's why I wanted to talk to you. Do you suppose your mother could take me in for a year? Of course I'd pay my board. I know you're crowded, but a year isn't so awfully long. After that—"

"Of course!" Liz broke in triumphantly. "That's the answer. I know Mother'll do it. She likes you better than any friend I have. We simply can't have you going off to Western wilds right before senior year. Imagine wasting Linda Hollis on a hick town! But do you think your mother will let you stay behind?"

"I don't know. If I have a plan to offer, perhaps she will. She had a taste last night of how Martin Stevens and I feel about each other."

"But won't you miss her awfully?"

Linda hushed the small voice that wanted to cry out inside and answered quietly. "I can get along on my own. I'll be all right."

Liz looked doubtful. "It's too bad this Martin person

couldn't have turned out to be someone you'd like. Of course I don't mean it would be nice to give up New York, or that I want you to go, but just the same it might be exciting to travel and meet new people, see new places."

"I don't imagine the people I'll meet in Cedarhill would be very exciting," Linda said dryly. "And I simply couldn't stand pretending that Martin Stevens was my father."

"Then what are we waiting for?" Liz demanded. "Let's go talk to Mother right away. If she agrees, it's practically settled."

Mrs. Johnson, however, was more doubtful than her enthusiastic daughter expected her to be.

"It isn't that we couldn't work it out, Linda," she said, doing neat things to the pie crust she was trimming while she talked. "But I'd want to talk this over with your mother and make sure it's what she wants. Fond as I am of you, Linda, it wouldn't be the same for you as having a mother here to go to with problems and troubles. I guess there are always problems and troubles, and no substitute for a mother."

Linda wanted to say, "I haven't any mother to go to now. He's taken her away from me." But she couldn't say that, so she fell back on the words she'd spoken to Liz: "I'll get along all right."

"But will your mother get along all right?" Mrs. Johnson asked unexpectedly. "Have you thought about the way she'd miss you?"

Linda remembered the moment last night when Joyce had come to sit on her bed and hold her close in her arms. Yet all the while, underneath the lovingness, Linda had known that her mother would do as she planned to do; that something of her had gone away. No, she told herself stubbornly, her mother would not miss her much, or for long.

Liz came to her aid before she had to answer. "After all, Mother, Linda's growing up. One of these days she'll go away to college, or maybe get married, and then her mother will have to do without her. So why can't it be a little sooner?"

But Mrs. Johnson did not mean to argue. She opened

the oven to test the heat and then popped the pie in and closed the door. When she faced the girls again, she had obviously made up her mind.

"You talk this over with your mother, Linda. If she's willing to consider the plan, then you have a home here."

The promise was enough for optimistic Liz. She caught her mother around her waist and gave her a quick hug. "It's going to be wonderful! I can't imagine anything nicer than having Linda Hollis right here under our own roof. My goodness! Maybe I can even work on her enough to reform her into using lipstick and growing more than two inches of hair."

Liz's confidence was contagious and they laughed together as they discussed future plans. But that evening when Linda faced her mother across the dinner table, she felt much less sure that she could convince her of the importance of the decision.

Mrs. Hollis listened gravely to her proposal and a brightness came into her eyes that hinted of tears.

"Honey, I do want to see this work out in a way that's best for you, but what you're suggesting is impossible. I couldn't possibly shove my responsibility as a mother off on another woman's shoulders."

Responsibility. What a cold word, Linda thought, pressing another thorn of self-pity into her hurt.

"I know it's difficult," Mrs. Hollis went on, "but you're making it harder than it really is. This isn't a real tragedy, any more than my leaving Cedarhill for New York was a tragedy. If you'll just give the town a chance, give the school and the new friends you'll make a chance, the change won't be so difficult. It will even be interesting."

"I want to stay here," Linda repeated. "I suppose you can make me go, but if you do I'll hate every minute of it."

Her mother reached across the table and touched her hand. "Perhaps I'm a little selfish," she said. "I want my daughter with me. I don't want to gain a husband and lose you. That's too high a price to pay."

Hope leaped suddenly in Linda. Too high a price? Did that mean—?

"And an unnecessary price," her mother went on. "I won't consider paying it. Last night in your first meeting with Martin we somehow all got off to a bad start. I think I was to blame more than either of you. When we settle down in Cedarhill everything will be better. You'll see, darling."

Linda shook her head, not wanting to see.

"You may not believe it now," her mother said, "but you might even miss me more than you think. And I know how much I'd miss you. Let's not hurt each other like this."

But it was Martin and her mother who were hurting her, Linda thought. She hadn't wanted to hurt anyone. She only wanted things to go on as they had before. There was one more argument she had not used till now.

"What would Dad think? Oh, Mother, how *can* you?"

Mrs. Hollis shook her head gently. "Linda dear, if you'd stop trying to think with your emotions and use that perfectly good head of yours, you'd know the answer to that. Your father always wanted people to be happy. He understood why they acted as they did and he never judged anyone harshly. Do you think he'd judge me harshly now?"

In her heart Linda knew he would not, but she could not bring herself to admit it. Somehow she wanted to demand for her father a loyalty not even he himself would have asked.

"Maybe he'd have wanted me to be happy, too," she said.

Her mother folded her napkin and got up from the table. "Let's not talk about it any more tonight. When I got off the bus I noticed that a good movie is playing at the Star. Let's be frivolous and treat ourselves to a show."

Linda knew by her mother's tone that nothing would be gained by saying a word more at the moment. But she was not ready to give up by any means.

4 The Uprooting Begins

In the days that followed a good many words were spoken. Linda brought every argument she could think of to her aid. She even brought Liz to plead her cause. Nothing had any effect. Her mother went quietly about the purchasing of her simple trousseau and Linda found herself going along to help.

It made her mother happy to have her advice, to have her approve, or disapprove the tilt of a hat, the hang of a skirt. And Linda herself had to have new clothes for fall wear in Cedarhill. Her mother took the adviser's chair in selecting them and there was comradeship in shopping together. If at night Linda still ached with the hurt inside, they were closer now than they had been since her mother's vacation.

Not that Linda was any more resigned to this uprooting than before, but momentarily she allowed the tide to sweep her along. Later, when she had something firm to cling to, she would turn against it. She promised herself that. Even out of Cedarhill there were roads that led to New York, and the time might come when both Martin and her mother would be willing to let her have her way.

As the day of the wedding drew near there was even a sort of excitement to buoy her up and make her forget now and then the upheaval that lay ahead of her. There were moments when her mother looked so pretty and happy and excited that Linda could not help but be happy for her and hope that her life would turn out well.

Martin came to New York for the quiet wedding.

Neither Mrs. Hollis nor he wanted the neighborly affair their friends in Cedarhill would have tried to make of the occasion, and the ceremony in the small church was not as difficult to get through as Linda had feared it would be. There was only one sharp pang when the minister pronounced his solemn words and Linda experienced a moment of complete loneliness and loss.

Nothing had been as bad, however, as the day when she and her mother moved out of the apartment. What with the apartment shortage, new people moved in the very day the Hollises moved out and Linda felt a little sick over that. The apartment reached back into the happy days when her father had been with them. In a sense something of Bob Hollis lingered in the rooms he had known, at windows from which he had looked. It was like another farewell to go out the door and know they would never come back.

Her mother felt that too. There was a moment when she stood in the familiar hallway waiting for the elevator, looking back at the closed door behind them. Linda caught the shine of tears in her eyes and tucked her hand quickly through her mother's arm to give it a little squeeze. The look of love her mother gave her brought a chokiness to Linda's throat and she wished desperately that there were some way for them both to be happy without this dreadful uprooting of her own life.

Then, almost before she could realize it, the wedding was over and her mother was Mrs. Martin Stevens. There was only one Hollis left now. The married couple took a train for Oregon on their honeymoon trip and Linda returned to the Johnsons for the remainder of the summer vacation.

The ten days of her stay with Liz were a mingling of pain and fun. You couldn't be under the same roof with a live wire like Liz and continue to suffer. Liz worked wholeheartedly at the job of keeping Linda cheered up, and she was full of gay advice.

"Just remember how lucky this Cedarhill place is to have you coming to town. You go on out there and show those Middle Westerners a thing or two. I expect to hear that you've stirred up Cedarhill High and walked off with practically all the class honors."

"Oh, stop it!" Linda cried, laughing. "I don't suppose Cedarhill is dying to meet me any more than I'm dying to meet it. I'm not going to waste my efforts on anything except a plan to get back here as quickly as I can. So keep the welcome mat out and the pot boiling."

But in spite of the bantering that went on with Liz, in spite of all they crammed into those last days—a trip to Bear Mountain, a ferry ride to Staten Island (which reminded Linda of the day her father had taken his famous shot of lower Manhattan, now carefully packed away in the collection of his pictures she had shipped ahead to Cedarhill), a last minute visit to the Metropolitan Museum (which would make Martin Stevens's little Museum look like a child's hobby)—in spite of all this, there were dark, falling-asleep moments when Linda ached over the change that was coming, that had already begun. As she said to Liz in a rare, sober moment which the other girl permitted, "My roots hurt. They come up so hard."

Nearly every other day air mail letters came from Oregon that glowed with happiness. But they were filled with Martin-this, and Martin-that, and Linda found that it hurt to read them. Her mother had gone so far away that she'd probably never get her back.

Then the time was up. Martin and her mother were flying to Chicago and going by bus to Cedarhill. They would be there a few hours before Linda arrived and her mother wrote that she'd be at the station to meet her. Babs had already returned from her aunt's and was "home" in Cedarhill waiting.

Liz and Mrs. Johnson came down to see Linda off. They helped her carry her bags and the unexpected going-away presents she had found herself loaded down with at the last minute. The girls from school, undoubtedly prodded by Liz, had given her a surprise party, and the "loot" consisted of everything from homemade fudge to a folding clothes-brush-coat-hanger contraption.

An anticipation she had not expected to feel was rising in her as they walked into the station. This afternoon she was no mere visitor to Grand Central, waving someone else off on a journey; she was one with the crowds that rushed and waited and milled about restlessly. But there was soreness, too, for Bob Hollis was with her again in the station, keenly, sharply. He was at her elbow, watching with eager, interested eyes. He'd loved crowds, people moving, intent on their own lives, yet part of a big pattern of which they were unaware.

He was part of Grand Central, just as he was part of so many other places in New York. In a little while she would go away, for good, perhaps, and no road she walked would be a road where Bob Hollis had ever set foot. That made everything lonelier than ever.

It was Liz who found that her train was ready and she could get aboard at once. No visitors were allowed on the platform, so she said good-bye to Liz and Mrs. Johnson at the gate and hurried in the wake of a redcap with her bags. In fact, she practically ran off, lest she break down and weep on Liz's sympathetic shoulder. Liz herself was sniffling and begging her to write soon, and suddenly Linda couldn't take any more.

Her car was apparently a thousand miles down the platform, but the walk gave her time to blink her eyes dry. Now there was excitement in the air, other travelers hurrying along the platform, dodging pillars and baggage trucks, searching anxiously for the right numbered Pullman car.

Linda's redcap found her car and she hurried breathlessly after him to her section. There was no one as yet in the opposite seat and Linda hoped it would stay empty the whole way to Chicago. The last thing she wanted was some chattering companion to disturb her thoughts. She tipped the redcap and seated herself on the brown plush seat. After the heat of the New York afternoon the air-cooled car was a relief.

Out on the platform the distant wail of "A-a-all abo-o-oard!" sent a thrill prickling down her spine. Even though she hated leaving New York, there was a contagious excitement about a train pulling out of a station and heading toward unknown adventures. She would not have been her father's daughter if she hadn't responded to the stir of anticipation.

Bob Hollis's favorite camera was slung over her

shoulder by its strap and she slipped it off and settled the camera carefully in a corner of the seat. Her mother had wanted to sell the bulk of Bob Hollis's photographic equipment, but Linda had protested so earnestly that she had given in and permitted all of it to be shipped to Cedarhill. The camera, however, Linda would take no chances on. It wasn't new, but it was an expensive make and had been her father's companion on many a picture hunting trip. Linda gave it a little pat, glad this one bit of her father was making the trip with her. Probably even in Cedarhill he would have found pictures to take and perhaps she could try getting a few shots for him.

She wished Roughy could be in this car with her. The little dog wouldn't think much of his baggage car quarters, and undoubtedly he'd be confused by the unusual things that were happening to him. But he'd just have to manage until they were both set down at the Cedarhill station. There'd be a change of trains out of Chicago and perhaps she could see him for a moment there.

Sunlight flashed across the window beside her as the train left its underground tunnel and sped along the elevated embankment. In a little while they were on the ground again, running beside the Hudson River. There were inlets and little green islands, the jutting brow of Storm King across the river, the Catskills hazy blue in the distance. It was lovely and peaceful in this familiar Hudson River country.

"New York," Linda thought to herself. "This is still New York. All the way to Albany it will be with me, and for a while after we turn west. But when I wake up in the morning I'll be in new country I've never seen before."

She made the swaying journey to the dining car early, forewarned by Liz's father. "If you don't get your soup by five-thirty," he'd told her, "you'll find yourself standing in line." So she bumped her way through Pullman cars, down narrow corridors past compartments and roomettes, and struggled with heavy doors which opened between cars to let in a roar of sound and heat from the unsealed world outside.

The dining car had not yet filled up and she followed the head waiter's beckoning finger to a seat at a table for two. Liz had said, "Dining on a train is fun. If you're lucky you can meet the most interesting people."

But the chair opposite her remained empty for a while. She wrote her order neatly on the slip the waiter left and then turned her attention to the wonderful river view speeding by outside the big window.

It was not until she had embarked on the reckless adventure of balancing a soup spoon on a train swaying at high speed, that the chair opposite her was filled. Her first reaction was one of pleasure when she saw the head waiter bringing the newcomer toward her table. She could so easily have drawn some stodgy older person, but this young man must be near her own age.

He glanced at her briefly without smiling and busied himself at once with the menu. She had an opportunity to study him while she juggled her soup and he chose his dinner. He was too thin for his height and didn't look particularly robust, but he was handsome in a dark, unsmiling sort of way. Certainly he wasn't very friendly. After his first quick glance he hadn't looked her way again, so she wasn't fortunate after all. She might just as well have sat opposite a bore as to have for a dining companion a stiff-necked young man who wasn't going to talk to her.

She considered the possibility that he might be more shy than unfriendly. There was even a chance that he might be fun, once the ice between them was broken and some sort of talk had been started. Well, she wasn't shy. She always got along fine with boys right from scratch, even if she didn't have a lot of silly notions about them the way Liz did. What had she to lose for the try?

"You'd better not order soup," she advised as he poised his pencil above the order sheet.

He glanced up as if he were surprised to find her still there, but he didn't follow up her opening. He merely looked at her until she felt an annoyed pinkness creep into her cheeks. No, she certainly hadn't been fortunate. This young man was a regular turtle.

"It's not that it's bad," she went on hurriedly to

break the awkward pause. "The soup, I mean. But getting it into the mouth instead of into the lap is rather a problem."

There was something odd about the look he continued to give her, almost as if he were waiting for her to say something further that he wasn't going to like. Then a surprising twinkle came into his brown eyes and a slow smile lifted the somber corners of his mouth.

"Coffee's worse," he said. "Just wait till you get to that."

The ice was broken. Or at least the top coating had started to melt. Linda gave him a friendly grin. "Oh, dear. I would try to give advice to a veteran traveler. Do you travel by train often?"

The smile disappeared and he began to scribble on the order sheet before him. She had a queer suspicion that he did not like her question. He shrugged vaguely and lapsed into silence again. But now she knew he wasn't wholly turtle and she didn't mean to let him crawl back into his shell.

"This is my first trip," she explained frankly, "so I'll probably do all the wrong things before I find out what the right things are."

"You sound as though you were having fun," he said.

She nodded. "Right now I am. That's because I'm suspended between two worlds. One I love and one—I don't. So I might as well have fun while I can."

The waiter came for his order and when the young man's attention returned to her it was plain that he meant to prod her with no questions, though she'd tried to make a conversation provoking remark.

Their talk was a curious skirting of surfaces for the rest of the meal. It wasn't that he was unfriendly, but just that he never for a moment talked about himself and managed somehow to keep Linda from talking about herself. On impersonal subjects he was interesting and well-informed. He knew some of the old legends about the Hudson River and he told them well. He made places they were passing take on new interest for Linda. But when she asked if he lived in New York, he

shrugged the question aside as if it were of no consequence and lapsed into silence again.

"Well, *I* live in New York," Linda said determinedly. "And I love every stone and tower of it. So here I
am going out to a one-horse Middle Western town
called Cedarhill that I know I'm going to dislike with
every inch of me."

This time he was startled into a response. "Cedarhill!
Why, that's where I'm going."

They stared at each other in astonishment for a
moment, then uttered the same original thought in one
breath: "Small world, isn't it?" and broke into laughter
together. The thing was one of those amazing coinci-
dences that could pop up in everyday life. There was
Cedarhill, a mere pinpoint on a map, and here was all
America to choose from for a destination. Yet here
were two New Yorkers headed for that same pinpoint
dining at the same table on a train.

Perhaps he'd have really thawed after that and they'd
have had a better chance to get acquainted, if something odd had not happened to spoil everything. At the
sound of their laughter a woman at a table across the
aisle looked up and glanced at Linda's companion.
Linda saw the look clearly since the woman was opposite her. It was a look first of curiosity, then of recognition. The woman nudged the man sitting beside her and
he looked up too.

"I think there are some people over there who know
you," Linda said softly to her companion. "The woman
looks as if she'd just recognized you."

A harmless incident, she'd have thought, to be recognized by an acquaintance on a train. Linda expected
the young man to look around and smile at the woman
across the way. Instead, a somber coldness seemed to
close down over his face. He turned his dark head to
look out the window beside him as if he had no interest in the world except the view. Now the entire table of
four opposite were whispering and looking at Linda's
companion. Their interested attention and the boy's
indifference to it made her uncomfortable.

"They must be your friends," she persisted. "Perhaps
you ought to speak to them."

He shook his head darkly. "I don't know them. I don't know them at all."

Which seemed to Linda a curious thing to say, considering that he had not once looked to find out whether he knew them or not. There was no further conversation for the rest of the meal. The turtle had gone back into his shell and was obviously going to have nothing to do with the dangerous outside world. A timid soul, Linda thought with distaste. She didn't care much for timid souls. But even while she labeled him, she wondered whether or not she was right. Was there possibly something here she did not understand?

She finished her dinner before her companion finished his, paid her bill and prepared to leave her place at the table to one of the standees already lined up at the rear of the car.

"Well," she said lightly, "I expect we'll meet again in the metropolis of Cedarhill."

This time he gave her no smile. "I suppose so," he said as if the thought gave him no pleasure. All the way back to her own car Linda found herself pushing doors with unnecessary indignation. If that scowling young turtle thought she meant to urge her friendship upon him out in Cedarhill, he was certainly mistaken. He could remain strictly to himself for all she cared.

At Albany a fussy lady with troubles and ailments came aboard to inhabit the opposite Pullman seat from Linda. Linda discovered the troubles and ailments at once, because unlike the turtle, the newcomer took pleasure in telling anyone who would listen all about her private affairs.

In self-defense, Linda had her berth made up and retired gratefully to its seclusion and silence. Something of a sense of adventure began to return, once she was tucked under the covers, with a pillow propped behind her and the cozy reading lamp turned on. She didn't feel like reading just then, but she did feel like starting a letter to Liz. Dramatically she launched into her story: "At dinner tonight I met a man of mystery. He wasn't very agreeable, but he was certainly mysterious." She went on from there, making the turtle sound more romantic than he had looked or acted, building up the suspense for Liz's enjoyment. Probably there'd be a sequel to write later on in Cedarhill that would be much less exciting. But for the moment at least she could be entertaining in her letter back to the New York that the pounding wheels were taking her farther away from every moment. Right now their song was still the same: "Still-in-New-York, still-in-New-York."

Later that night, tossing restlessly in a berth that was comfortable, yet did not induce sleep, Linda knew that the song had changed, but she could not tell when, or be sure of the words.

Now and then she raised herself on an elbow and pulled up the shade an inch or two to peer out at the rushing darkness. Sometimes it was so black that it seemed no world could exist out there and they must be rushing through emptiness. Then the train would whistle its way through a town where lamps shone in windows and lights marked the streets. Just a flash and the scene was gone. Down would come the shade and Linda would go back to tossing on her pillow.

In the long hours she wondered about many things. About Babs Stevens, who would now be a "sister." She had not warmed to the pretty face that had looked out at her from the snapshot Martin had shown her. But she recognized honestly that her own prejudice might have blinded her. Perhaps Babs wouldn't be so bad. Perhaps she'd even prove a friend in a strange place. That was one thing to hope for.

5 Arrival in Cedarhill

Sure that she would not sleep a wink all night, Linda was startled to open her eyes and find gray daylight shining at the edges of the shade and hear the porter's voice telling someone in the car that the train would arrive in Chicago on time.

She got up and found that she was early enough to have the ladies' room to herself. Balancing in a swaying train while you dressed was something of a trick and she was glad to be alone.

The wheels sang of Ohio, then of Indiana. Dunes piled yellow sand along the tracks and there were glimpses of Lake Michigan, gray and choppy in the morning light. It was definitely not a cheerful morning to be starting a new life, Linda thought.

In Chicago a hot wind blew through the streets, and Linda, who had thought she might try for a picture or two, as her father would have done in her place, decided to stay by her bags in the station, rather than check everything and go exploring in the damp heat. A brief reunion with the unhappy Mr. Roughneck, who could not understand what was happening, served to pass the time a little.

She was weary enough of travel by the time she had boarded her second train and was on her way to Cedarhill. The only thing she cared about now was the thought of her mother waiting at the station to greet her and the expectation of a tub of warm water at Martin Stevens's house to wash away the travel grime.

When the conductor called out "Cedarhill," she gathered her belongings together and hurried to the end of the car. What the town itself looked like she could not tell, and did not particularly care. The threatening gray gloom of morning had resolved itself into a drizzling afternoon, and her spirits matched the day. She had not seen the "mystery man" of the night before during her wait in Chicago and had wondered if he were taking a different train. But now she saw him descend to the platform from a car ahead and go toward an elderly woman who had apparently come to meet him. He did not glance her way and she forgot him at once in her own concern at finding no one she knew there on the platform to meet her.

Since neither her mother nor Martin Stevens was in sight, she gave her attention to making sure that the Roughneck had been unloaded from the baggage car. Shoving her bags under the shed roof out of the wet, she ran to release him from captivity. He greeted her with yaps of joy and had to be restrained from trying to leap into her arms from the station platform.

"Down boy!" she said. "Down, Roughy! Behave! I can't find Mother with you jumping around like that. Stand still so I can fasten your leash."

She had just managed to snap the catch when a small boy voice spoke behind her: "Boy, oh boy! Genghis Khan isn't going to like *him!*"

Linda straightened quickly and looked into a freckled, impish face that wore a broad grin. Beside the boy stood a tall young man, with gray eyes and fair hair. Before the boy could burst into words again, the tall young man put a restraining hand on his shoulder and spoke to Linda.

"You're Linda Hollis, aren't you?"

Linda nodded, her bewilderment increasing. The small boy must be Roddy Stevens, but who the other was she had no idea. And why were these two here to greet her, instead of her mother? Dismay must have risen in her eyes for the young man went on quickly.

"Don't worry. Everything's all right. Your mother's plane was grounded because of a storm and they're coming on by train. That means they won't be here for a couple of days. I'm Peter Crowell, across the street from the Stevenses, and this is Roddy Stevens."

"Babs went out," Roddy announced. "She didn't want to come to meet you."

Linda sensed that his widening grin was one of interested anticipation, rather than welcome—anticipation perhaps of trouble to come?

"Whoa there," Peter said, his hand pressing the boy's shoulder. "That's no way to make Linda feel at home. Babs had an appointment to keep. She couldn't make it this afternoon, so I offered to pinch hit."

"She won't like that either," Roddy said and regarded Linda frankly. "My sister doesn't want you to come to our house."

Weariness, the disappointment of not finding her mother there to meet her, coupled with the unexpectedness of Roddy's words, was too much. She could feel tears come up in her eyes and she bent above Roughy again, blinking rapidly to conceal them.

Peter Crowell reached down to pat the little dog as if he did not notice. "Good fella," he said, and the Roughneck responded to this offer of friendship with all his small wiggling person.

"Genghis Khan'll scratch his eyes out," Roddy prophesied cheerfully.

Linda picked the Roughneck up in her arms, suddenly angry. "Anything or anybody who hurts Roughy will get personally settled by me. Just remember that."

"Wow!" said Roddy admiringly. "You get mad fast."

"Are these your bags over here?" Peter asked hastily. "Dad let me take the car, so we'll put them in the back, and you won't have to get wet at all. Say, that looks like some camera you've got there. Do you go in for photography?"

"A little," Linda said. "It was my father's camera."

"That's swell. Maybe we can use you in this town."

He picked up the bags and Linda did not trouble to ask what he meant as they started toward the car. Whether or not the town could use her was of no importance. She felt increasingly sure that she could not use this town, nor anyone in it, not this impossible small boy, not Babs, who didn't want her here any more than she wanted to be here, nor Genghis Khan, the cat who constituted a threat to her darling Roughneck.

"It's too bad it had to rain today," Peter went on, determinedly cheerful as he shoved her suitcases and parcels into the back seat and opened the door in front. Roddy started into the front seat and Peter collared him casually. "You're getting in back, youngster. Company rides in front today."

Roddy looked for a moment as if he might object, but evidently the expression in Peter's eyes quelled him and he gave up and climbed into the back seat.

Linda held Roughy on her lap and rested the camera carefully on the seat between her and Peter. She had no intention of trusting either dog or camera to the tender attentions of Roddy Stevens.

"As I was saying," Peter went on as the car pulled away from the curb, "I'm sorry it had to rain today. Cedarhill's a pretty town; it's too bad you can't see it look its best the first time. Anyway, we'll drive past school so you can see what it's like. Back to the grind tomorrow, you know. You going to be a senior, too?"

She wished he wouldn't try so hard to make up for the unpleasant things Roddy had said, and the disappointment of not finding her mother waiting. She knew he meant well, but she felt too limp and unhappy to respond.

School tomorrow. She'd known she was arriving with no margin of time, but she had not wanted to get to Cedarhill a single minute ahead of her mother. Now Joyce and Martin were coming the slow way by train and she would have to do all this breaking in by herself. She'd have no one friendly around to help. Roddy was worse than she'd expected, and apparently Babs already resented her coming.

"There's the high school building," Peter said. "Not bad for a small town, do you think?"

Linda looked out the car window indifferently. Dinky, she thought. Could that little thing be a high school? Why, it would fit into a corner of her New York school and be lost in a minute. Nevertheless, the grounds around it were more spacious than any she had ever seen about a school. Even in the rain the lawns looked green and neatly kept. There were no iron railings, only the softness of shrubbery growing against the walls.

"I suppose it looks small to you," Peter went on, "but I guess small schools have some advantages big schools don't have."

What they could be Linda did not know, and she certainly didn't care. Large or small, Cedarhill High held no promise of interest for her.

"Let's go past Dad's museum!" Roddy requested suddenly from the back of the car.

Peter nodded and turned down the next block. How countrified it all looked, Linda thought. Wide streets with big trees arching overhead. That might make a good picture—she pulled her thoughts up sharply. She did not want to find so much as a good picture in Cedarhill.

"There it is!" Roddy announced proudly. "They've got an armadillo, too. A stuffed one Dad just got up here from Texas. Wait'll you see!"

Linda felt she could contain her impatience to see the armadillo, but she found herself looking at the old brick building with curiosity. One thing was obvious— the town needed a new museum. If this was what Martin Stevens directed it wasn't much. No more than two stories high, with thick green vines growing all over it, even creeping their way across some of the windows where nobody had bothered to cut them back.

"I like vines, don't you?" Peter said.

For the first time she took a good look at Peter himself as he sat next to her on the seat. Certainly she would not be able to describe him as good looking when she wrote to Liz Johnson back home. Liz had said, "Wait till you fall for one of those husky, handsome country boys—you won't even want to come back to New York."

Peter was tall, but he wasn't husky. He had a nice, ordinary sort of face, but he wasn't anything even Liz (who had a romantic bent) would go dreamy-eyed over. As far as she could like anything in this town, she liked Peter. He'd been kind about coming to meet her and he seemed to be trying awfully hard to make up for the complete lack of welcome which had been offered her.

But he was just a small town boy, naively proud of his little corner, and that was that.

"Vines?" Linda said. "Well, I suppose so. Don't they collect a lot of dirt and shut out the light?" You wouldn't find New York harboring much in the way of clinging vines—not of any kind.

Peter glanced at her. "I guess you're right," he said. "I mean about the dirt and shutting out light," and after that he made no further attempt at conversation. Oddly, she wished she had been less critical about the museum vines.

The car turned down a quiet side street and again tall trees arched their leafiness overhead. Rambling old houses, set well back from the street, added to a sense of spaciousness with their broad lawns and uncrowded flower beds.

"That's our house!" Roddy was playing guide again in the back seat. "See—the white one down there on the right with the swing on the porch. And there's ol' pickle-puss Burr peeking out the front windows."

Mrs. Burr, Linda knew, was the housekeeper, and Roddy was probably right about her peeking because as she looked toward the house a curtain moved at a window. So this was Martin Stevens's home? There was obviously nothing up-to-date about it. It was as old-fashioned as the museum building, but it was not as big as some of its rambling neighbors, and the lawn looked trampled, the flower beds weedy and neglected.

In a sudden wave of longing Linda wished for the neat, well-ordered apartment back in New York, modern and convenient and compact. Home? This house could never be a home to her as long as she lived.

She laid her cheek against the Roughneck's coat and held him close until he turned his head and licked her cheek with a reassuring pink tongue. "We've got each other, pal," he seemed to be saying, and she stepped out of the car feeling as if the little dog was the one friend she had in the world.

6 Stepsister

Roddy ran ahead down the walk and then turned back at the steps. "You'll hafta tie your pooch outside, you know. You can't bring him inside where Genghis Khan can see him. The Khan's the best old fighting cat in this town."

Linda held Roughy all the tighter in her arms. "My dog goes where I go," she said firmly and walked up the steps. "You'd better shut up your cat."

"Not me!" said Roddy. "I want to see this. Anyway, he's not my cat—he belongs to Babs."

"How about being useful and bringing in a load from the car?" Peter suggested.

Roddy hesitated a moment and then raced back down the walk to return with unbelievable speed carrying a single small parcel.

Peter pushed the doorbell and the housekeeper took her time in making her appearance, wanting perhaps to give the impression that she had not been practically hanging out a window waiting for them.

It was odd sometimes the way people fitted their names, Linda thought. This woman looked prickly all over. Her iron gray hair seemed all fuzzy ends, with a hairpin or two adding to the thistle effect. Her starched dress stood out in sharp pleats and her nose and chin jutted to sharp little points.

"I'm Mrs. Burr," she told Linda. "Too bad there was nobody here to give you a proper greeting, but that's the way it is with those planes, I always say. Never can be sure of getting where you want to go. If it hadn't been for Peter here, I don't know what we'd have done."

"It's all right," Linda said. "It couldn't be helped." She turned to Peter, who'd made another trip to the car and had set down her bags in the front hall. "It was awfully nice of you to come to my rescue."

He turned a little pink around the ears. "Don't mention it. I just got to thinking how I'd feel if I was coming to a new town and my father and mother weren't on deck to—" he broke off, apparently remembering that Martin Stevens was not her father, blushed the brighter and backed out the door. "Well, see you in school tomorrow," he said and went off whistling.

Countryish, Linda thought, smiling. But at least he was nicer than anyone else she had seen in Cedarhill.

"Oh, boy! Look at that!" came Roddy's hushed voice behind her.

Linda followed the direction of his gaze to the top of a narrow stairway that led upward from the small hall. On the top step was poised a furious ball of orange fur. Ears were laid back wrathfully, feline lips drawn away from sharp white teeth, orange tail puffed to giant size, and every bright hair on end with indignation.

This was the Khan! He certainly looked every inch the outraged emperor. Roughy wiggled in Linda's arms and gave funny little hushed barks in a well-trained apartment house manner.

"Stop it, Roughy. Be still," she whispered.

"That cat can lick your old dog with one paw," Roddy said scornfully and Linda rather suspected he was right. The Roughneck had never encountered anything like this before, though his mischievous interest in cats was of long standing.

Mrs. Burr flapped her apron in the direction of the stairs. "Shoo, you! Get out! Behave yourself!"

The Khan did not condescend to look her way. His baleful yellow eyes never left the little dog and he drew himself back like a crouching tiger preparing to spring. Linda decided that retreat was a better choice than valor, and ended the tension by carrying Roughy through a door into the living room.

"I told you to leave your pooch outside," Roddy cried excitedly. "The Khan likes fights."

Mrs. Burr's voice was sharp. "You go get that cat and shut him in the basement. Right away now. I don't want any cat and dog fights in this house." Roddy went off reluctantly and she turned back to Linda. "I'm sure I don't know how we're expected to have two animals that hate each other in the same house. The cat was here first and I know Babs won't give him up, so I guess something will have to be done about your dog. Probably you can find him a good home somewheres if you try."

Linda patted Roughy and held back the quick answer she was tempted to give. If they were going to find the Roughneck an outside home, they could find one for her, too. But it wasn't for this woman to decide about that. Once her mother was here there'd be no question about giving up Roughy. Her mother knew how she felt about him and she'd stand by her, in spite of Babs or Roddy or anyone.

"I wonder if I may go up to my room now?" Linda asked Mrs. Burr. "I feel grubby after my trip and I'd like a hot tub."

"Mmm," the housekeeper considered this. "You can go up to your room, of course. But I don't know about hot water right away. The heater's been acting up lately. I'll see what I can do. Just take up what you want, and when Roddy comes back from shutting up that cat, I'll send him upstairs with the rest of your bags."

Linda slung the strap of her camera over her shoulder, clutched Roughy under one arm, and picked up her overnight bag in the other hand. Mrs. Burr, apparently, had no intention of helping with anything. She marched up the stairs ahead of Linda, her starched shell rattling as she moved.

At least, Linda thought, they could shut themselves away in her own room, she and Roughy. She could lie down and rest a while, till the hot water was ready. It would be something to have privacy again. Train travel in a Pullman gave one little of that.

The stair carpet was worn and not too clean, she

noticed as she followed Mrs. Burr, and the same could be said of the runner in the upper hall. A door on the left opened upon the untidiness of what was obviously Roddy's room, and then Mrs. Burr opened a door on the right.

"Of course, properly speaking, you won't have a room of your own," she said. "That's one of the things Babs is so mad about—having to share. But it seems to me she's got to be reasonable about this. You've got to sleep somewheres, goodness knows. Well, there it is— make yourself at home. I'll go see about the heater."

Linda crossed the threshold into the room and then turned to swing the door shut behind her. There was a brass bolt placed shoulder high and she thrust it across. Then she set the Roughneck down and let him go exploring. She felt stunned by this latest bad fortune. Not having a room of her own was the worst blow of all.

For one girl, the room would have been of ample size, bigger perhaps than her room at home. (Home! It didn't exist any more. It belonged to someone else and she'd never see it again.) But for two girls, especially one who had as many possessions as Babs seemed to have, it was crowded indeed. An effort had been made to furnish it fairly and equally for two, but Babs's belongings had been here first and the new furniture did not match.

Not even my own room, Linda thought as she walked to the bed which occupied the emptier side, and therefore obviously her side of the room, and dropped onto it. She sat there numbly looking around. So clearly had the division been made that it was as if someone had drawn a chalk line down the middle of the floor. Even the two windows were evenly spaced, one to each side. But despite the balance, there were differences.

Babs went in for fuss and frills, something Linda disliked, and she was none too tidy about her possessions. A lipstick lay open on the powder smeared top of her dressing table, numerous snapshots and photographs were tucked around the edge of the mirror. On the wall hung an assortment of pencil sketches and water colors. Blue gingham bedspread, dressing table flounce and window curtains matched and must have been attractive when they were crisp and new. They had faded in many washings and now hung dejectedly limp.

On Linda's bed the spread was a bilious India print, her dresser merely a small table with a single drawer, which no one had tried to dress up. Above it hung an oval mirror, not too well placed for light. Each section boasted a small bureau, but these were no better matched than the other things. The one on Babs's side was a nice looking maple piece and certainly new, while Linda's was an ancient golden oak affair, old-fashioned, battered and scratched.

She took the new one and gave me the old, Linda thought, liking Babs less and less as she continued the inventory.

Roughy had begun an investigation of his own. Over against the wall on Babs's side, Linda had discovered a flat gingham pillow which he was sniffing with obvious indignation. That, she surmised, would be the Khan's bed.

Someone tried the door of the room and then banged on it lustily. "Hey, there! Whatcha got the door locked for? Here's your stuff."

Linda opened the door and Roddy came in with the remainder of her bags. Roughy, naturally friendly, bounded over to sniff at the small boy, but Roddy drew back from the touch of his nose.

"He won't hurt you," Linda said. "He just wants to get acquainted. Don't you like dogs?"

"The Khan doesn't like 'em," Roddy said, as if that answered everything.

Roughy began to bound around the boy, whining excitedly.

"I'm afraid he smells cat," Linda explained. "Thanks for bringing up my things."

She wished he would satisfy his curiosity and go away, but he stood where he was, looking about the crowded, unbeautiful little room. Whatever his thoughts were, however, he did not speak them.

"Will your mom be like Mrs. Burr?" he asked unexpectedly. "I mean will she be bossy and crabby? I saw her a couple of times, but you can't tell about people from just the outside."

Tired as she was, Linda roused herself. For the first time Roddy Stevens seemed more a person than a pest. A young person with a need for reassurance. That was something she herself could understand just now.

"Mother's nice," she said. "She hardly ever stops being cheerful and smiling. You'll like her. And I know she'll like you. She's always wanted a little boy."

Roddy thought about that with apparent skepticism. "In stories," he said, "stepmothers are mean."

Linda nodded. "I know. Stepfathers aren't so good either. That's what your father will be to me. Maybe I'm just as worried about that as you are about my mother."

"That's silly," Roddy assured her quickly. "My dad's swell. There isn't anybody in this town smarter than he is. Sometimes he has to tell the mayor what to do, and even the principal of my school."

Here, certainly, was a case of hero worship and Linda found herself wondering what there was about the unimposing Martin Stevens to arouse such admiration as this. Probably small boys always felt like that about their fathers; especially when there was no mother to claim a divided allegiance.

In his interest in talking about his father, Roddy had forgotten the Roughneck, but Roughy had not forgotten either the boy or the dreaded Genghis Khan, whom for the present the boy probably represented in the little dog's eyes. Without warning the Roughneck came out of the corner into which he had retired and nipped at Roddy's ankle.

The boy's reaction was quick and angry. He drew back his foot and kicked the dog sharply in the side. The Roughneck yelped in pain and amazement and Linda, without stopping to think, put her hands on Roddy's shoulders and shook him hard.

"Don't you ever dare kick my dog!" she told him grimly. "Don't you ever dare!"

Roddy wriggled himself free. "He bit me! Your old pooch bit me! My dad'll make you get rid of him. You wait!"

"Roughy never bites," Linda said sharply. "Let me see. Stop yelling and let me look."

But Roddy squirmed out of reach and ran off, protesting loudly that he had been bitten, that he had been shaken. Linda did not trouble to close the door after him. She flung herself full length on the bed and when Roughy came to put his forepaws on the spread and nuzzle her shoulder with his friendly and repentant little nose, she pushed him away.

"You're no help," she said. "You ought to have better sense. Down! Lie down and stay there!"

Roughy obeyed shamefacedly and Linda threw an arm over her eyes. She was beyond coping with anything more, come what might. She was too tired to think clearly, too depressed and confused to try. Everything was so much worse than she had expected it to be.

Downstairs Roddy's uproar and accusations died away. Nothing happened about the bath water and after a little while fatigue, emotional as well as physical, won out and Linda fell asleep.

When she opened her eyes she saw that rain still ran in rivulets down the windowpanes and that gray daylight had shaded into early dusk. She turned her head to search for Roughy and was startled to see a girl standing in the middle of the room looking at her. She struggled dazedly to a sitting position, fighting the languor that tried to pull her back.

The girl, seeing that she was awake, crossed the room to the light switch and Linda blinked in the sudden glare from the overhead lamp.

"H-hello," she said fuzzily.

The other girl did not answer her greeting. She dropped into the room's most comfortable chair—which was on her side—and crossed her gray-slacked legs. Her eyes appraised Linda frankly, openly—eyes that looked surprisingly like Roddy's except that they were greenish in hue. Linda, accustoming herself to the light, returned her look levelly, weighing the other girl, just as Babs weighed her. What she saw she did not like.

The snapshot Martin had shown her of his daughter

had not done her justice. This was no mere prettiness of face—this girl was beautiful, or would have been had she worn an expression less sulky and watchful. Her glossy black hair hung in soft waves to her shoulders, caught back from her ears with a green ribbon that matched the hue of her eyes. Her lips were full and soft and wore a dissatisfied pout. It was a beautiful face, but it was not a pleasant one.

"Well," Babs said when the silence had gone on long enough to satisfy her, "you've got off to a good start. What's all this about you biting Roddy? Or did he bite you?"

Linda smiled ruefully. Her nap had refreshed her, and she felt better able to deal with this new world which wanted her no more than she wanted it.

"I shook him," she said. "I shook him good and hard and if necessary I'll do it again."

The other girl swung a red sandaled foot back and forth comfortably. "For that I don't blame you. I'm always shaking him myself, but it never does any good. What did he pull this time?"

"He kicked my dog," Linda said. "I'll admit Roughy wasn't polite. He didn't like the cat smell and he went nipping at Roddy's ankles. But Roughy's never really bitten anybody in his life, and I don't believe he bit your brother. He just scared him."

She bent to look under the bed, continuing the search for the Roughneck her discovery of Babs had halted.

"If you're looking for your dog," Babs said coolly, "I took him out on the back porch and tied him up. You can't keep him here. This is the Khan's place."

She nodded toward the gingham pillow and Linda saw the great orange cat curled upon it regally. Genghis Khan blinked his yellow eyes at her once and ignored her from then on. Obviously in his opinion she was a creature of no consequence. The outrage to his domain had been rectified and his reign was again unchallenged.

Linda stood up, shaking out the crumpled skirt of her suit, brushing back her short hair with careless fingers. Somehow she felt better standing on her feet, looking down at this other girl.

"Roughy can't stay out on the porch in this dampness," she said. "In a minute I'll go down and bring him in. But first perhaps we'd better get a few things straight."

"Good enough," Babs said. "You can't go shaking *me* for what I do to your dog."

No she couldn't, Linda thought. Not even if she might like to, which seemed very possible. What was the matter with her today? She'd never had such belligerent impulses before.

"Look," she said, "the first thing we'd better understand is that I hate coming here to this house just as much as you hate having me. Roddy told me how you felt. He told me you had to give up part of your room to me. I don't like that any better than you do. I'd supposed of course that I'd have a room of my own as I did at home."

There was that word again. Home. She wished she could forget it. Just saying it made her feel weak and miserable, when she needed most of all to be strong.

"Go on," Babs said curtly. "This is all very interesting."

Linda folded her arms in front of her and set her feet slightly apart. "If it's any comfort to you, I don't want to stay in this house, or this town one minute longer than I have to. I belong in New York and if there's any way at all to get back there, I'm going. In the meantime, I have to stay here. There isn't anything you or I can do about that. So maybe we'd better draw up a—a sort of charter."

"Armed truce?" Babs said. "That suits me. You're not as bad as I expected. For a New Yorker. But let me tell you—I don't like this town any better than you do. If Dad hadn't gone all over romantic—at his age!—I could have stayed in Chicago and finished school with the other girls. Now because he's got this sickening big-happy-family idea I'm going to have to finish at dinky little Cedarhill High."

Dinky. That was the word she had used, Linda thought. She had not expected to hear it echoed by

Babs Stevens. And the big-happy-family didn't appeal to her either. It was queer to find that she and Babs were, in a sense, on the same side.

"Maybe we can work together for what we want," Linda said thoughtfully. "Maybe they won't be able to stand against two of us."

Babs nodded. "That's a thought. You don't look as if you'd fit a one-horse town like this any better than I do. By the way, how did you get here from the station today? I was supposed to do the honors, but I walked out on the job."

It was a statement, not an apology. At least this girl was frank and direct, even if her directness was not very pleasant.

"I managed all right," Linda said. "Peter Crowell met the train and got me home in his father's car."

For a second the other girl was quiet. Linda suspected she did not approve of the fact that it was Peter who had come to the rescue. Then Babs tossed back the heavy dark hair that had fallen across one shoulder in a gesture that was somehow defiant.

"Peter! I'll bet he showed you the glories of Cedarhill like any town father. You'd think this whistle stop was to be preferred to Chicago to hear him talk."

"I thought he was nice," Linda said quietly. "At least he was more thoughtful than anyone else has been."

"I know Peter," Babs said tartly. "I know just what a do-gooder he is. And if that last remark was aimed at me, save your breath. I'm not going to spend my time trying to be thoughtful about anybody but Babs Stevens. I've found out that you have to look out for yourself in this world."

What had almost amounted to a sense of comradeship was gone. Linda picked up her suitcase and put it on the bed. As she opened the locks she spoke coldly over her shoulder.

"Is there any possibility of getting a bath in this house? I asked Mrs. Burr when I arrived, but she said something was wrong with the heater."

Babs pulled herself up from her chair with a snort of impatience. "Old Prickles has a complex about the water heater. She's afraid of it. I'll go have a look and get you hot water in a jiffy."

She swung out of the room, moving with a long-limbed natural grace that was pleasing to see. She'd make a good model, Linda thought with a flash of professional objectivity. Photogenic—if she'd get that sulky look off her face.

Well, Babs Stevens's disposition, or how well she might photograph was not her problem. Linda had more pressing affairs of her own. She took her clothes from the suitcase and began to hang them in the room's single crowded closet. There had been no attempt at division of space in the closet. Babs's things occupied all the space and Linda had to shove her dresses aside on the hanger rod to fit her own things in at all. The two overhead shelves were heaped untidily high and Linda resolved that one of the first things she was going to try for was a rearrangement of the closet.

But before she undressed for her bath, she'd go downstairs and bring Roughy in out of the dampness of the back porch. She threw Genghis Kahn a look of disliking as she went out of the room, but the big orange cat did not even open its eyes.

7 House Divided

Dinner that night was a strange affair. Roddy's bad table manners went unchecked, except for a weary protest now and then from Mrs. Burr and snorts of disgust from his sister, both of which he ignored. Babs had sunk into gloomy silence and Linda had no desire to make bright conversation. This, however, did not discourage Mrs. Burr, who apparently liked a bit of sprightly chatter, and was only too willing to furnish it herself.

"I see by the *Hill News* tonight that Mrs. Kenyon finally got that grandson of hers home," she said, helping herself to a second spoonful of lumpy mashed potatoes.

Apparently no one was interested in this astonishing information, but Mrs. Burr pursued the subject to her own satisfaction.

"She's right, too. She's got good sense, Grandma Kenyon. That kind of life only spoils a boy. Imagine— at his age! Exploiting—that's what I call it."

Roddy, reaching for more bread, knocked over his glass of milk and Mrs. Burr fussed and scolded and mopped. Babs said, "Clumsy!" in cutting tones and Roddy made a face at her. Linda wanted to push away from the table and leave her food uneaten. The meal was tasteless anyway, and the company added nothing on the pleasant side. But there was nowhere to go where she could be sure of privacy, except maybe down in the basement where she had put Roughy.

When the milk puddles had been sopped up and a napkin thrust under the damp place, Mrs. Burr returned to her subject as if she had never been interrupted.

"I suppose he'll be going to your school, Babs. The paper said he was a senior. That ought to cause a stir."

"Why?" Babs asked indifferently.

"Because he's a celebrity, that's why. If you'd sit up and take an interest once in a while, you'd find lots of things happening in Cedarhill."

"What's a celebrity?" Roddy asked. "And who's one?"

"It's somebody famous," Mrs. Burr told him. "If you'd listen you'd know. It's this Gordon Kenyon I'm talking about."

In spite of her lassitude, Linda's interest pricked to attention. Gordon Kenyon? The name had a familiar ring.

"Nobody famous would come to Cedarhill," Babs said. "What's he supposed to be famous for?"

"I know!" Linda broke in. "He's been in the New York papers a lot because of his parents' divorce case. There was an awful scrap and it hasn't been settled yet. His grandmother was awarded temporary custody. He's a musical prodigy of some kind—a pianist, I think."

"That's right," Mrs. Burr nodded. "But Grandma Kenyon's against any more of that stage stuff till he's of age. She wants him to have a taste of normal American life."

Babs began to laugh softly and the sound was not pleasant to hear. "That makes three of us!" she said. "Three of us who don't want to be in Cedarhill. We ought to start a club. We might call ourselves the Normal Americans. Want to join, Linda?"

Somehow it wasn't very funny. Linda felt suddenly sorry for this Gordon Kenyon who had no more to say about his life than she had about hers. He was from the East too, New York. Why—why, of course! That boy on the train who had seemed so strange and who had been coming to Cedarhill—that boy had been Gordon Kenyon. The identification explained many things. His indifference to being recognized by people at the table across the aisle was now understandable. Probably he was used to being recognized by strangers and didn't like it very much. She could understand too his reluctance to talk about himself. He hadn't been unfriendly, just reticent. Who wouldn't be after all that publicity about his family's troubles? She could forgive him, now that she understood. She could look forward to seeing him again at school. There was even the possibility that they might be friends. She needed a friend in this town, for certainly she'd never find one under the Stevens roof.

Thinking about her loneliness in this house, she forgot about Gordon Kenyon. If only her mother could have been here this first night everything would have been so much better. But there was no use wishing. No word had come to say exactly when Martin and her mother would arrive; just a telegram to announce the grounded plane and a change of plans. Even with good train connections it would probably be another day or so before they could get here.

Tomorrow meant starting to a strange school alone. Babs would be no good at helping her get acquainted. In a sense this was a strange school for Babs too, though she probably knew most of the girls and boys. But Babs had already stated her philosophy, to take care of her own interests and let the other fellow look out for himself.

When the unsavory dinner was over, Linda took the dress she meant to wear to school the next day down to the basement laundry for pressing. She got some kitchen scraps from Mrs. Burr to feed Roughy and the moment she opened the basement door the little dog greeted her with joyous affection. The Roughneck's love was without reproach. Even though he did not understand the strange things that were being done to him, or the unfriendly people who had handled him, his loyalty had obviously never wavered. Even in his hunger he paused to lick Linda's wrist to indicate his love before he fell upon his dinner.

Linda watched him for a moment, glad of his presence and support, and then set up the ironing board and plugged in the iron. While she waited for it to heat she inspected the pile of trunks and cartons her mother had shipped ahead from New York. The ones which

interested her most were those which contained her
father's mounted photographs and his photographic
equipment. Everything appeared to be in good shape,
but she couldn't be sure until she unpacked them. She'd
need tools for that. Later on would have to do.

The iron hissed at the touch of a damp finger and
Linda spread the dress on the ironing board. Having
finished his dinner, Roughy wriggled over to sit as close
as possible, evidently fearful of losing her again.

It was raining harder than ever. At several places the
high basement windows leaked and thin streams
trickled down cement walls to dampen the floor. This
was no better a place for the Roughneck than the back
porch. A dog confined down here might develop rheu-
matism. Something would have to be done about Babs
and that cat as soon as Martin and Joyce got home.

The doorbell shrilled upstairs and Linda wondered
who could be out on a night like this. Babs went to
answer it and Linda heard another voice—it sounded
like that boy from across the street, Peter Crowell. A
moment later the door at the head of the basement
stairs opened and someone came down. She did not
look up from her ironing until Babs's scornful voice cut
through her concentration.

"Peter thinks two frail young things like us won't be
able to walk to school alone tomorrow morning. So he's
come to offer his assistance."

Linda looked up to see Peter standing on the steps
behind Babs and grinning good-naturedly over her
shoulder. Apparently her mocking words had not disturbed him in the least.

He said calmly, "I thought you might like somebody
who knew the ropes to show you around the first day.
Babs can take care of herself all right, but you're a
stranger here."

Babs came the rest of the way downstairs and again
Linda noted her easy, long-legged grace of movement.
Roughy growled deep in his throat. Linda spoke to him
quickly and he hushed, though he watched Babs suspiciously as she went across to perch herself on a corner
of one of the Hollis packing cases.

"I told you Peter was a do-gooder," Babs said. "You

can always count on him in a pinch, or even when there isn't a pinch."

Linda glanced at Peter, lounging against the stair rail. His wet black slicker shone in the light and there were droplets of rain on his fair hair.

"Thanks a lot." Linda ignored Babs and spoke directly to Peter. "I was a little worried about breaking in tomorrow and I'll be grateful for a few steers."

"I'd have looked out for you," Babs said sulkily.

Peter chortled. "The only trouble with that, Barby, is that she'd never be able to guess ahead of time that you would. You'd let her worry up to the last minute before you'd offer any help."

"She looks strong and healthy," Babs said. "I doubt if worry is breaking her down."

Linda went back to her pressing, running the iron over a pleat she had already pressed three times. So this was what it was like to have a sister! She was going to have to live in the same house with this girl, share a room with her, listen to her sharp tongue day in and day out. It was for this she had had to trade her happy life in New York.

"One of these days," Peter said gently, "gran'pappy will have to spank again. Remember the last time I spanked you, Barby? We were all of eight years old and I did a very good job."

Babs tossed back her mane of black hair and hopped down from the packing case. "If you ever lay a finger on me again, Pete Crowell, I—I'll—" but she did not finish her threat. Instead, she ran past him up the stairs and they heard the basement door bang sharply behind her.

Linda blinked her eyelids and ironed furiously. Unwanted tears burned under the lids, but the last thing she wanted was to shed them before Peter. All this was so unpleasant, so disturbing. It had been bad enough to have had to leave New York and everything she loved. Now to have everything turn out so miserably here made the move just that much worse.

Peter seated himself on the bottom step and snapped his fingers at the Roughneck. The little dog bounded over joyously, recognizing a friend in a world that had turned unpleasant for him too. Linda was grateful for his interest in the dog, not only for Roughy's sake, but because it gave her time to blink back the threat of tears.

Peter's fingers scratched behind Roughy's ears and he did not look at Linda when he spoke. "I don't know what your mother's like, but she's going to be good for this house. Barby doesn't know it, but she needs a mother. She needs a sister too. You're going to be good for her."

"I don't know if I want to be good for her," Linda said stiffly.

Peter let that go. "What I really came over for was to find out how things had worked out between the Roughneck and Barby's Khan."

"You can see for yourself," Linda told him. "The cat stays upstairs. Roughy's been banished to the basement."

Peter looked at the trickles of water running in around the windows and at the spreading dampness on the floor. "Not so good," he said. "Maybe you'd let me take him over to my place for a couple of nights till you get something worked out?"

"Oh, would you?" Linda cried. "That would be wonderful. I'll miss him like anything, but until Mother gets home, perhaps that's the best way. I have been worried. What about your mother? I mean will she mind—"

"I checked on that before I came over. It's okay. Mom said to tell you if there was anything else we could do to help make you comfortable, just to let us know."

Linda's spirits rose a little. At least there were good neighbors in Cedarhill.

"Maybe you could help me," she told him. "I've been wanting to get into these cases of my father's things. Not to unpack them—just to see if they've made the trip all right."

"As good as done!" Peter announced, pulling himself up from the step. "Wait till I shed this wet coat and I'll get at them. Mr. Stevens has a tool box down here somewhere."

While Linda pulled out the iron plug and arranged

her dress on a hanger, Peter found a claw-headed hammer and went to work on the first case. When Bob Hollis's big enlarger came into view he whistled reverently.

"Wow! Isn't that something! Do you do any of this kind of thing yourself?"

"A little," Linda admitted. "I used to help Dad a bit. We had a darkroom in a closet at home. It wasn't very big, but some awfully good things came out of it. I've brought all Dad's pictures with me, but I don't want to open them up till I've found a place to put them."

"A couple of years ago I built a darkroom in the basement at home," Peter said. "Any time you want to use it you're welcome."

He was nice, this Peter Crowell, but opening up these cases made her ache still more for the old life. There was something melancholy about thinking of days that were done.

She shook her head in refusal. "Thanks, but I'm not much good at photography and I don't expect to use any of this stuff just now. I only wanted to make sure nothing had been damaged."

"Well, I guess everything's all right," Peter said when the cases had been opened to Linda's satisfaction. He got into his coat again. "Come along, Roughneck, we're going to get you out of the damp for tonight. Tell Linda good-bye."

Roughy never liked that word. It made his ears droop and his tail stop waggling. But at least he trusted Peter and accepted him as a friend, so he made no objection to being tucked inside the slicker with just his head sticking out.

"See you in the morning," Peter said, as Linda went upstairs with him to the front door.

In the living room Linda could see Roddy curled up in a big chair with his nose in a book, while Babs stretched on her stomach on the long shabby couch, listening to the radio. Neither looked up, though Peter called, "So long, kids," as he went out the door.

Linda stepped into the rainy dampness of the big front porch and watched as Peter and the Roughneck made their dash across the street through the downpour. The street lamp at the end of the block shone on a streaming world. Linda stood on the porch for a moment, sniffing the unfamiliar smells of the night. She knew how a city smelled in the rain. She knew the pounding sounds rain made on roof and wall and sidewalks. Here both the odors and the sounds were different. The smell of wet earth and fresh green things was unfamiliar. The thudding of drops falling onto soft ground had a sound less harsh than raindrops striking pavements. In the garden the trees whispered as if they spoke a gentle, rustling language of their own, but it was a tongue Linda Hollis did not understand. She turned away from the strangeness of the rainy garden and went quickly inside to shut the door behind her.

She did not pause to glance into the living room at Roddy with his comic book, or at Babs by the radio, but ran upstairs and into the room she shared with this stepsister she liked so little. "Barby," Peter had called her, almost affectionately, though goodness knows she didn't deserve his liking. Barby, he had said, who needed a sister. That was a joke, if ever she'd heard one. Babs needed no one but herself.

Linda turned on the light and winced as the confused, unattractive little room sprang into view again. The photographs that crowded the edges of Babs's mirror caught her eye, and she crossed the room to look at them more closely.

That was Peter there in a rowboat waving an oar. In fact, Peter appeared in more than one picture, so Babs must think something of him, despite her rudeness.

In a place of honor on the dressing table top was a small framed photograph of a beautiful woman with heavy dark hair like Babs's and a smile like Roddy's. Linda bent to look closer. That would be their mother, of course. For the first time Linda found herself considering the similarity between the situation in which she and Babs found themselves. Babs had lost a mother, just as she had lost a father.

In her absorption she heard no step at the door and started in surprise at the sound of Babs's curt tone. The other girl stood in the doorway, her hands resting on slim hips, elbows set akimbo. In her eyes there was no liking for Linda Hollis.

"I hope we won't have to build a fence down the middle of the room," she said. "Maybe there's something else we'd better get straight right away. This side of the room's mine and I don't want you in it. Stick to your own side and maybe we can get along. And another thing—I don't like snoopers. You tend to your business, and I'll tend to mine. You leave my things alone and I'll leave yours alone."

Linda could feel the flush of indignation rising in her cheeks, but she held her words in check. Not for one moment did she mean to put herself on the same ill-bred plane with this Cedarhill girl.

"I was looking at the picture of your mother," she said quietly. "I'm sorry I trespassed. I won't again."

She took her pajamas from her suitcase, got out her toothbrush and cold cream and went down the hall to the bathroom. She did not glance at the other girl again, but out of the corner of her eye as she left the room she saw her fling herself full length on the bed, and realized in surprise that Babs Stevens was crying.

Downstairs she could hear Mrs. Burr calling vainly to Roddy to get to bed because there was school tomorrow. Roddy apparently had no intention of obeying, and after a while Mrs. Burr gave up and came up to her own room.

What a strange, unhappy household this was, Linda thought as she went into the haven of the bathroom and locked the door behind her. What sort of man was Martin Stevens to have made such a thorough mess of things? Everything she saw in this house made her estimation of him drop a little lower.

8 Gordon Speaks Up

During the night the rain stopped and Linda awoke with a sense of being startled by something unnatural and disturbing. For a moment she did not know where she was, but lay there in the darkness, pulling herself up from drowsiness, groping for reality.

Then she knew what was wrong. It was the utter quiet that had awakened her. No familiar taxi horns shrilled, no brakes screeched, no garbage cans banged across the sidewalk, no hum of a city that never slept. The quiet was so intense it seemed to throb. Then small sounds began to emerge from the muffling blanket of stillness; sounds so faint that they seemed part of the quiet themselves.

The dripping of wet leaves, the tiny cracklings of garden life, the distant barking of a dog, all suddenly took on a thunderclap importance. She sat up in bed to listen and saw that moonlight streamed in at the window, calm summer moonlight flooding a quiet world.

"What's the matter?" came a whisper from the other bed.

"I can't sleep," Linda said. "It's so quiet."

"I know." The return whisper was unexpectedly understanding. "I feel like that too, after Chicago, even though I grew up here. I hate the quiet."

"I don't hate it," Linda said. "I'm just not used to it."

She lay down again and pulled the sheet over her ears to shut out the throbbing stillness. The girl in the other bed went quickly back to sleep and her soft breathing made one more unfamiliar sound to listen to in the night. Then Linda herself fell asleep and when she awoke again Mrs. Burr was calling from the head of the stairs. Everybody had better get up and get going, she shouted. First day of school today!

Getting going was a frenzied series of clashes for the bathroom, with Roddy winning out for first place. Then the smell of burning breakfast toast and the taste of lumpy oatmeal. Somehow everyone got through more or less at the same time and when Peter rang the doorbell the two girls were ready to leave.

For some unaccountable reason Babs had decided to be helpful this morning. She smiled at Peter sweetly and he grinned back with his usual good nature.

"Roughy's homesick for you," he told Linda as they started down the block.

"I'll stop in to see him right after school," Linda said.

Babs looked surprised. "You mean Peter's got your dog? Wasn't he all right in the basement?"

"It was too damp down there," Linda told her stiffly. Somehow, now that Babs was making a tardy effort to be pleasant, she herself felt less friendly than ever. Yesterday she could have done with a small welcome. Today she didn't care. She didn't care about anything— not about the shared room, or how Babs behaved, or that the sun was shining brightly over a newly washed Cedarhill, or that she was going to a new high school.

The last was especially unimportant. Today back in New York Liz and the rest of the crowd were starting their senior year. Since New York time was an hour ahead they were already at classes by now. Was Liz thinking about her today, wondering how things were going out in this small town?

In spite of not caring, Linda had dressed carefully this morning. Her tailored dress was a soft forest green with nice lines and fit. Her mother had picked it up at a discount at the store and it was a good make. Linda had noted Babs's quick eyes registering its details that morning and though the other girl had made no comment, she sensed a grudging approval.

As the neat, clean building of the high school came into view, Linda, in spite of herself, felt her heart begin

to thud a little faster, though she knew anticipation was
foolish. There was no reason to feel like a child going
to school for the first time. After New York, this little
school was a joke. She should be able to take it in her
stride without a silly flutter.

As they joined the others converging on all sides
toward the two main doors, a tall, rather thin boy went
up the steps ahead of them, and Linda recognized the
boy on the train.

Babs nudged Peter. "Who's that? Somebody new in
town?"

"Looks like our celeb," Peter said. "His picture was
in the paper. Why don't you keep up with what's
happening in Cedarhill?"

Babs sniffed. "As if I cared! Well, there's another
hope shot. He may be famous, but he doesn't look like
much."

"Oh-oh!" Peter chuckled. "Looking for new game?
Going to give the rest of us the air just for a little fame?
There's a woman for you—fickle. Don't you be like
that, Linda."

Linda smiled vaguely, but she was paying little attention to this banter. Gordon Kenyon hadn't seen her,
but later when they had a chance to get acquainted, she
meant to look past the surface that was evidently all
Babs needed to judge by and find out what he was
really like.

They were early enough for the two newcomers,
Babs and Linda, to register and be assigned to a room.
Peter disappeared with a group of senior boys and the
girls did not see him again until they reached their section room.

"Markham!" Babs whispered to Linda as they
reached the door. "We would have the bad luck to land
him for a section teacher. Now we'll have to be under
his thumb through our whole senior year."

"Don't you like him?" Linda asked.

"He's a friend of Dad's, but I don't like what I've
heard about him as a teacher. Hey, look who's with
us!"

Linda looked and saw that Gordon Kenyon had
taken a seat nearest the window and was engrossed in

the open pages of a book before him, paying no attention to the commotion going on in the room about him.

"He's not bad looking at that," Babs whispered. "I wonder if he's really as important as Mrs. Burr said? Come on—let's get seats near the windows."

But others were before them and Linda found herself in the next to the last seat of the second row from the windows, several seats behind Gordon Kenyon, and a seat away from Peter Crowell. Mr. Markham came in and some of the seething commotion in the room began to die down.

"We'll have him for English," Babs whispered gloomily over her shoulder to Linda in the seat behind. "He's a Shakespeare fiend, or something just as desperate. We'll have fun."

The room quieted and the first term seniors gazed expectantly at the teacher, who stood beside his desk, tossing a bit of chalk in his hand. He was a stocky young man who looked as if he might be more interested in football than English literature, but, as Linda remembered her father saying, you could never tell about people, it took a clever photograph to show more than the outside. His sandy hair was the sort that resisted restraint and managed to give him a slightly excited look. As he waited for the rustle to still, his eyes traveled from face to face with a keen gaze that seemed to look for more than lay on the surface.

In spite of Babs's remarks about "old Markham," Linda found herself inclined to respect him. He might be a small town teacher, but she suspected that he liked his job. His gaze rested briefly on Linda and she returned the look steadily. We're an adventure to him, she thought, a little surprised. We're new territory and he's an explorer. Then she saw that he was gazing at the bent head of the boy who was so interested in a book that he had not glanced up with the others when the room came to order.

Mr. Markham's attention rested there and did not move on. Something in the quiet of the room, the focus of its attention, must have reached Gordon Kenyon, for he lifted his eyes for the first time. If it disturbed him to find himself suddenly the center of attention, you could not tell, for he merely glanced at the teacher and then calmly out the window beside him as if it made little difference whether people looked at him or not.

Mr. Markham set the bit of chalk on the blackboard rail and launched into routine instructions for the beginning seniors. When the bell rang and the class filed out to follow its various schedules, Linda was surprised to have Mr. Markham stop her.

"You're Martin Stevens's new daughter, aren't you?" he asked.

New daughter! She could feel that slow flush she hated creeping into her cheeks. She was Bob Hollis's daughter—no one else's.

"I'm Linda Hollis," she said stiffly, knowing she was being childish and that this man had only meant to make her welcome.

"I'm glad to have you in my class." His tone was grave. "Martin is a good friend of mine and I've met your mother. I realize this is quite a change from New York. If you run into any snarls, let me know if I can help."

Before she could thank him, he had turned away to stop Gordon Kenyon who was going out the door. Linda slipped into the corridor, to find Babs waiting watchfully.

"Martin Stevens's new daughter," Babs echoed and there was a bite to her words.

Linda put a quick hand on her arm. "Listen! My father is Bob Hollis. I haven't any other. You keep your father and I'll keep my mother."

"Ouch!" said Babs. She drew her arm away and abandoned forthwith any effort to be helpful.

It was Peter who saw that Linda was stranded and set her on the way to the next classroom. Her surge of irritation began to die down, but now she felt more determined than ever to find as little that was good in Cedarhill High as possible. The Markham incident only pointed up the small town aspects. No big city high school teacher would know personal details of new students' lives on the first day of school. She liked the impersonal flavor of the city better. New daughter indeed!

She walked through the rest of the day without very much interest in where she went or what happened. At lunch time in the cafeteria she slipped away from Peter and ate by herself. Babs went home for lunch, but Linda had no wish to sit at Mrs. Burr's table any oftener than she had to. Mother simply had to get home by tomorrow!

There were other seniors at her table, but they laughed and talked among themselves and made no effort to open their circle to receive her. Once or twice she caught a glance directed her way, but she turned her head indifferently and each time the girl swung her attention quickly back to her companions.

Linda had never particularly enjoyed the echoing reaches of the big bare lunchroom of her New York school, but now she felt almost nostalgic for the bigness and the clatter. Sound had actually been deadened in this room and an effort made to give it the more gracious appearance of a dining room. Bright draperies hung at the windows and there were plants along the sills. But to Linda, in her mood of resistance, it looked unnatural and fussy for a school cafeteria.

- Not until she was finishing the piece of chocolate layer cake she had chosen for dessert, did she notice another lone diner occupying a solitary place in the midst of companions who paid no attention to him. Gordon Kenyon had a book open beside his plate and again his attention was absorbed by the printed page. Maybe that was a good idea, Linda thought. If you had a book to read the time would pass more quickly, and you wouldn't have to bother avoiding curious glances. There was a bookcase in the Stevens living room. Tonight she'd investigate and see what might be readable.

Now and then she found herself in a classroom with Gordon Kenyon, but for the most part their paths did not cross. If he recognized her as the girl on the train, he gave no sign. Oddly enough, considering that he was a musician, he was majoring in science, while Linda was taking the academic course. Not until last period in sociology did the boy from New York suddenly make his presence felt.

Miss Atwater, the teacher, had thrown the period open for discussion of current events and the class was not responding with any particular enthusiasm. What happened on the other side of the world did not interest them at the moment and Linda was listening a bit scornfully to the apathetic discussion, though not attempting to join in herself. Her father had always been vitally interested in world events and he had talked about them to Linda even before she had been able to absorb much of his conversation. Newspaper reading, the reading of editorials as well as news, had long ago become a daily habit with her.

But there was a warm September somnolence in the air, unlike the cool of early morning, and the first day of school was proving too much for the students of Cedarhill High. The teacher, a small, lively little woman, had done her best to stir the lagging interest of the class without result. Into this sleepy atmosphere of droning voice and inattention, Gordon Kenyon's quiet tones were like an electric current, whipping everyone to startled alertness.

My goodness, Linda thought, he was contradicting the teacher! Courteously, firmly, but in a manner of quiet conviction, he was pointing out errors he felt she had made in her statement about the recent occurrences in Greece.

Without exception the class craned to look at him, but he went on calmly as if not an eye were upon him. Good for him! Linda cheered silently. Here was the East Coast showing the Middle West a thing or two. She wished she hadn't been so lost in her own personal concerns for the last few weeks so that she scarcely knew what was going on outside the range of her immediate surroundings. Maybe she could have jumped into this too.

It was good just to listen to him speak. No flat Middle West "a's" in his words, no slurring of a single "ing." He sounded like home and she loved it. Somehow, she had to get better acquainted with Gordon Kenyon.

Proud because he was from New York, and a little amused at the astonishment and sudden interest which swept the room, Linda looked at the faces around her. There was interest in Peter's eyes, and something like admiration. Babs looked both interested and annoyed, and Linda wondered what the other girl was thinking. It was probable that Babs was more interested in the boy than in foreign affairs. Miss Atwater was plainly delighted.

"You've put the case very well, young man," she said crisply. "I'm not sure that I agree with you, but I'm glad to see that one member of the class knows that there are events which concern him going on beyond the confines of Main Street. May I ask the authority for your opinion?"

Gordon explained quietly, undisturbed by the sudden attention riveted upon him. He mentioned the name of a diplomat with whom he and his father had had lunch before he had left New York. It was no secret, he explained, but a matter that would soon be in the papers.

Miss Atwater accepted his contribution and turned back to the class. "I want every one of you to interest yourselves in this affair in Greece. Watch the papers. See what you can find in recent periodicals. Prepare a report for me by the end of the week and then perhaps we can take up a sensible discussion with the rest of you joining in."

The bell rang in the middle of the groan that went round the room and she waved her hands at them in dismissal. The seniors thronged toward the door, buzzing over the incident.

Linda found herself walking behind Babs and Peter.

"Did you ever hear anything like it?" Babs demanded of the world in general. "His father moves in diplomatic circles. But naturally. There's New York snootiness for you!"

What Peter answered, Linda did not hear, for she dropped back and let the others go ahead of her out of the room. She hoped Babs's remark had not reached the ears of Gordon Kenyon, but she was afraid it had. He had picked up his books in a leisurely manner and was moving toward the door as if he walked in a world he occupied alone. He'd have gone by without seeing her, Linda was sure, if she had not gathered her courage and spoken to him quickly.

"Good for you!" she said. "I'm glad you showed this small town something."

He had gray eyes, she noted as he glanced at her. Rather a cool, remote gray. "Thanks," he said briefly and went past her out the door without a second look. You'd never have guessed they'd been dinner companions on a train.

Linda could feel anger rising inside her. She had only meant to offer her friendship, like one outsider to another, but he had shown plainly that he wanted no intrusion of that sort upon his privacy.

Babs had turned back to watch. "Maybe he thought you wanted his autograph," she said in a tone that carried the length of the corridor. "I told you he was snooty."

"Sh-sh," Peter warned. "Papa will wash your mouth out. You're sore because he was the only one in the room who hadn't dropped back to first grade."

Babs sniffed and hurried down the corridor toward their section room.

Peter smiled wryly at Linda. "Problem child, isn't she?"

"Oh, I don't know," Linda said, a little surprised to find herself coming to Babs's defense. "He was pretty superior, don't you think?"

Peter shrugged. "Perhaps he had a right to be."

"Maybe. But he didn't have to be unfriendly too."

"I wonder," Peter said. "I wonder if he really is unfriendly."

That was too much for Linda and she followed Babs feeling thoroughly disgruntled. The first day in Cedarhill High was over. It had not been a pleasant day. She thought of Liz and the others back in little Old Manhattan and a sore place throbbed deep inside her.

9 The Khan Attacks

The fight between the Roughneck and Genghis Khan—
if so one-sided an affair could be called a fight—took
place after dinner that night.

On the way home from school Linda stopped at
Peter's and met his mother, a plump, sparkling little
woman who reminded her faintly of Liz's mother. Then
she went out to the back yard to greet Roughy. The
little dog was moping in the shade of a tree, his head on
his paws, his tail listless. But at Linda's whistle he
turned into a ball of ecstasy, leaping at her with little
yaps of joy.

"I couldn't get him to eat a thing," Mrs. Crowell
said. "I think he was lonesome for a friend."

Linda picked the little dog up in her arms and held
him fiercely close. There had been enough banishment
for Roughy. He was *not* going to be put in a damp
basement and he was not going to be sent away from
her again.

"I'm taking him with me," she told Peter and his
mother. "I know he'll eat for me."

They went straight across to the Stevens house and
out to the kitchen. She paid no attention to Mrs. Burr's
half-hearted objections, but raided the icebox for tidbits
that would please Roughy. There must have been battle
in her eye, because not even Roddy said a word about
Genghis Khan's possible displeasure.

Warm afternoon sun streamed through the windows
over the sink and made a bright square of light on the
green linoleum, spotlighting Roughy while he gobbled

the food ravenously and wagged a furious thank you
with his tail at the same time.

"What are you going to do with him now?" Roddy
asked.

Linda looked up from where she knelt on the floor
beside the Roughneck. "He's going to stay in the house.
He's not going to be put in the basement and he's not
going to be sent across the street. I'm going to keep him
with me. If your sister's cat doesn't like dogs, he'd
better stay out of the way."

Roddy widened his blue eyes to circles of astonishment. Apparently no one had ever questioned the
Khan's reign before. But he offered no objection, and
after a moment he went outside whistling, having lost
interest in the affair.

Nevertheless, in spite of her bravado, Linda was
reasonably cautious until dinnertime. She did not take
Roughy up to Babs's room (she could never think of it
as being *her* room too). When she went into the living
room to study the bookshelves, she kept him carefully
beside her. He was so glad to have her back that he
made no effort to leave her side. Finding nothing
among the books which appealed to her at the moment,
she settled down in a big chair with her school assign-
ments for the next day, and Roughy stretched out on
the floor with his nose against the tip of her shoe.

Babs had disappeared after school, but she showed
up at dinnertime and commented at once on the Roughneck's presence in the house.

"He can't stay inside," she announced. "There'll be
trouble."

"All right, there'll be trouble," Linda said lightly. "If
they get into a row your cat will learn to leave my dog
alone. I'm not going to have Roughy treated like an
outlaw any longer."

Babs shrugged indifferently. "Okay. But whatever
happens is on your head."

Supper was as gloomy an affair as it had been the
night before, with Mrs. Burr chattering animatedly, but
dully about matters of interest to her, and no one else
paying much attention.

They were just getting up from the table when the

uproar started. Roughy had gone into the hall and was at the foot of the stairs barking wildly.

"There they go!" Roddy cried excitedly and rushed to the front of the house so as not to miss the show.

Linda hurried after him, but everything seemed to happen at once. Before she could pick Roughy up he had started yapping up the stairs toward the Khan who stood his ground on the top step, every tawny hair on end, until he was twice his already regal size.

"Sic 'em!" Roddy shouted. "Sic 'em, you!" There was no telling which animal he was urging into the fray, probably both.

Before Linda could so much as call the Roughneck back, Genghis Khan launched his attack. From the top step he flung himself downward like a streak of tawny lightning, to land on Roughy's neck. The dog yelped in pained astonishment and came sliding and slipping back down the stairs, trying to shake off the spitting, furious creature which clung to him with embedded claws.

Babs stepped back out of the path of the whirling dervish the Roughneck had turned into. "Serves your dog right. I told you what would happen."

Linda started for the spitting, yelping mass and might have been bitten or scratched if Mrs. Burr had not come to the rescue and separated the two with the armed force of a broom.

Even when shooed to a distance, the Khan showed no willingness to retreat, but stood on his tiptoes, his back arched in indignation, ready to take on the enemy again if the opportunity offered. Linda gave him no chance. She swept Roughy into her arms and carried him upstairs to examine his wounds. Roddy followed her to the bathroom and stood in the doorway watching interestedly while Linda knelt on the bath rug beside the little dog.

"I guess our Khan's the champ all right," Roddy said. "I guess he can lick your ol' dog any time he wants to."

Linda hated the angry tears that sprang into her eyes. She wanted to do something furious and desperate—take that horrible cat out and drown it, or box

Roddy's ears until he screamed. She had never been so violently angry in all her life, yet she could only kneel here and cry. It was awful to be angry and helpless at the same time.

"Serves him right!" Roddy echoed Babs's words. "Guess you'll keep that ol' dog out of the way after this. Guess you'll tie him up outside some place. Guess you'll—"

"Stop it, Roddy!" Surprisingly, that was Babs's voice. "Stop it right now! How would you like to have a cat land on your neck? Stop being so mean!"

Babs dropped to her knees beside Linda and reached gentle hands to the Roughneck.

"Is he badly hurt?"

"What do you think?" Linda demanded stormily, brushing the back of her hand upward across a cheek to stop a rolling tear.

So carefully that Roughy scarcely winced, Babs separated the hair on his neck to show the claw marks. "I don't think they're deep," she said. Then she looked up at Roddy who was still staring in astonishment at this changed Babs. "You know that disinfectant the vet gave us the time the Khan got hurt on a nail? It's in the basement. Go get it. And hurry!"

Linda held the trembling little dog in her arms and wished that Babs would go away. It didn't make it any better for her to be helpful when it was too late. When Roddy brought the bottle from the basement, she took it quickly from his hands.

"If you'll just leave us alone, I'll take care of this," she said. "Having so many people around makes him nervous."

Babs hesitated for a moment and then pushed Roddy ahead of her out of the room. When they'd gone, Linda read the directions on the bottle, got some cotton from the bathroom cabinet and went to work on Roughy's wounds.

When the ordeal was over, she carried him downstairs and set him on the walk in front of the house. He seemed a little subdued, but not very much the worse for wear. It was she herself who was on the verge of trembling collapse. Her anger had left her emotionally spent. All she wanted at the moment was to get away from this house, away from Babs and that unpleasant little boy with the cruel streak in him. She didn't even want Peter Crowell to look out and see her here, and perhaps come over to sympathize because of what had happened. She wanted to put distance between herself and anyone she knew in Cedarhill. What she'd have liked best would have been to put distance between herself and the very town. But that wasn't possible, not at the moment.

She picked the Roughneck up, but he squirmed and wanted to be set down. Probably carrying him hurt his sore neck. So she put him down again and walked slowly out to the sidewalk. He trotted along after her, willing enough to go for a walk.

The evening was soft and pleasant. The sleepy warmth of the day had given place to the coolness of wide-awake early evening and a little breeze ruffled the leaves of the big elms that arched above the street.

There was something soothing about the quiet, broken only by the sound of radio music drifting through open windows, and the shouts of children playing outside. Gradually Linda's inner trembling died down. She couldn't feel peaceful and she was far from contented. The moment she allowed her thoughts to stray back over the events that had happened since her arrival in Cedarhill, she began to grow angry again. But an old trick her father had taught her came to her aid. She could almost hear his voice advising her. Almost. It was strange and a little sad about voices. They were such a distinctive part of a person. Yet, while you could remember a face that was gone, remember the expression of the mouth and eyes, and recall exactly the familiar gestures, the tone of a voice escaped you so quickly. She would know her father's voice anywhere, yet when she tried to remember how it had sounded, she could not. But the words remained. She would never lose them.

"When you're upset," he'd say, "it doesn't do much good to try to think things out right then. You need to wait till you're in a calmer, more sensible state. You have to find a way to shove all the troublesome

thoughts out of your mind temporarily until you're
ready to look at them. You can't do that just by will
power. They won't go away."

That was true. She'd been trying now to shove them
back, but they crowded in helter-skelter—angry
thoughts that stirred her up again.

"Think about little things," he'd said. "Think about
the pattern a crack makes in the sidewalk. Wonder
where that ant is going. Wonder who lives behind that
window up there where there's a geranium on the sill.
It'll work because you can't think of two things at the
same time."

She tried it now. They'd turned away from Elm
Street, and the road they'd chosen wound downhill in a
curve. She wondered where it led and why it broke
away from the straight crisscross pattern of the other
streets. She studied the graceful drooping of a willow,
trying to understand the feathery pattern of many twigs
that made the whole so lovely to the eye. If the sun was
right and there were contrasting lights and shadows,
that tree might make a good picture.

Someone ought to spank Roddy good and hard. She
almost wished she *had* boxed his ears. He ought to be
shown what pain was like so that he would not find the
pain of a small dog a matter for entertainment.

Whoops! That was the wrong trail for thoughts to
take. Quick, back to the scene around her.

"It looks as if there might be a park down there,"
she told Roughy. "Want to go down and explore?"

Aside from moving a little gingerly, the Roughneck
seemed to have recovered from the experience better
than she had. He wagged his tail, willing enough to cut
away from the beaten path.

They crossed a weed-grown vacant lot to a crum-
bling stone wall near the willow. Linda lifted Roughy
over and then found a toe hold and pulled herself to
the top. The drop to the soft earth on the other side was
a short one and she turned to look downhill toward the
glint of rosy sunset on water. What she had taken for
the open area of a park was in reality a river.

The bank slanted steeply down and bushes and
shrubbery crowded the water's edge. Beyond their

green tops she could see the narrow strip of water cutting through the town. Here was a perfect hideaway for a girl who wanted to be alone until she got her perspective straightened out.

"Come along, Roughy," she called and plunged down the bank, catching at bushes, to keep from slipping, her feet sinking here and there into muddy patches which a day's sunshine had not had time to dry out.

There were rocks along the water's edge and they followed them upstream for a way, until shrubbery cut in again to bar their path. The exploring fever was strong in Linda now, so up the bank they climbed again, to circumvent the bushes and slide down to the water's edge beyond them.

But this time they reached the bank to find someone there ahead of them. A few yards away a boy sat with his back to the bank. He had a pile of small stones beside him and he was flinging them one after another out across the water. Linda recognized the gesture. He was trying clumsily to make them skip.

"That's not the way!" Linda called impulsively. "You've got to throw a stone so it sort of skims across the surface before it lands."

He turned to look at her and they both stared in surprise. The boy was Gordon Kenyon, the last person in the world to whom she'd have cared to offer advice.

For a moment she thought he would turn away as he had that afternoon in school, but instead he gave her a slow smile that seemed a little uncertain around the corners.

"I guess I looked pretty silly," he said. "But I've never been around water much, except the ocean, and that's not such a good place for stone skipping."

Somehow, with his words and that odd little half smile, her feeling toward him softened. After all, he was someone from home, even if he had behaved in so superior a fashion.

"Look," she said quickly, "I'll show you how."

She selected a flat stone and drew her arm back in a boyish throw that sent the stone zipping out across the water in three distinct skips.

"Neat," he admitted. "I guess you need to learn that when you're about ten. You must not have spent your summers in New York as a kid."

"Oh, but I did," Linda said. "You know where I learned how to skip stones? In Central Park. My father taught me."

Gordon Kenyon gave up his effort at stone skipping and stretched himself on the grassy bank, his long legs out before him. Apparently he wasn't going to run away this time. Linda dropped the second stone she'd been balancing in her fingers and perched herself on a big smooth rock near the water's edge. The Roughneck looked at them inquiringly for a moment and then bounded off to investigate something in the underbrush.

"Ever been out in this part of the country before?" Gordon asked. It was the first time he'd shown any interest in asking a question.

"No!" She shook her head emphatically. And then, without entirely meaning to, but because the resentment boiling up in her needed a release, she added grimly, "I hate it here."

He looked surprised. "Why? What's wrong with Cedarhill?"

It was her turn to be surprised. "You don't like it here, do you? Don't you want to bet back home as quickly as possible?"

He considered her words soberly, as if it were not his habit to give quick answers before he'd had time to think them out. "I don't know. I think I rather enjoy being in a small place for a change."

She studied him curiously, no longer angry with him, or ill at ease. "You didn't behave as if you liked it today in school. You kept your nose in a book most of the time and didn't talk to anybody until you burst out in sociology last period."

"I didn't mean to do that." He looked away from her, plainly embarrassed. "I suppose it seemed a show-off sort of thing to do. But I did know an angle that Miss Atwater couldn't know about and I thought I ought to tell her."

"Of course. That was all right. But you acted as if the rest of us weren't there. And afterwards when I tried to talk to you—because we'd met on the train and you were from New York—well—" she couldn't tell him all the piled up reasons for her resentment against him, so she let the sentence drift off unfinished.

The sun had gone down and its red and gold cape was fading away on the horizon. From the east a darkening navy blue spread up the sky and Linda watched a first star come out, and then another. Gordon had not spoken again and she began to wish that her words had been less critical.

"You can see so much sky out here," she said. "So much all at once."

He tipped his head back to look and she watched him again. He was different from any boy she'd ever known. There was a subtle difference about him that she couldn't quite put her finger on. He seemed older, more thoughtful, but that wasn't all.

"Probably it's the goldfish influence," he said.

For a moment she was confused. What had goldfish to do with the expanse of sky? Then she realized he was answering her criticism and waited for him to go on.

"Grandmother came to visit us in New York one time when I was about nine," he said. "She didn't approve of Mother's ambitions for me. She thought if I wanted to play the piano I should be allowed to play for myself and let alone. She said something to my father about putting a child in a goldfish bowl. It took me a while to figure that out."

He picked up a stone from the pile beside him and threw it out over the water, not attempting to skip it, but tossing it in a high arc the way boys did sometimes on a baseball field. Irrelevantly she wondered if he'd ever had much chance to play baseball.

"I used to study the goldfish in the bowl at home after that until I could understand what she meant. People could watch them all the time. They were always out on a stage. But they didn't seem to mind. In fact, they didn't seem to know that creatures who weren't goldfish existed, and I thought it would be a good idea to use the same technique. Then I could just go my own way, no matter how many people looked at me as if I were Exhibit A."

He had not explained to her who he was. He had taken it for granted that by now she knew, and yet there was no conceit in his attitude. He was used to having people know about him.

"Don't you suppose the goldfish get lonely sometimes?" she asked. "Don't you think they ever want to get acquainted with the people who stare?"

He smiled and even in the growing dusk she liked his smile. He was rather a grave person. He wouldn't smile too often. He probably wouldn't kid and offer casual insults, and bounce around the way the boys she'd known used to do. He was different. And she liked the difference.

"I don't think they get lonely," he said. "I'm not sure I do either. But I'm not quite a goldfish. I can only imitate them."

"You shouldn't do it so well," she told him. "You're nicer when you—well, when you're like you are now."

The smile went away, but he didn't seem unfriendly. "Let's talk about you. Why don't you want to like Cedarhill?"

It was funny the way he put it. He hadn't said, "Why don't you like Cedarhill?" but, "Why don't you *want* to like it?" That struck to a core she hadn't recognized before. She didn't want to like it. She hadn't wanted to like it from the moment she'd first heard she was coming here.

He folded his hands behind his head and lay back on the grass, waiting as if he knew she would tell him. Perhaps if it had been bright sunlight she wouldn't have been able to talk about herself. There was something relaxing about the soft air of the September night, with a few fireflies left over from August flitting above their heads, and the liquid whispering of the river at their feet; something relaxing to all the guards she had tried to keep up against the world. It didn't seem strange that she could talk quite easily to a boy she scarcely knew. Perhaps in a way it was easier to talk to a stranger than to someone far closer to her.

She told him about her father's death and about her

mother marrying again. About Martin Stevens, who could never replace Bob Hollis. About Babs and Roddy, who'd be the last choice she'd make for a sister and brother. Even about the fight between Roughy and Genghis Khan. While she was talking Roughy came back and stretched himself at her side, resting his head against her hand, as if he wanted to listen too.

When she finished there was a long silence. Then Gordon said, "Look at the stars!"

She tipped her head back and looked up at the millions of them bright against the deep blue of the sky. You never saw stars like that in New York. The nearer, man-made stars shut out their light. For a moment she felt a little hurt, even a bit ashamed of giving her confidences so easily when he made no comment. But the feeling went away as she looked at the sky. There was nothing Gordon could say; nothing she wanted him to say. She had needed someone to listen. He had recognized her need.

"I've got an idea," he said, jumping to his feet and extending a hand to pull her up after him. "It's a grand night for a ride and I've got Grandmother's car parked back there. Let's get acquainted with Cedarhill."

She tried to see her watch, but the dusk was too thick by now. She had a feeling that more time had slipped by than she realized. If her mother had been home, she'd have phoned to let her know where she was and that she'd be out a while longer. But who at the Stevens house would worry about her, or care what she did? Probably the longer she stayed away, the happier they'd all be. She made her decision quickly.

"We'd love it," she said. "That is, if Roughy is invited too."

Gordon made it clear that any and all of Linda's friends were welcome and they climbed the bank to the street and the waiting car.

10 Reprimand

The ride with Gordon was wonderfully satisfying. Not that it made her like Cedarhill any better. New York streets hid adventure around every corner. She and her father had found miracles in junk shop windows, hilarious misfits in swank Park Avenue shops. Cedarhill's streets were quiet, lacking in excitement of any kind.

The stores downtown on Main Street were closed and no life stirred except around the corner drugstore and the town's one movie house. The lighted shop windows looked dull and second-rate, unimaginative.

"Wait till you see Main Street on Saturday night," Gordon said. "Broadway at the theater hour has nothing on this. Farmers bring their families in and everything comes to life. Every parking spot is taken and they practically turn out the police force to handle traffic."

Linda recalled a phrase she'd read in a story: "Saturday night town." Cedarhill would be one of those.

"On my left," she said in her best tourist-guide manner, "you'll find the town square and the courthouse. I presume that's what that red brick monstrosity must be."

Gordon looked out the car window and nodded. "I expect so. But don't be so hard on town squares. I like the tradition. And somehow I like old buildings with vines growing all over them. Maybe that one's not exactly pretty, but it's a solid citizen. It belongs."

"You and Peter!" Linda cried. "I'm afraid I lack the sentimental small town spirit. This ride's been fun, but it hasn't sold me on small towns. I want to get back to tall spires and bright lights as soon as I can."

But while the small town aspects only added to her dissatisfaction and the general scorn with which she regarded Cedarhill, she enjoyed Gordon's quiet companionship. She could talk to him as she could talk to Liz, and yet there was something satisfying in the fact that he wasn't just another girl. She'd never particularly wanted to talk to a boy before. Mostly they were so busy with their own interests they didn't bother to listen anyway. You just listened to them. Gordon had real ideas about things and he knew how to express them, but he gave her a chance too, and really listened when she talked.

When he drove her home and left her in front of the Stevens house, she was sorry the evening was over. She wanted to let him know how much he had done for her. When she'd set off on her walk earlier in the evening with Roughy, she had been in a state of quivering emotion. It had been as if the Khan's claws had torn her as well as Roughy. Then she'd met a boy sitting on a rock throwing stones in a river, and a healing had begun. It didn't make any sense. It didn't have to. It just was.

Only now when she wanted to tell him what he'd done for her, wanted to thank him, she felt shy and ill at ease. And oddly enough, the moment she opened the car door and stepped out he went abruptly back to his goldfish bowl.

"Th-thanks a lot," was all she could manage.

He nodded remotely and she realized that she was standing stupidly beside the car and that he couldn't drive away until she turned up the walk. She wished he would say something about seeing her again, though that was silly because of course he would see her again. He'd see her the very next day in school.

But he said nothing, so she waved a little too energetically and turned to set Roughy down on the sidewalk. When she straightened again, the car was halfway down the block. She looked up to note with surprise that the Stevens house was ablaze with light. There were lights upstairs and downstairs, even a light on the porch. She glanced at her watch as she went up the steps and saw that it was nearly ten o'clock.

A vague misgiving stirred inside her. Ten o'clock wasn't an alarmingly late hour, but she had gone off without leaving word with anyone. And even if Mrs. Burr was not especially interested in her welfare, she did have a responsibility in the matter of running the household while Martin Stevens was away.

Roddy, who should have been in bed long ago, came out on the veranda dressed in his pajamas.

"Oh, boy!" he cried when he saw her. "Are you ever going to catch it! Oh, boy!"

Suddenly she realized the meaning of the brightly lighted house and pushed past Roddy, with the Roughneck bounding at her heels. She knew what all those lights meant now.

"Mother!" she called. "Mother, are you home?"

Martin Stevens was coming down the stairs and he looked at her gravely. "Hello, Linda. We've been worried about you."

She didn't care how worried he had been, or anything about him. "Where's Mother?" she demanded. "I didn't know she was going to get home tonight."

"She's upstairs——" he began, but there was the rustle of a taffeta housecoat behind him and Linda saw her mother at the top of the stairs.

She took the steps two at a time and caught her up in an embrace that made her gasp for breath, even though she was laughing, her eyes bright with tears Linda knew were happy tears. The Roughneck leaped and yipped around them, demanding his own share of the welcome.

"Why weren't you here before?" Linda demanded, knowing her words were unreasonable even as she spoke, but not caring. "I needed you! I needed you so much!"

Her mother looked past her down the stairs to where Martin stood leaning against the banister and wiggled her fingers at him. "See you later. Linda and I have to visit. Come along, honey."

Linda experienced a brief sense of triumph because Martin had been dismissed for the moment in favor of herself. She followed her mother into the big front room that she and Martin were to share and when she dropped into an easy chair Linda curled up on the floor at her mother's knee, just the way she'd done for special talks ever since little girl days. Roughy lay down nearby and regarded them both with loving, unblinking eyes, while his tail thumped the floor joyously.

Her mother pulled her head down against her knee and Linda felt her fingers stroking back of her ears and down to the nape of her neck in the old soothing way.

"I can't tell you how distressed we were when the plane was grounded," her mother said, "and we knew we wouldn't be here in time to give you a proper welcome."

Linda stiffened against that "we." She wanted it to be "I"—just her mother alone. Martin didn't count. What he felt, or thought, or said, or did, wasn't ever going to count with Linda Hollis.

"Nobody even met me at the station," she went on stormily. "That is, nobody from this house. If it hadn't been for the boy across the street there'd have been no one at all to meet my train. Babs doesn't want me here. And the little boy is horrible. Roughy has no place to stay and they have a cat who's scratched him all to pieces."

Her mother made little hushing, soothing sounds and went on stroking her hair. "I'm sorry, honey. This wasn't the way we planned it. Of course we'll find a place for Roughy and I'm sure you and Babs will get along fine once you've had time to get used to a new situation."

Linda raised her head and looked up at her mother with eyes she knew were stormy. "I don't even have a room of my own! Babs and I have to be practically in each other's laps whether we like it or not."

"I know," her mother said gently. "The disadvantages of a change always look bigger than anything else at first. But there are advantages. You'll see, honey. Let's move softly for a little while and give things a chance to work out."

Linda shook her head. "They'll never work out! I want to go back to New York. I want to be with people who know me and like me. It's easy for you—you want to be here. Everything's ready for you to just walk in and be at home—but they don't want me!"

The fingers paused in their stroking. "*Is* everything ready for me to walk in? I wonder."

Again Linda looked up at her mother.

"Perhaps it isn't as easy for me as you think," Joyce went on. "Babs and Roddy didn't give me any warmer a reception when I arrived tonight than they gave you. And, Linda, I have to make good at this new job I've taken on. There can't be any running away for me. And maybe I'm a little bit scared. Maybe I need some help from my own daughter."

Linda got up and moved restlessly about the big bedroom. She didn't want to listen to this kind of talk. She didn't want to find herself enlisted in some quiet little campaign of her mother's before she knew what had happened to her. She mustn't go soft and start getting her mother's viewpoint, or she'd be caught here for good.

"You knew you'd be stepping into this situation when you married Martin," Linda said coldly. "You asked for it—with all the attached problems. I didn't. Well, I guess I'll run along to bed. There's no use trying to work anything out tonight. See you tomorrow."

"Linda—" she heard the catch in her mother's voice, but she went out of the room quickly before she might find herself giving in to it. Above all, she mustn't go soft. Not if she didn't want to be caught in this stupid little town forever.

She was dismayed to find that Martin was waiting for her in the hall.

"I'd like to talk to you for a moment, Linda," he said. "Will you come in here?" He opened a door on his right and turned on a light.

Linda snapped her fingers at Roughy as a summons to follow her and went into the small room. She could see now why there could be no extra bedroom for her. The room that might have been hers was Martin Stevens's study. There were more bookshelves here, running across one end of the room, and other shelves filled with a mixture of odds and ends—rocks and pieces of wood, cases of mounted specimens, animal and vegetable. All this she noted with a single resentful glance.

Set out from the side wall of the room was a huge desk, piled untidily high with papers, folders, books. On the wall above it hung a framed charcoal sketch of a woman's face. It was the same face which looked out from the picture on Babs's dressing table. Now that Martin Stevens had married again, Linda thought, the least he could do would be to take down all pictures of his first wife.

He saw that she'd noticed the picture and nodded in its direction. "Babs did a sketch of her mother from an old photograph. Pretty good, don't you think?"

So those sketches and water colors that adorned Babs's room had been done by Babs herself. But Linda had no particular interest in whether the sketch was good or not. She seated herself stiffly in the chair Martin pulled out for her opposite his desk, while he took the swivel chair behind the desk. It was just like being interviewed by the school principal, Linda thought, and just as unpleasant. She waited in an unfriendly silence, broken only by the sniffing sounds Roughy made as he investigated the room.

"I won't keep you long, Linda," he said, smiling at her uncertainly, as if she had been a child whom he did not quite know how to handle. "It's late and this is our first night home. But I do want you to know how much your mother and I hope to build this household into a happy, affectionate family. Babs and Roddy need a mother and I hope you and I—"

She made a quick little sound of rejection and he paused. There was a brass paper knife on the desk and he picked it up, tapped its handle against his palm as if the gesture might help him to find the right words.

"I hope you and I will be friends," he concluded quietly.

They wouldn't be, she thought, staring at him coldly. She could never be a friend of this man who had cut in between herself and her mother and upset the happy pattern of her own life. He was foolish if he thought she could ever regard him as a friend.

He must have recognized her complete resistance to his words, for he sighed and tossed the paper knife back on the desk. When he spoke again his manner was as stiff as her own.

"Your mother was really very concerned tonight," he said, "and so was I. Mrs. Burr had no idea where you'd gone."

"I took Roughy for a walk," Linda informed him. She had no intention of telling him all the details of that walk. She'd tell her mother about Gordon Kenyon later on. But all that was none of Martin's business.

"Three hours seems a very long time for a walk," Martin pointed out. "I won't make an issue of it this time, but we do have a rule in this house which applies to Roddy and Babs, and which will have to apply to you as well. After this, when you go out, let someone know where you are going and how late you expect to be."

He was actually disciplining her! As if she'd been ten years old, instead of a beginning senior in high school. It was humiliating.

"Is that all?" she asked.

He looked at her as if she might have been some especially curious bug from a specimen case and she had that museumish feeling again that she'd experienced with him before.

Then he nodded. "That's all as far as I am concerned. But perhaps you'd like to say something, Linda. I understand things haven't gone too well since you arrived. Perhaps there are requests you'd like to make?"

She seized the opportunity quickly. "There is one. I want a place where Roughy can stay without being clawed by that cat. I won't have him put down in the basement where it's damp and unhealthy. A dog house in the back yard might be all right while it's warm, but it won't do when it gets cold. Look! Look what that cat did to him!"

She called Roughy over and parted the hair on his neck to show the claw marks. Martin bent to look at them.

"He chased the Khan up the stairs, didn't he?"

Of course, she thought. Put the blame on poor Roughy. Everyone in the house was against them.

"What do you expect of a dog?" she demanded.

"It's too bad," he said, not unkindly. "But I think things will be all right now. He won't chase the cat again."

"You mean I'm just to let Roughy run around the house without any protection?"

"Why not? After all, you can't furnish him with a police guard. He'll have to learn to take care of himself. I think it will be all right."

She was so indignant she couldn't answer. She snapped her fingers at Roughy and walked to the door without even a good night. Out in the hall Roddy was waiting at the top of the stairs. He grinned at her in impish delight.

"Bet you caught it!" he chortled. "I told you he was sore. I bet——"

"You stop it!" Linda told him sharply, not caring in the least that Martin might hear, not caring about anything at all because there seemed so little left in her immediate world to care about.

She picked the Roughneck up in her arms and started for the head of the stairs. She wasn't quite sure what she meant to do, but she wasn't going to be parted from her one friend tonight. Since he couldn't sleep in that cat's den, she would sleep down on the living room couch, with Roughy on the floor beside her. Martin had not come out of his study and there was no one to stop her. Not that anyone could stop her, short of using force. She didn't mean to take one single order from anyone tonight.

Oddly enough, it was Babs who changed her plans. She came to the door of her room in her pajamas and with her hair up in pin curls.

"You go back to bed!" she told Roddy across the hall. "If you don't, I'll tell Dad that you've been up three times tonight."

Roddy scampered out of sight and Babs turned to Linda. "You can bring your dog in here, if you like," she said in a completely matter-of-fact tone. "I bedded Genghis Khan downstairs. He can stand it for once."

She did not wait for an answer, but disappeared into her room without a backward glance. Linda experienced a moment of complete limpness. It seemed queer not to have to defy anyone, not to have to resist or fight any more. From the last quarter she had expected had come a reprieve. She didn't understand why Babs had made this concession, but she was too weary to worry about it.

Later when both girls were in bed and the Roughneck curled up on the rug beside Linda's bed, Babs spoke in a whisper from the darkness across the room.

"I was looking out the window," she said, "and I saw you come home. That was some car. Who was the boy?"

Somehow she didn't mind telling Babs. In a way she was a little proud of being able to tell her.

"It was Gordon Kenyon. Roughy and I went for a walk down by the river and he was there. He took me for a ride all around Cedarhill."

Babs's low whistle was admiring. "You're a fast worker. What's he like?"

"Nice," Linda said. "He—he's not like any of the boys I know. But he's nice."

"He sure didn't act it in school today," Babs said.

Somehow Linda didn't want to explain about the goldfish technique. That was Gordon's affair. She wouldn't discuss it with another girl. It was safer to change the subject than to answer.

"I saw the charcoal sketch you drew of your mother," she said. She could regard that sketch in a pleasanter light now. "I suppose you drew the things in this room too? You're really good."

"Oh, that!" There was a curious lack of interest in Babs's voice. "I just have a knack. It doesn't mean anything."

"Don't you want to do anything with it? Go to art school or anything?"

"You mean be a career girl? Not me! Too much trouble."

There was no more talk after that and Linda was glad enough to lie there in the quiet darkness with confused thoughts running through her mind, thoughts of resentment and hurt, until she grew sleepy. She longed for a return to the old comfortable relationships with her mother that now seemed so far in the past. She resented the man who had tried to step into her father's place. She felt irritation against Roddy and a strange mixture of half liking, half disliking toward the strange girl, Babs. And finally, just as she fell asleep, a comfortably warm, dreamy feeling that centered about Gordon Kenyon, whom she liked better than any boy she'd ever known, swept over her.

11 Linda Gets Involved

Perhaps breakfast the next morning was not a huge success, but at least it was a change from the Mrs. Burr variety.

When Linda came downstairs with the Roughneck at her heels, there was a tense moment during which she was afraid there'd be another dog and cat fracas. The Khan happened to be passing regally through the lower hall, but when he saw the Roughneck coming down, he stood his ground with arched back and made ready for battle.

The Roughneck remembered defeat, however. He took one look and scooted across the hall and out of sight toward the kitchen. The Khan's indignation subsided. Pursuit was evidently beneath his dignity.

Linda went into the dining room to find her mother bustling about, looking rested and cheerful and pretty in a gingham house frock tied with an organdy bow. It was one of Joyce's homemaking rules that no female had to look untidy just because housework was in order. After Mrs. Burr, she was a treat to the eye. Even Roddy seemed to be regarding her with a wary, but admiring gaze.

" 'Morning, honey," she greeted Linda as if nothing had gone amiss the night before. "It's nice to be home."

Linda winced at the word "home," but her resentment toward her mother had died away in the night. Martin was to blame, not Joyce.

She slipped an arm around her mother's shoulders.

"I'm glad you're back. You look good to me. I want to hear about your trip and how you liked Oregon."

"We'll have a visit the minute you get home from school," her mother promised. "Do you want your usual poached egg this morning?"

For a change there was no burnt toast or lumpy cereal. Under Joyce's supervision Mrs. Burr spent less time talking and more time attending to the food. Just the same there was a strained uncomfortable feeling about the breakfast table.

Babs and Roddy watched and were cautious. They didn't respond to the new Mrs. Stevens's efforts at banter. In fact, when she tried to tease Roddy with a little joke about the way he gobbled his food, he stared at her solemnly and waited to see what would happen next. There was a sort of waiting feeling about the entire meal. Babs and Roddy watched the newcomers and waited. Linda watched Martin and waited. An armed truce, Linda thought. No warfare right at the moment, but trouble was waiting under the surface, ready to break out. The house was a camp divided against itself. Linda could not be sure for the moment whose side she was on, or whether she stood alone.

Only Martin seemed unaware of any tension. He treated the three younger members of the family as if they were all the same age, Roddy's age, which meant paying little attention to them and not including them to any extent in the conversation. He wanted to talk to his wife, and talk to her he did. Stuffy talk about his Museum and plans to get the town more interested in it; make it more a part of Cedarhill life. Roddy listened raptly, but Babs and Linda ate their breakfasts in silence, letting his words drone over their heads.

Linda caught the word "diorama" now and then. The Cedarhill Museum did not own a single diorama and Martin considered this method a far more dramatic way of presenting natural history than any other which had been devised.

"What's a diorama?" Roddy demanded.

Martin explained with more enthusiasm than he usually showed. "It's something like a miniature stage set. It has special lighting and there's a painted background and a foreground scene made of real objects. When it has been skillfully done, you can hardly tell where the real things blend into the painted ones. You can show a woods scene and put in small animals, or modeled figures so that the whole looks very convincing."

Roddy and Linda's mother were the only ones interested.

Later, when they started for school, Babs and Linda found Peter waiting for them again. This was not, he assured them cheerfully, to be regarded as a permanent habit.

"Beginning tomorrow you find your own way to school," he announced. "But today plans are under way. Big plans, though nobody knows it yet but me. I need a couple of confederates."

Babs yawned as if she were not yet quite awake. "Beware, Linda," she warned. "When Peter wants a confederate it means he's going to put you to work. Just say 'no' without going any further and you'll be playing safe. Or don't bother—I'll say it for us. No, Peter, *no*. We are not going to take up stamp collecting, or selling magazines, or organizing civic groups for the betterment of downtrodden freshmen. Whatever it is, the answer is 'no!' "

Peter grinned, unabashed. "That's the trouble with growing up across the street from a girl. She knows all about you before you open your mouth. But this plan is irresistible. Anyway it will be to you, Linda."

How young and bouncy and enthusiastic he seemed beside Gordon, Linda thought. He was nice, this Peter Crowell, but he lacked the poise and the deeper thoughtfulness of the other boy. He was just too young, that was all. He hadn't grown up yet to match his years, while Gordon had grown ahead of his years.

"This isn't my irresistible season for plans," she told him. "But go ahead. We'll listen at least."

Babs shrugged graceful shoulders. "As if we could help it when he gets started. Get it out, Peter, before you burst."

Peter moved ahead of them, walking backwards on the sidewalk, so he could face his audience and get the full benefit of the stunned admiration he apparently expected them to register.

"Photography!" he announced dramatically. "I'm going to start a photography club at school. There's never been one in this town and this is the auspicious moment."

"Shutter-snappers!" Babs mocked.

Peter did not look in the least hurt. He dropped back to walk beside Linda, paying no further attention to Babs.

"You'll be interested, won't you? I mean with all that wonderful photographic stuff lying idle, and your father being Robert Hollis, and——"

She shook her head at him gently. She didn't want to hurt Peter's feelings, or treat him the way Babs did, but a photographic club in a small town was the last thing in the world that could interest her. For one thing, the thing she couldn't explain to anyone, there was the hurt that lay in so much as looking into a camera finder. All that part of her life was tied up with her father. Without him, it was impossible to consider. She didn't want to be constantly reminded and hurt by handling his things.

"I'm sorry," she said, "but I'm not going to have much time this year for extracurricular stuff."

"Nuts!" Peter exclaimed ungallantly. "Of course you'll have time. What do you think you're going to do, make yourself into a one-sided character? The well-rounded personality—that's what we strive to develop in Cedarhill."

Linda felt tempted to join Babs's scornful laughter. As if any personality could be well rounded in Cedarhill!

"Look," Babs went on, before Linda could search for a further way of saying "no," which would still be a pleasant way, "Linda's father was a professional. She's used to being around real picture takers. A bunch of amateurs, kids at that, isn't going to interest her. Can't you see she's trying to let you down gently? Now leave her alone."

"Oh?" Peter said. And after that was silent.

For a half block they walked along without speaking, and then Babs took up the fight again, as if she hadn't already won. "Anyway, photography is a feeble sort of thing. There's nothing creative about it, as there is about painting a picture. You simply point a camera at something, snap the shutter and that's that. If you get a good shot it's accidental. There's no art about picture taking."

"Linda," Peter challenged, "are we going to let her get away with that?"

Linda shook her head. "I'm staying out of the argument," she said, but Babs's words irked her a little. This was the eternal argument the artist flung at the photographer. But photography was no imitation of a painter's art; it was a special sort of art in itself and few really good photographs were the result of chance. You had to have the sort of creative imagination Bob Hollis had had to see a picture in everyday surroundings. You had to choose the right time of day to take the picture. You had to be sure the balance of darks and lights was right and then you had to decide on exactly the right camera angle. Nevertheless, she had no intention of getting embroiled in any of this because Babs was talking of something she knew little about.

She was aware of Peter's eyes upon her hopefully and she shrugged her indifference, wishing he wouldn't look so disappointed. If he wanted to start a camera club in school, that was his affair. If she hadn't come to Cedarhill, he would have started it anyway. So why should he look at her reproachfully? She owed nothing to this small town school.

"Maybe you'll change your mind," Peter said as they reached the steps of the school. "I know Babs is right and we'd be beginners to you, but that's the very reason we need you—because you know so much more about it than the rest of us. Anyway, think it over."

She found herself thinking it over the rest of the day, trying to thrust down the prickings of her conscience. She remembered all too well that one of her father's pet hobbies had been the photography group in a New York City boys' club. He'd never hesitated to give his time and sympathy and advice to the beginner when it was wanted. She stilled the prickings by reminding herself that *she* was no professional. She was not an authority to give advice to beginners. Even though she'd been soaked in a hypo atmosphere all her life, she was only a beginner herself. The whole thing was foolish as Babs said, and she didn't mean to give it a moment's serious thought. Besides, she had other things to think about.

Gordon Kenyon, she discovered, had not gone entirely back to his goldfish bowl. He wasn't exactly oozing cordiality in all directions, but he cocked an eyebrow at her in greeting and gave her a smile that was friendly enough. She experienced a faint disappointment when he didn't seek her out, or find an opportunity to talk to her. There was no reason to mind, but she did a little.

Later in the day when Peter bore down on her in English Lit with a triumphant grin on his face, she was glad to see him. At least a girl knew where she stood with Peter.

"Guess what?" he demanded like an eager little boy.

"You've got your club," she said. "It's written all over you."

"Well, anyway, I've got us a teacher sponsor, so we're on our way. I had to have that first. And who do you think—it's Markham!"

He nodded toward the desk at the front of the room where Mr. Markham was poring over some papers.

"I thought he just went in for Shakespeare and art and stuff," Linda said.

"He does, but I've just discovered that he dabbles in darkrooms, too. He thinks the club is a good idea and we're calling an organization meeting to talk over plans right after school today. Aw, Linda, be a good scout and come. We need you."

He waited as anxiously for her answer as though the entire project hung on her acceptance, and it was impossible to steel herself to refusal.

"All right," she sighed. "I'll come. But don't count on me to take any active part. Honestly, I—I don't care much about picture taking just now."

His smile was as wide as if she had presented him with the photographic award of the year. He put a hand on her shoulder and gave her a little shake of approval.

"Good girl. Gosh, I'm glad you've come to this town," and then he was off down the hall after the next victim.

Linda looked ruefully after him. He was an engaging sort of boy, this Peter Crowell. If only he wasn't so terribly young.

Apparently his persuasive enthusiasm had made itself felt in a number of quarters because when Linda waited in their section room after school to watch the meeting shape up, she discovered that not only a number of seniors, but a sprinkling of lower classmen were interested. To her surprise, Babs put in an appearance, looking a little bored and scornful of the whole proceeding.

She regarded Linda with a cynical eye. "So he bullied you into coming, did he?"

Linda nodded. "You too?"

"Not me," Babs denied languidly. "I have an ulterior motive."

She glanced meaningly toward the door and Linda looked around to see Gordon Kenyon coming in with Peter who was talking volubly in his ear.

"The stranger in our midst interests me," Babs muttered and Linda was aware of a sidelong look from the other girl's eyes. She smiled sweetly. Not for anything would she rise to Babs's bait. After all, she had no stakes claimed in Gordon.

Mr. Markham took a back seat and left the running of the meeting entirely to Peter, a gesture Linda approved. She had known of school clubs which turned into nothing more than another class because some sponsoring teacher insisted on running everything and airing specialized knowledge. Mr. Markham seemed to feel that this project belonged to the young people and that he was there to give advice only when it was needed.

When the group was assembled and reasonably quiet, Peter stood up in front of the room and told them the details of his plan. He was no oratorical spellbinder, but his sincerity and his enthusiasm for his subject were impressive.

"This seems to be the right time for starting this sort of club," he explained, "because the Weston Camera Company has just announced a national contest for amateur groups. Several Weston enlargers are being given as prizes and we could sure use one if we set up a darkroom here at school. I've got some entry blanks and the contest rules. There are several classifications: portraiture, human interest, animals, outdoor scenes and night photos. We've got three months to come up with something worth entering."

"Where are you going to put a darkroom?" asked a boy in the front row.

"We've got a promise of that big closet back of the chemistry lab," Peter told him. "If the fellows in the carpentry shop are willing to build cabinets in the lab to hold the equipment that's been kept there, we can have the room. If we get busy right away maybe we can get a darkroom going in a couple of weeks."

"Photographic equipment costs money," someone else pointed out. "Where do we get the stuff to start out with?"

"We don't have to have the best there is," Peter said. "We'll have club dues and they'll help a little, though we don't want to make them high. Maybe some of us have stuff at home we can contribute temporarily as a loan. I've got some pans and an extra developing tank and I'm willing to lend my homemade enlarger for a while. We can buy paper out of the dues and if anybody feels especially flush——"

Linda heard her own voice breaking in unexpectedly. "I have an assortment of paper you can have."

Peter rewarded her with a pleased grin, but she felt annoyed with herself for having spoken. She had meant to do nothing but sit and listen, and here she'd gone offering the last of her supply of paper. Not that it was anything she wanted to keep. Photographic emulsions went stale and before long the stuff would be no good anyway. Nevertheless, the offer made her to some extent a participating member and she didn't want to be that.

"Thanks, Linda," Peter said. "Maybe some of you don't know, but Linda's father, Robert Hollis, was one of the country's best known news photographers. It's a real break to have Linda here because she can give us tips about the finer points of photography that would be beyond most of us."

"Beyond most of us is right," Babs put in. "Not that I'm going to be an active member. But I'll bet a lot of us don't know the ABC's of so much as developing film."

"You'll learn," Peter said cheerfully. "This sort of thing is like smallpox—it's catching. There are books in the library, and those of us who've played around with printing and developing can give a few demonstrations once we get a darkroom set up. And we can count on Linda Hollis for help."

Oh, he could, could he, Linda thought rebelliously. He really had a lot of nerve, this young man. She had been soft-headed to let herself get caught up in something like this. One step led to another and the first thing she knew—oh, goodness, he was talking directly to her again, asking for suggestions right now, of all things. She was aware of necks craning and eyes turning in her direction, and was once more aware of being an outsider, the girl from a big Eastern city who didn't belong in a small Middle Western town. Only Gordon Kenyon was really her own sort. She remembered Liz's words: "Go on out there and show 'em!"

But she didn't want to show anyone anything. All she wanted was to be quiet and go unnoticed, so that she could go on disliking Cedarhill because, as Gordon Kenyon had said, she *wanted* to dislike it. But the room was waiting. She had to say something, and suddenly she was more keenly aware of Babs's attention than that of anyone else in the room. Babs who thought photography a feeble pastime. She had a sudden desire to answer Babs that she had lacked before. Perhaps she wanted to show Gordon as well as Babs.

"Of course there's more to picture taking than the mechanical end of developing and printing and enlarging," she began. "Those are the easiest things to learn. But it takes a really creative touch to get good pictures and that means learning something about composition and about recognizing the elements of a good picture. You don't just point your camera at something and snap the shutter."

Peter nodded his approval and Linda saw his eyes meet Babs's across the room. "That's right! We have to get some angles on the artistic side too. Especially if we want to stand a chance for one of those prizes."

Babs said, "Artistic side!" under her breath and once more Linda found herself speaking up with more feeling than she intended.

"We could take some field trips, perhaps. Get out and conduct a—a sort of picture hunt."

There was a bustle of interest over that. Apparently it sounded like more fun than darkroom dabbling. The darkroom magic would get them later on, Linda suspected. Peter had to rap for order and for the first time Mr. Markham, who had been listening, entered the discussion.

"Linda's idea is an excellent one. If we get out on a picture taking trip we can hold some discussions afterward concerning the finished prints and learn a lot by our mistakes. I'm a beginner too, and I can use some criticism on my final results."

So the Photographic Club was launched on a surge of enthusiasm. A quick election of officers followed. Peter, of course, was uncontested as president. Then Gordon Kenyon asked for the floor.

"I'd like to nominate Linda Hollis for vice-president," he said quietly.

There was a stir and once more Linda was aware of the concerted gaze of strangers. She shook her head violently, but Peter was calling for a second to the nomination and the election flowed over her head as if she were not really concerned in it. There was no opposing nomination, and although Linda refrained from voting for herself, she found that whether she liked it or not Linda Hollis had been elected vice-president of the new club.

Peter beamed as if he'd invented her himself, Babs nodded cynically, and Gordon looked amused. Oh, darn! Linda thought in annoyance. She had certainly been caught that time.

Next the secretary and treasurer were voted in. A girl named Nancy Loomis became secretary and a boy they called "Owen" became treasurer.

At least, Linda tried to comfort herself, a vice-president would have few duties with so active a president as Peter on the scene.

Babs waited for her when the meeting was over. Her comment was brief and pointed. "Wow!" she said inelegantly. "Are you ever a sucker! Vice-president of the shutter-snappers!"

Peter heard her and echoed her words. "Shutter-Snappers! Barby, you're a genius. There's the name for the club. We'll vote on it first thing next meeting."

12 Musical Moment

On Saturday Linda visited the Museum for the first time. She was drawn to its doors by no irresistible urge, but only because she could not avoid the visit without turning her mother's request down flatly.

Her mother of course was familiar with the Museum and nothing would do but that she must go on Saturday and take Linda with her.

It was a clear bright day with a snap of cold in the air and they walked along briskly, Mrs. Stevens lifting her head to breathe deeply of tangy autumn scents, walking with a lift to her step that Linda had not seen for a long while. Certainly Cedarhill agreed with her mother. She was reacting to it the way Bob Hollis and his daughter had always reacted to the stir and excitement of New York. In spite of herself Linda experienced a pang. How lonesome her mother must have been for her small town all these years! Not that she'd suffered because of city life—she was always one to make the best of any situation. But there was a bloom on her now that no one could miss. As Linda had no desire to give Martin Stevens the least credit for the bloom she decided it must be due to getting back to scenes where she'd had fun as a girl.

The Museum vines looked even more dusty close up and Linda gave a superior little sniff as she walked up the steps with her mother. Peter and Gordon and their moth-eaten old vines!

Her mother led the way quickly upstairs. The walls above the stairway were hung with old prints of what Linda judged to be Midwestern scenes. Upstairs she had a brief glimpse of an art gallery on the left and a combination exhibit room and workroom on her right. Ahead, across a small hall containing tables of glass cases, was an open door to a smaller room, Martin Stevens's office.

At the moment he was engaged in a spirited discussion concerning some sort of mess in a pan on the desk before him. Every now and then he would poke it experimentally with a stick to emphasize his remarks. Beside his desk stood a little fawn of a woman regarding the sticky wet mess with alarm. "Fawn" was the word which occurred to Linda at first glance. She was a soft gray-brown color from her neat oxfords to the top of her smooth brown head. There was a shy flyaway look about her, as if she tolerated the haunts of man, but did not entirely accept them. At any moment she might be startled and disappear into some woodsy hiding place.

So engrossed was Martin in the contents of the pan that he did not notice Linda and her mother in the doorway. It was the fawn who saw them first. She smiled shyly, gently, as if she were not quite sure whether or not these newcomers were harmless.

"Good morning, Miss Foster," Mrs. Stevens said. "This is my daughter Linda. Linda, Miss Foster is the Museum librarian. Hello, Martin. What on earth is that?"

Martin nodded to them absently and gave the mixture another stir. "You see before you in embryo a diorama. An imaginative eye can detect in this pan a woodland scene, peopled with small animals."

"Flexibility," Miss Foster murmured, sounding much less woodsy than she looked. "That's what it takes to work in a museum. You are employed to do research work, to catalogue books and find ways to enlarge the reading collection. You end up digging rocks out of a mountainside or stirring up messes of papier-mâché."

"As Hallie says," Martin agreed, "we're jacks of all trades around here, but it so happens that none of the staff has gone in for making papier-mâché before. We've been experimenting, but I'm not sure we've got it right. Joyce, do you think you could run over to the public library and see if they have a book that tells how to make this stuff properly? Charge it out to the Museum."

"I'll be glad to," Mrs. Stevens said, at once the efficient and very flexible wife of a museum director. "Linda, would you like to look around while I go to the library? It isn't far. I'll be back before long."

Linda agreed uneasily. She wondered if Martin would insist on taking her about the Museum himself, explaining everything in the sort of lecture tour he had given her mother. But she realized quickly enough that she needn't worry. The moment his wife went off on her errand Martin forgot everything except the proposed diorama. He went on expounding his plans to Miss Foster, who looked at Linda with a gentle twinkle in her brown eyes.

"I have all the artistic ability of a—a flea," she murmured. "And he wants *me* to make something out of *that*."

"Child's play," Martin snorted. "If I had time I could make the thing myself. Anyone with an ounce of imagination—" his eye fell on Linda and grew alarmingly speculative. "I'll bet you could turn out the sort of thing I want if Hallie here is afraid to get her fingers sticky. There's an old smock around someplace, Linda. Hallie, get it for her and—"

Miss Foster wriggled warning fingers at her. "Run! Run for your life and leave me to my fate."

Linda backed hastily out of the room. It was not the fawn-like Miss Foster who was going to take flight, but herself.

"Oh, no!" she gasped. "I couldn't possibly. I wouldn't know the first thing—"

She saw the brief disappointment in his eyes as she moved toward the door, but knew it was not directed personally at her. He was disappointed because he hadn't been able to coax a new victim into one of his projects, not because his stepdaughter had refused to help him. Probably he didn't even remember who she was, Linda thought unreasonably as she crossed the hall and walked through the door nearest at hand. But she rather liked that little Hallie Foster, who was not nearly so much the startled fawn as she looked.

It was the art gallery she had fled to, she discovered, and began automatically circling it, looking at one picture after another, without really seeing them because of her preoccupation with her own thoughts. She had been drawn into that ridiculous photography club against her will and she was certainly not going to become involved in anything else. Especially not anything Martin Stevens wanted her to do.

At least there was some point to photography. That was something she knew a little about. But dioramas—! And she hadn't worked with papier-mâché since— well, since her first year in high school when they'd experimented a bit in art class. That could scarcely count as workable knowledge.

"She must have been quite a gal," said a familiar voice behind her.

Linda whirled, startled, to face Gordon Kenyon. "Goodness, but you frightened me! I didn't know there was anyone within miles. Who must have been quite a gal?"

"The lady in the picture," Gordon said. "I thought you were making her acquaintance."

Linda looked back at the wall. A gray-haired woman with chilly blue eyes, a firm mouth and obviously iron will, returned her gaze disapprovingly.

Linda winced. "Do you think I ought to beg her pardon? I hadn't even noticed her and I think she's annoyed. I was thinking THOUGHTS. The capital letter kind. Among other things about how a certain party nominated an unwilling lady for vice-president of a club she didn't even want to belong to."

Gordon was unabashed. "You'll have fun. And you'll do the club good too."

"I will not," Linda contradicted. "I mean to let Peter do all the work. I'm going to play hookey from every meeting I can."

Gordon pushed the matter no further, but the faintly amused look was still in his eyes.

"What are you doing here?" Linda asked. "I'm related to the place now, so I had to come and look at

their collection, but you must have walked in by your
own free will."

"I like places like this," Gordon said. "I came to
explore. Want to come along? I'm just starting."

She didn't want to especially. She felt too contrary at
the moment to fit in anywhere, but she had to kill time
till her mother came back and this was as good a way
of doing it as any. He led her about the small gallery
and she began to notice the room for the first time. It
was interestingly irregular in shape, entirely without
windows, as an art gallery should be, with fluorescent
bulbs lighting the exhibit. Gordon, she discovered
quickly enough, knew something about art. In fact,
Gordon seemed to be informed about almost everything. His reading had been vast and everything seemed
to arouse his interest. When they crossed the hall to
examine glass cases filled with an assorted array of
objects, he was always able to make intelligent com-
ments. He even knew a lot about a subject as obscure
as turtles, for instance. There was a collection of shells
and he could point out the markings and tell her about
the species, its home and its habits. Somehow he made
it interesting too.

Next they carried the exploration to the main floor
where there was a temporary exhibit of model airplanes
built by Cedarhill boys. From there they descended to
the basement and found themselves in a long room
ruled across with rows of folding chairs. At one end
was a small stage with curtained wings, and there were
more paintings and prints about the walls.

"There's nothing much to see here," Linda said.
"This must be where the local ladies' club meets."

But Gordon paid no attention. He walked directly to
the stage end of the room and Linda saw the object
which drew his interest, a small grand piano, the top
down, the keys hidden. There was a look about him as
absorbed as the expression Linda had seen on Martin
Stevens's face upstairs.

"Grandmother has an old-fashioned upright," he
said. He lifted the lid from the keys and, still standing,
played two or three soft chords. "Good tones. This is
an old piano and a good one."

Linda glanced toward the door and then eagerly back at Gordon. "Play something! There's no one else down here and I don't think anyone upstairs would care."

He needed no coaxing. In a moment he had the piano open and without self-consciousness had seated himself on the bench. He seemed to forget Linda altogether the moment his fingers touched the keys. There was magic in the sounds he wove. Lullaby magic at first, gentle and appealing, quickening into something exciting and stormy, then falling away to a minor melody that touched Linda's heart as she listened.

Linda closed her eyes and let the pictures the music wove move before the eyes of her mind. Somehow sadness was predominant, even when the musician set his fingers scattering gay ballet notes on the staid museum air.

Gordon was much more than a merely good musician. Perhaps it was an awareness of that fact that tightened her throat as she listened. Gordon Kenyon could never be lost for long in a small Midwestern town. Talent like his belonged to the world and sooner or later he would go back to the world to give to it the thing he had to give. Music would always come first with him and he would always be able to shut everything else away. Without putting her consciousness of these things into words, Linda was somehow sharply aware of them; aware too that the knowledge frightened her a little, though she couldn't be sure why. It was as if, deep in the loveliness of Gordon's playing, there lay some threat of future hurt to Linda Hollis.

His fingers crashed into a rousing martial bit that all but drew Linda to her feet and set the room to roaring with a sound that was too loud for its small confines. Gordon laughed and broke off in the middle of a measure to swing about on the bench and look at Linda.

"Sorry," he said. "It sort of got away from me. Anything you'd like? I can do popular stuff too, though they throw a fit back in New York when I try it. Mother acts as if I'd been caught reading a comic book."

Without waiting for an answer, he turned back to the piano with a lively arrangement of a popular tune that brought Linda to her feet. She went lightly down the aisle, curtseying to an imaginary partner, swinging to the left and then to the right, while Gordon watched her over his shoulder until she dropped back again in a front row seat, laughing and out of breath.

"You'd better not let Cedarhill High discover that you can do that," she gasped. "You'll find yourself with a job on your hands."

"I'll be careful," Gordon said. "Now what about that selection of yours? Just call 'em out, ladies and gentlemen! A large black see-gar to the party who can call a number I can't play!"

Linda's response was impulsive, unthinking. "*Oh, What a Beautiful Morning!*" she cried.

He looked around at her. "It is, isn't it?" he said. Beneath his fingers the music hushed. It was almost as if he sang to her through his playing—sang about the kind of morning that tingled with life when you were young and there was a girl you liked, and you knew all your dreams for the years ahead simply had to come true.

In a moment Linda was back in memory in a quiet, darkened theater in New York and her father was on one side of her, her mother on the other, as the curtain went up on the opening song of *Oklahoma!* Linda was scarcely surprised when someone slipped into the chair beside her and tucked a hand through her arm and she knew her mother had come into the basement room. They listened together, Linda with her eyes closed and her lashes wet on her cheeks. She knew her mother was feeling what she felt. They were close together again, as if Martin Stevens had never taken her away. Always this song would bring Bob Hollis back to them as warmly and clearly as if he were alive. No changes could ever spoil that. In that moment something of Linda's resistance to Cedarhill began to crumble and it was Gordon Kenyon's music which started the healing.

"Thank you," she said softly when his fingers paused above the keys.

He glanced at her keenly, as if he sensed a deeper

thanks than the playing of a popular tune might warrant.

"Mother," Linda said, "this is Gordon Kenyon."

She caught her mother's slight start of recognition at the name and was glad she would never be the type to acclaim or gush.

"Are they going to send the guards down to put me out?" Gordon asked. "I should have asked permission first."

Mrs. Stevens smiled. "You did raise the echoes, rather, with that polonaise piece. Even Martin came out of his flour and water mixing long enough to hear that. I'll admit he looked a little startled, but I think it did the Museum good."

It was pleasant, Linda thought, to laugh and be a little foolish after so nostalgic a moment.

"It's nearly lunch time," her mother said. "Perhaps we'd better get home before the hungry brood arrives. I do hope you got to see something of the Museum. The library search took longer than I expected."

"Gordon and I did the place together," Linda explained. "Which was a lucky break for me because he's practically an encyclopedia."

They started back upstairs to tell Martin they were leaving for home and parted from Gordon at the door.

"Nice boy," her mother said. "He deserves a better break from his family than he's been getting according to the papers. That's a pretty large portion of talent he has."

Linda nodded silently. Somehow she didn't want to discuss Gordon just now; not even with her mother. She wanted to hold a very special experience quietly to herself. Then she could take it out and look at it now and then as if it were all happening again and feel both the sadness and the sense of healing.

As they left the Museum and went outside again the sun was shining brighter than ever in the brilliant light of approaching noon. The old trees arched leafy and green above the streets of Cedarhill, speckling sidewalk and pavement with their faintly moving shadows.

Oh, it *was* a beautiful morning!

13 Disaster

Roddy was sitting on the front steps when Linda and her mother got home. He was stormy-eyed and tense and about him was placed an array of live turtles, two snakes in bottles and one dead frog. It was the lifeless frog which had apparently aroused the storm and brought a quiver to his chin.

"Look what your old pooch did!" he accused as the two reached the steps. "Gulliver was practically tame. He'd got so he'd sit right on my hand and let me feed him flies. And your old dog bopped him on the head with his paw."

For just a second Linda was fiercely glad. Good enough for Roddy to see what it was like to have something of his own hurt. But in the same flash, and still under the spell of the mood Gordon's music had aroused in her, she knew her reaction was that of a child, not an adult. No matter what had gone before, Roddy was the child, and this accident spelled tragedy to him.

"Oh, Roddy, what a shame!" her mother was saying. A clean white hanky with a delicate lilac scent had found its way into Roddy's grubby paw for the purpose of nose blowing, but he resisted this gentling feminine influence with every inch of his small, defiant person.

Linda glanced at her mother and nodded in a way that meant, "I'll have a try at this." Mrs. Stevens patted Roddy's shoulder and went on into the house. Matter-of-factly Linda sat down on the step and looked at Roddy's collection.

"It's too bad about the frog," she said. "The Roughneck didn't understand. We'll have to teach him better. He probably only wanted to play. Maybe we can go down by the river and catch another one."

"It wouldn't be Gulliver," Roddy said gloomily.

Linda touched one of the glass jars, thrusting back a natural repugnance for its reptilian contents. "Do they have names too?"

"That one's Slithery," Roddy told her grudgingly, "and the other one's Slathery."

"I guess I like turtles better," Linda said, pushing a small turtle back from the edge of a step with a finger that made him draw in his head until only a small nose showed under the shell. "I used to buy them sometimes at the dime stores in New York. Did you ever build card houses for turtles to walk through?"

For a moment Linda thought Roddy would unbend. Then, like the turtle, he retreated into his own shell.

"Nope," he said curtly and began gathering up his pets, dead and alive. The turtles went into a dented pan, while the frog was wrapped carefully in Joyce's scented handkerchief.

"Are you going to have a funeral?" Linda asked, remembering the elaborite rites with which her father had once helped her to bury a deceased canary. But Roddy was too grown-up for such make-believe. He snorted scornfully and went off toward the back yard with his menagerie.

Roughy came leaping down the hall to meet her as she went into the house and Linda bent to pat and cuddle him. But she scolded him a little too about the frog. A cat and a dog in one house made things complicated enough, but that Roddy should go in for a natural history collection of the live type added to the difficulties.

How did you win over a small boy, she wondered as she went upstairs? It was a little surprising to find herself concerned. Gordon's music had certainly soothed the savage spirit in her breast. She was not safe, she knew, from all the sore, hurtful things that would crowd back upon her at any moment. But for just a little while the tension had eased and Cedarhill did not seem so forsaken and unfriendly a place. She could even look outside herself enough for the moment to see a rather lonely, mixed-up little boy who needed help even more than she needed it.

In the room she shared with Babs she stood before the mirror and began to brush back her short hair with quick, vigorous strokes that brought out the shine in it. She was thinking about Roddy as she brushed; remembering the inquiring little boy who had brought her bags up to this room when she'd arrived and asked those hesitant questions about her mother. Every now and then his watchful guard went down and you could glimpse his need. If you could get that guard down long enough to interest him in something.

"Why on earth don't you let it grow?" Babs asked from the doorway. "That crew cut certainly doesn't do much for your personality."

Linda stopped brushing and looked past her own reflection in the mirror to Babs's sulky face. Somehow not even this girl's effort to sting could irk her this morning. Besides, her words had a familiar ring.

"It isn't quite as bad as a crew cut, is it? Though I've a friend back in New York who is always screaming about my hair. It's comfortable this way and easy to take care of."

Babs whisked back a strand of her own somewhat tumbled mane. "Well, it's your business if you want to look like a worn-out shaving brush. But you won't get any place with Gordon Kenyon if you go around looking like another boy."

"I don't want to look like anybody but myself," Linda said a little sharply. "Why should I want to get anywhere with anybody?"

She went back to her brushing more energetically than was necessary, while Babs crossed the room behind her and picked up a lipstick from her dressing table. After a moment Babs asked a deliberate question.

"You mean you, personally, are not interested in Gordon Kenyon or in what kind of impression you make on him?"

Drat the girl anyway, thought Linda. Her new-found calm was beginning to crack around the edges.

"Gordon seems to be nice enough," she said. "But I've yet to see a man who can make my heart go pitter-patter—if that's what you mean."

"Mm," Babs said, smoothing the texture of her too bright lips by pressing them together. "Glad to know it. I don't like to poach on reserved property. I thought you saw him first, so I was going to keep hands off."

"Don't be foolish!" Linda snapped. "Go right ahead if you're interested."

"Thanks, I will. Naturally it was because of Gordon that I joined that idiotic photography scheme of Peter's. But I wouldn't have done anything very active about it, Madam Vice-President, until I got the go-ahead sign from you. I play fair."

It was just as well that Babs tossed down her lipstick and went airily out of the room because Linda was experiencing a new surge of irritation. There was no sense to being irritated, of course. Gordon was just a boy she'd like to have for a friend. There wasn't the slightest tinge of romantic nonsense in her feeling about him. Her irritation against Babs, she assured herself, was due to the other girl's shallow self-conceit, her arrogance and her tendency to be unkind. It had nothing whatever to do with the fact that she meant to make a play for Gordon, who could undoubtedly look out for himself and would never be taken in by someone who was outwardly stunning and inwardly empty.

But she suddenly bent upon her own reflection a gaze more intent and seeing than before. How would she look if she tried her hair in a style less severe? Did she really seem as plain and uninteresting as Babs implied? The girl in the mirror was certainly a lot less vivid and vibrant than the one who had just walked out of the room. But the face that looked back at her was frank and honest. There was an unhappy droop to the mouth that surprised her a little and she straightened her lips self-consciously. That helped a little, and she tried to be satisfied with the improved effect.

An interesting face, she thought in wry amusement. That was what people always said about a face when there was very little else to say for it. Well, it was hers and she would have to get along with it for some time.

She simply mustn't let Babs rub her the wrong way so easily.

Meals at the Stevenses had improved decidedly since that first breakfast when Martin and his wife had come home. In fact, the atmosphere of the entire house had changed subtly. Mrs. Burr and Mrs. Stevens had been digging into dusty corners which had probably not been dug into in years, and though Mrs. Burr grumbled, there was no resisting the tide of housewifeliness which had rolled down upon the household with the arrival of Joyce.

There were flowers on the table at mealtime, and small treasures that Linda remembered from New York had begun to appear around the house, a bowl here, a water color there, a ceramic horse with a saucy look prancing on the bookcase. Curtains and draperies had come down and weekday mornings the dining room hummed with the whirr of the sewing machine. Only Linda's and Babs's room had not been touched by this onslaught of activity and Linda wondered about that. Even Roddy was getting new curtains, but not a finger had been laid upon the faded draperies and mismatched bedspreads in the girls' room. Oh, well, her mother couldn't get to everything at once. But Linda found herself stifling a faint hurt.

When she sat down at the table that noon, Linda gave Roddy a cheerful smile which he returned with a look so dark that it startled her. Goodness, she thought, he looked positively revengeful. And a bit guilty too. After that one black look of warning that said "Stay away; I bite," his eyes refused to meet hers again. Something would have to be done about Roddy.

As usual Martin was absorbed in his museum projects and seemed oblivious to the undercurrents at his own table. The subject was still the experiment in constructing a diorama, and this time not even Roddy seemed interested.

"Don't you have to make a background first;" Joyce asked. "What's the use of turning out a papier-mâché foreground if you don't know what you're going to match it against?"

"We're only experimenting now to see what the possibilities are," Martin explained. "With amateur talent like ours we have to learn all the steps from the beginning."

It was just as they were finishing their dessert that the blow fell on Linda's unsuspecting head. Mrs. Burr had gone down to the basement for something and a few minutes later they heard her running upstairs. She burst into the dining room, breathless and excited.

"Maybe you better go down and look at that stuff of yours, Mrs. Stevens! Something's got into it. Everything's in an awful mess."

Linda reached the stairs before any of the others. She plunged down so quickly that only her hand clutching the rail at the bottom saved her from a fall. The moment Mrs. Burr had started to speak she had known with certainty what had happened.

Now her horrified gaze corroborated her suspicion. A quite terrible destruction had been wrought in the basement. Roddy had had his revenge for the murdered frog.

Weakly Linda clung to the railing, afraid to go nearer and check the appalling details. Near her feet were strewn the contents of a package of photographic paper she had intended to give to the school club, its value destroyed by wanton exposure to daylight. Some tangled rolls of unused film had been treated in like manner. Bob Hollis's darkroom equipment had been dumped around helter-skelter, a pan dented here with an angry heel, a ferrotype plate hopelessly scarred by scratches across the surface.

Hazily she heard the others coming downstairs, heard Joyce's voice exclaiming in dismay, Martin's angry tones, even Babs's shocked murmur. But Linda's eyes skimmed hastily over the nearer destruction. None of this mattered. Nothing mattered except her father's pictures.

Swiftly she picked her way across the littered basement, turning on lights as she went. That case with the mounted photographs—it wasn't in its accustomed place. Where—oh, he'd gotten into that too! There it was over behind the trunks and cases. Tugging furiously she began to bring out the pictures. The first had been torn ruthlessly across, the second had a hole punched through its center, the third—but Linda could bear to look no further.

She dropped down on a workbench near the wall and wept silently into the closed fingers she pressed against her face.

She felt her mother's arm about her shoulders as she knelt beside her, whispering vain comfort in her ear. Dimly she heard Martin go upstairs and in a little while the sound of Roddy screaming in rage came down to them. A lot of good it would do to spank him now, Linda thought numbly. She pushed away from her mother and after a moment Joyce went upstairs, following the sound of the screaming.

Only Babs offered neither consolation for her, nor criticism of Roddy. Linda heard her poking around among the wreckage and after a moment she took her hands away from her face in order to see what the other girl was doing.

Babs, having caught her interest, proceeded to hold it. "If it's the pictures you're most worried about, it isn't as bad as it might be. Looks as though he'd just got started on these when he was called to lunch. Only three have been hurt. Say, your father was really good, wasn't he?"

One by one, Babs was taking out the mounted photographs, lining them up around the baseboard of the basement like an exhibit. Dully Linda watched her. Dully her eyes found each familiar scene, boys fishing off a city dock, a grizzled oldster with broken teeth and a pipe in his mouth, shadows on a Manhattan pavement, a sharply arresting shot of a truckman at his wheel.

"The mess isn't as bad as it looks," Babs went on in the same offhand manner, turning away from the pictures to fish among the odds and ends around the floor. "It looks as if he didn't get into more than one box of paper, and the film isn't so important, is it? The big box with the enlarger was too heavy for him to get at, so that's all right. How about our picking this stuff up?"

But somehow Linda could only stare about her in dejection. This was what a beautiful morning could turn into a few hours later. All because of that vicious little boy who was now screaming his head off upstairs.

Suddenly Linda left the bench and started for the stairs. She paid no attention to Babs's startled, "Where are you going?" but went up through the kitchen, brushing past her dismayed mother and Mrs. Burr. Not even a yap of greeting from Roughy could distract her and she was scarcely aware of Martin's awkward apology as she passed him on the way to the second floor.

The screams had subsided and only muffled sobs came from beyond the closed door of Roddy's room. Linda heard Martin pause on his way downstairs, but she marched resolutely toward Roddy's door.

"You'd better not go in there," Martin called after her.

She gave no sign that she had heard, but put her hand on the knob and pushed open the door.

14 Linda Takes a Hostage

Roddy lay face down on the bed, his head buried in his arms, his body shaken by sobs, more of indignation than repentance. Quietly Linda looked about the room. It was a tidier room since Joyce had taken over the household, so things were easier to find. It took only a second to spot what she had come for in its place of honor in the middle of Roddy's dresser. Just a few days before she had noticed Roddy's pottery giraffe and asked about it. He'd told her proudly that his mother had made it for him when he'd been a very small boy. It was undoubtedly his most valued treasure.

Roddy heard her as she moved across the room and out of the corner of her eye she saw him sit up to watch, his breath coming in tight gasps. Her indifference to him, her concentration on the dresser must have caught his startled attention.

It was the pottery giraffe she reached for. In the mirror she could see Roddy launch himself for physical attack and she raised the giraffe quickly above her head.

"If you come near me," she told him quietly, "I'll throw this against the wall and smash it into bits."

He dropped back on the bed, staring at her in horror. She crossed the room, the giraffe in her hands, and paused at the door to speak to him again.

"This is a hostage," she said. "Do you know what a hostage is?"

She could tell by his expression that he knew.

"You can't do that!" he shouted at her. "My mom

made that. If you hurt it—" he broke off, tears welling up in his eyes.

"Those things you destroyed downstairs were my father's," Linda told him. "Maybe they meant just as much to me as this giraffe does to you."

"Your dog hurt my frog," Roddy accused.

"So then you hurt me. If those are the rules, then it's my turn now to hurt you. Maybe I ought to just smash this right away without waiting."

The threatening look settled over Roddy's face again. "If you do, I—I'll do something awful. I'll do something to your dog. That's what I'll do."

"You won't do anything," Linda said with a calm that belonged to the surface only. "You won't do a thing because I'm not going to smash your giraffe. At least not right away. I'm just going to keep it for a while as a hostage. If you behave yourself, then maybe I won't have to smash it at all. If you don't—" she left the threat hanging unspoken and went out of the room.

Martin was still on the stairs, looking like a very unhappy father. On a sudden impulse Linda thrust the giraffe toward him.

"Will you please lock this in your safe?" she asked in tones Roddy could not miss hearing. "I may want it back later on."

For an instant she was afraid that he would not take the thing from her hands and if he didn't she had no idea what she would do with it. She certainly didn't want Roddy breaking into her possessions looking for it, and it was too large to carry around with her.

After a moment's troubled consideration, Martin came up the last few steps, took the giraffe and went off to his study. She had no way of knowing whether he was angry over what she had done, or whether he approved the action, and she didn't particularly care. The thing she wanted most of all at the moment was to sit down. The outward calm was very much a fake and her knees felt like soft macaroni.

She went into the room she shared with Babs and dropped weakly down on the bed. She wasn't at all sure her lunch meant to stay down. In spite of her victory over Roddy she felt anything but happy. She had a feeling that this entire incident came under the heading of unfinished business and that it should not be left in its present hanging-fire state. She had the upper hand at the moment, but only because of the threat she'd hung over his head. Somehow, now that her anger was spent and the wild temptation to hurt Roddy as he had hurt her had faded out, the victory seemed a petty one.

She lay back on the pillow and closed her eyes, trying to recall an elusive memory that kept escaping her. It had been something in which her father had figured. Bob Hollis had been wonderful with boys; he'd have known right away how to handle Roddy. Why, one time when they'd been out for a walk in the wintertime—

She had it now! She could recall the whole scene clearly. Four or five young toughs had started throwing snowballs at the two of them. Not soft, snowy, good-natured snowballs, but dangerous icy ones. She'd been a lot younger then and when one struck her in the back she'd been frightened.

Her father had gone into a surprising act on the spur of the moment. When a snowball struck him he went down on the icy sidewalk full length while the boys laughed and loaded up with ammunition. Then Bob had struggled to get to his feet, only to drop back on his knees with a gasp of pain. Linda had been really frightened, until her father caught her eye in a secret wink.

"Hey, fellows!" he'd called. "How about a hand? Guess I've hurt my ankle, and the little girl here is too small to help me up."

The boys had halted with arms upraised, their surprise evident, and their suspicion too.

"Just one of you will do," her father called confidently. "Come on and be a good sport."

Strangely enough the whole gang had come over. The project of getting Bob Hollis back on his feet and escorting him the couple of blocks home, limping realistically while he leaned on two hard young shoulders, took their entire attention. The two groups had parted friends and thereafter the Hollises were never pelted with snowballs, either soft or hard, by that particular gang.

"Get a fellow to do something for you," her father had said. But this was different. Roddy Stevens hated her. He probably hated her twice as hard because he'd injured her. You always resented a person you'd hurt. But she had a weapon in her hands she could use if she chose.

The prospect of action sent the sick feeling away, she discovered as she sat up. Almost cheerfully she went back to Roddy's room.

"If you're through crying," she said, "you'd better get up and wash your face. Then you can come downstairs with me."

He turned his head and stared at her in astonishment. "What for?"

"You don't think I'm going to clean that mess up by myself, do you?" she said. "You're going to come along and help me." She could see the possibility of flat refusal coming into his eyes.

"You'll come," she told him quietly. "You'll come because of that hostage."

By the time they reached the basement, Babs had made a bit of headway into cleaning up some of the destruction. When she saw them on the stairs she glanced up without surprise and went right on with what she was doing.

"I didn't think anybody was coming to help me," she said calmly. "I've got the worst of it up by now."

"Roddy's going to help with the pictures," Linda said with equal casualness. This was news to Roddy. In fact, it was practically news to her, since the idea had come to her on the way downstairs.

Roddy said nothing. He stood sullenly in the middle of the basement, obviously at odds with the universe.

"Can you do anything about those?" Babs asked, indicating the three damaged pictures. "I mean replace them or anything?"

"Not as they were," Linda said. "My father did the work on them himself. He enlarged them and did the finishing and mounting. So nothing I could do would ever make them quite the same. But I hope they can at least be replaced. I don't have the negatives to everything my father did, and I can't tell about these."

She opened a small carton that was inside a larger one and took out a cardboard box.

Babs watched with curiosity. "Oh? A filing system for negatives, is that it?"

"Right," Linda said. She handed the box to Roddy. "Look under the heading of *Portraits—Women*," she said. "That's what that bashed-in one is. You'll have to go over by the window and hold the films up to the light one by one till you get it."

Her tone was neither friendly, nor sharp. She was trying to be matter-of-fact and confident as her father had been that other time. For a second Roddy hesitated, but there was no need to mention the hostage again.

He took the box and went over to one of the high basement windows as she had directed. She watched him a moment as he held one film after another up to the light. Then she stopped him.

"No, wait! Not like that. When you're handling negatives you must be careful not to get your fingers all over them. That leaves smudges and scratches. Take each one like this."

She illustrated by holding a negative delicately up by the edge and then replaced it in the box. Again Roddy did as he was told. Linda turned her back on him and went over to help Babs. The other girl looked as if she were about to say something, then changed her mind, but there was an odd smile about her mouth that Linda could not fathom.

Linda gathered up the ruined paper with a sigh. It had been a box of extra fine enlarging paper. A cheaper box of print paper had gone untouched. She dropped the lot into the trash basket beside Babs and turned her attention to the scratched ferrotype plate. A sudden cry from Roddy made her look around.

"Hey, I've got it!" he announced. "Here's your old film!"

She went over to look and approved the find. But though Roddy searched through other headings for the two remaining negatives, he had no further luck. By that time the basement was back in order.

"Wait a minute!" Linda said as Roddy started upstairs. "We're not through yet."

She searched through a carton until she found another box of enlarging paper. She tucked it under her arm and then beckoned to Roddy.

"We're going across the street to see Peter. Come along."

He followed her, not docilely, but without open resentment. She wondered how long it would be before he snapped the finely spun thread by which she led him, hostage or no hostage. If only Peter were home! She really needed him now.

Mrs. Crowell came to the door at Linda's ring. "Peter's in the darkroom," she said. "You can go down if you like. He's rigged up a red signal light over the door. If it's on, don't go in."

There was no light over the door, but Linda tapped on the green painted surface just to make sure. Peter opened the door and grinned at the sight of his company. He noted the box of photographic paper under Linda's arm at once.

"Hi, Linda. Hi, Roddy. Want to borrow my darkroom? I've just taken some prints out of a fixing bath. Come on in."

The familiar smell of hypo brought back a surge of old memories to Linda. For just a moment she wanted to turn around and rush back to fresh air that was burdened by no painful recollections. But she dared not release the weak strand by which she held the small boy at her side.

"Roddy wants to try his hand at an enlargement," she explained cheerfully.

Peter poked the prints about the pan of rinse with a glass rod. "Good enough. I didn't know you were interested in this sort of thing, Roddy."

The boy opened his mouth, probably to announce that he was not interested, but Linda got her words in first. "He is for the moment," she said firmly. "Very interested. Do you suppose you can show him how your enlarger works?"

Peter seemed not to notice Roddy's reluctance to be there at all. "Sure I can. Just let me set these washing and we'll get at it. Glad you came over."

As he worked, Peter explained about the enlarger. It was homemade and had a few gimmicks you had to watch out for that a really good enlarger wouldn't have. But it did the job all right.

There was a high stool near the linoleum covered worktable and Linda perched herself upon it. She held the negative Roddy had located up to the light and speculated about the time it should be given for a satisfactory enlargement. She hadn't worked in a darkroom for so long that she felt all thumbs.

Peter stood behind her to look and pointed out the various factors to Roddy. "It's kind of dense in places so we'll have to give it enough time to bring out the detail in the shadows. Let's have a look at it in the machine."

He showed Roddy how to fit the negative into place, then turned on the enlarger light and switched off the hanging bulb that lighted the darkroom. Roddy came over to look at the blurred reflection that fell on the plate where the paper would go.

"It's fuzzy," he complained.

"Here," Peter said, "turn this and you can focus it yourself. See if you can get it good and sharp."

The glow of light from the enlarger was reflected back into Roddy's intent face as he bent to examine the picture. For the moment he seemed to have forgotten that he wasn't interested.

"Is that right?" he asked. "Have I got it right now?"

"I think that's about as sharp as you can get it," Linda said. "Peter, what about this paper I've brought? I'm afraid it's too contrasty—the lights will be too light and the darks too dark, with nothing much in between."

Peter switched on the light again and moved to the wooden shelves on which boxes and equipment were arranged. "Maybe I've got something that will do a better job. What about this?"

The paper was decided upon and then Peter selected

the proper chemicals for the developing solution. Roddy watched the process in grudging surprise.

"All that just to make one old picture?" he demanded.

Peter nodded. "All that."

Then he switched on the red darkroom light which had no effect on film or paper emulsion. At Peter's direction Roddy took a piece of paper from the box and lined it up correctly on the enlarger table. Peter set the timer that would tick away the necessary seconds for the enlargement and let Roddy turn on the enlarger and turn it off. In the room's dim red glow that followed the turning off of the enlarger, Roddy blinked his eyes in disappointment.

"But there's nothing on the paper. It's still blank."

"Sure," Peter said. "It goes into a developing bath next and we have to watch so it won't get too much or too little. Come over here and have a look."

Linda watched as the paper went into the developer and felt the old twinge of excited anticipation as a dim image began to come out on the paper.

"Gosh!" Roddy breathed in heartfelt wonder. "It's coming out! You can see the picture."

"Okay," Peter said. "Into the fixing bath it goes."

There was excitement in Roddy's voice. "Can we turn on the light now? Can we see how it looks in a real light?"

"Not yet. It has to have time to get fixed first so it won't fade. Then we'll wash it a bit and have a look. Linda, there's a ferrotype plate on the table over there. It's just been cleaned so it's all right. Can you bring it over?"

She searched in the dimness and felt the plate cool beneath her fingers. When Peter turned on the light she set it on the worktable beside him. Now they could have a look at the enlargement. Linda's experienced eye recognized at once that neither the timing nor the paper had been altogether right, but to Roddy's enraptured eyes it looked wonderful.

"How do you get it dry?" he asked.

Peter pulled over the metal plate. "That's what this is for. And you have to be sure it's clean and unscratched.

Otherwise your finished picture will have marks across it."

Roddy looked up at Linda quickly and then away and she knew he was remembering the sharp scratches he had made across the plate in the Stevens basement.

Peter put a roller into his hands and showed him how to smooth the picture on the plate and roll the surplus water out of it. "You can come back and have a look after a while when it's dry," he said. "Is that one of your father's pictures, Linda?"

"Yes," Linda said, but she offered no further explanation. "And thanks a lot for helping us out. I'll try and get together some stuff for your club before school Monday."

"*Our* club," Peter said.

He went upstairs with them to the door and watched Roddy and Linda cross the street. The excitement had died out of Roddy and he scuffed his feet along as he walked. Linda made no effort at conversation until they reached the steps. Then she spoke quietly.

"You can have your giraffe back, Roddy. I don't want to keep it. And I wouldn't have smashed it anyway. I know how you feel about it. I know because of the way I feel about those pictures of my father's that I can't replace."

Roddy kicked each step with his toe as he went up, releasing feelings he couldn't put into words. Linda walked quickly into the house ahead of him, not waiting for an answer.

15 Home Town Contest

It was not at a meeting of the Shutter-Snappers, oddly enough, that Gordon Kenyon presented the idea that set camera bugs young and old buzzing around the town. The thing came out much more casually during a school dance one Friday afternoon in the gym.

The autumn days had rolled along, no longer bright blue and gold, but touched with the browns and reds of changing foliage, and the hazy gray of smoke from burning leaves. The nights were frosty and fires burned in the open grates of Cedarhill. There was something about logs in a fireplace, as Linda had to admit, that you could never get by turning on a steam radiator back in New York. Not that she had given in to Cedarhill, but just for the moment she had stopped fighting it. The longing for New York and old friends was like a sore tooth that ached whenever she touched it. But now she did not touch it quite so often, and she was not quite so often at odds with Cedarhill.

Their relationship with the Stevenses was certainly not all that her mother would have liked it to be. Roddy still held himself apart from the newcomers. The brief interest he had shown in Peter's darkroom had grown into nothing stronger, though Linda had found an old box camera that she'd used as a child and had given it to him. The film she'd put in it had gone unused. Roddy had taken not so much as a single snapshot. His eyes were distrustful when he looked at her, as if he felt that she had been guilty of playing a scurvy trick on him and he meant to take no more chances. The giraffe was back in its place of honor on

140

his dresser, but he gave her no thanks for placing it there. The brief moment of elation she had experienced in the hope that Roddy had been won over, had long ago died out. Roddy meant to have none of her and that was that. But at least there had been no further serious warfare.

Babs was as unfathomable and unpredictable as ever. There were moments when Linda would have been ready to like her, but Babs seemed indifferent to the fact. She was alternately sharp and gentle and there was simply no figuring her out at all.

But while Linda might have been ready to accept Roddy and Babs in a more friendly relationship if they had shown any sign of accepting her in return, she was no closer to accepting Martin than she had been in the beginning. Now and then he made awkward, rather self-conscious overtures in her direction, as if he considered it his duty, but she knew them for the artificial attempts they were and turned coolly away. Somehow she could never avoid comparing Martin with her own father, and each time the comparison left her more bewildered then ever as to what Joyce could see in him. As far as Linda could tell, he had been a total loss with his own children. Roddy adored him, and yet Martin seemed to wield no influence for the better over the boy. Babs seemed to regard her father with a cool indifference that had a touch of crossed swords in it. Always she seemed ready to raise a defense against him, or to prick him with some small attack. Linda, thinking of the wonderful companions she and Bob Hollis had been, pitied the girl. Babs had missed so much.

But if, with the exception of his wife, Martin was not too happy in his human relationships, he slipped with utter absorption into the affairs of the Museum. "He doesn't need any human beings in his life," Linda thought more than once. "He only needs his work to keep him happy." In that he was certainly the opposite of Bob Hollis who had loved anything that lived and breathed—even when the object of his interest might seem unlikely to anyone else.

Sometimes Linda was almost sorry for her mother

who had been helpless when it came to cracking the hard, resistant surface of the two younger members of the Stevens family. It had been easy for Joyce to turn the cold, rather bare old house into something warm and almost gracious. Not entirely so, because human graciousness was needed to complete the picture, and that she had not been able to get from the occupants of the house. Certainly life was more comfortable and went along with less friction than when it had been in Mrs. Burr's indifferent hands. But good food at a table, clean, bright surroundings, a general air of attractiveness were not enough to turn a house into a real home. You needed affection and a one-for-all spirit to accomplish that. This was a house divided into enemy camps, all watching one another suspiciously; each with a private goal of its own that might be in direct opposition to the purpose of another member of the family.

There were other matters, too, which disturbed Linda more than she liked to admit. The matter of Gordon Kenyon, for one. There had been no more breathless moments like the one in the basement meeting room of the Museum. At school he had been friendly, but as casual as ever. He never seemed quite a part of things, but always a visitor from the outside world. Even Linda herself had been caught into activities more than he had. Her determination to remain a very inactive vice-president of the Shutter-Snappers had done her little good. Peter dragged her into every discussion, and even Mr. Markham asked her opinion when the group got into an argument. Gordon was safely out of things, having no knowledge of photography and being thus able to remain an innocent bystander.

He had come to none of the after-school dances that were now in swing. Every other Friday there was an informal dance in the gym and Linda had been willing enough to go to these. She loved to dance and she had found that there were as good dancers in Cedarhill as there had been in New York. She also found that boys were about the same everywhere. A few would be out on the floor the moment the music started, dancing because they really enjoyed it. The rest would hang around on the outskirts and watch, joining in now and

then, but for the most part letting the girls dance together. Linda didn't mind. She liked to dance, no matter with whom. But Babs said she'd never be seen
dancing with another girl. Consequently, after attending
one dance and looking over the field, Babs had not
come again.

Until today.

And today Gordon was here too. Linda knew it was
Babs who had persuaded him to come. The two were
out on the floor now dancing together and it was easy
to see that they were both experts. Babs had lost no
time in making good her threat to go after Gordon, and
as far as anybody could see she was succeeding. Babs
could be clever and entertaining when she chose. In
fact, Linda rather suspected that she could be altogether fascinating when she put her mind to it, and apparently she considered Gordon worthy of her best efforts.

Linda danced with Peter and listened to endless talk
about the Shutter-Snappers. Peter ate, slept and
breathed photography these days, and Linda was a
little bored. Peter would be a moderately good dancer if
he'd try, but most of the time he pushed her around the
floor in an absent-minded way, giving his real attention
to the line his thoughts followed so endlessly.

"Sorry," he murmured absently as they grazed another couple rounding the end of the gym beneath the
basketball basket. "The trouble is the real interest we
want isn't coming to life. Attendance isn't too good at
club meetings and the kids aren't really getting to work
with their cameras."

Linda nodded, half listening, her eyes on Gordon
and Babs, easily the best dancers on the floor. He'd
danced every dance with her so far and she wondered if
he'd follow that pattern right through the afternoon.
Once he'd smiled at her over Babs's shoulder, but
though she had certainly not danced every dance, Gordon had not come near her or any other girl.

When the music ended Peter said, "Next one?"
promptly, but she suspected it was because he was in
the middle of his problems and didn't want to let her go
till he'd finished.

She shook her head. "Let's just stop and talk. It's simpler."

"Swell," Peter said, so obviously pleased that she wanted to shake him.

They found a quiet corner and leaned against an exercise horse while Peter continued as if there'd been no interruption.

"I thought I could stir up some interest in Weston's big national contest," Peter went on, "but everybody's afraid to try. They all think they're not good enough."

"That's probably true," Linda said, feeling contrary and unsympathetic.

"*You'd* be good enough," Peter told her. "But you haven't so much as pointed a camera lens at anything."

"No interest," Linda admitted. Peter was always so good-natured about everything that she had a willful impulse to see if she could prick him into a state of annoyance. An idle glance over the floor showed her that Babs and Gordon weren't dancing this one. In fact, they were coming right toward this corner.

"You haven't any right not to be interested," Peter said as patiently as if he hadn't already said it a dozen times. "Your father's daughter—"

"My father's daughter knows just how much it takes to make a good photographer," Linda snapped, discovering that she was the one who was getting annoyed. She turned her back on the floor and the two coming across it. "It's really pretty silly for a bunch of amateurs who aren't even good beginners to try to get into a big national contest."

"But how else can we stir anybody up?" Peter demanded. "And how can we know we can't if we don't even try?"

Linda could sense Gordon and Babs at her elbow before she looked around, but she kept her head turned. She didn't want those two to think she had the slightest interest in them.

"Why don't you work up a local contest?" Gordon said over her shoulder. "Something beginners wouldn't be afraid to get into and that would be more fun than struggling for something as tough as a national prize."

"For instance?" Peter asked.

Babs said, "For heavens' sake, Peter, can't you talk about something beside that silly club?"

Gordon went on as if she hadn't spoken. "I've been thinking about it myself and an idea occurred to me. How about a home town contest? Pictures taken in and around Cedarhill. You could make it bigger than just a high school affair by taking entries from people outside school too. If you worked up a little publicity, a little interest—"

Peter had been listening with his mouth open and now he reached out to clap Gordon on the shoulder. "Pardner, shake! You've just done something for this town. East meets West. Linda had me thinking New Yorkers were all hopeless, but now I'll have to change my mind."

The grin he gave Linda took any possible sting out of his words, but she had no intention of yipping for joy about the new suggestion just because Gordon Kenyon had made it.

"Oh, fine!" she said a little sharply. "You'll have ten-year-olds competing with adults. A nice, fair contest that!"

"Ten-year-olds!" Peter echoed, looking at her rapturously. "Why not? We could run the thing in three classes—make it town wide. Grade school entries, high school entries, and an adult group. The editor of the *News* will give us a write-up, and the art class can do some posters we can set up around town."

Linda and Babs looked at each other and sighed together. "Men!" their eyes signaled and for an instant there was one of those comradely moments between them that occasionally flashed unexpectedly into being.

Then Babs waggled a finger at Peter. "Being as how I love to wet-blanket things, I have an offering to make if you'll shush the ecstasy for about a minute."

Peter turned his broadening grin in her direction. "Don't be shy. Go right ahead."

"What are you going to do for prizes?" Babs asked. "What are you going to do for incentive? How are you going to persuade people that they ought to go out and take pictures of Cedarhill? For what?"

Peter turned the grin into a thoughtful scowl.

"Maybe we could dig up a couple of prizes. Not very big ones, of course, but—"

"Three dollars for first prize," Babs chanted mockingly. "Two dollars for second and fifty cents for third. That's about what the club treasury would stand and that will be just ducky. I'm going right out and use up five dollars' worth of materials to see if I can win third prize."

Linda looked at Gordon. There was a mild interest in his eyes as if he wanted to see what these Cedarhill folk would do with his idea, but he was offering nothing else; he was still the outsider. In some curious way the fact annoyed Linda a little. It was as if she had begun somehow to belong to Cedarhill and resented any suspicion of patronization from a New Yorker. Besides, she had a perverse desire to set herself in opposition to Babs. She wasn't quite sure why. Maybe the fact that Gordon had danced with no one else was a good enough reason.

"I don't know that money prizes are so important," she said lightly. "Maybe you could work out something with a bit of glory to it that would be even more intriguing."

"Atta girl!" Peter cheered. "I knew you had it in you if we could ever get you started. Go ahead."

"Don't think you're going to mix me up in this," Linda said quickly. "I'm just thinking out loud."

"Well, do it some more," Peter urged.

"Sh-sh! The idea is elusive. I haven't quite captured it yet. But if you get a set of judges, important town fathers maybe, to decide on the blue ribbon winners, and then if we had an exhibit and hung all the photographs entered, providing they were properly mounted, of course, and—"

"Glory be!" Peter cried. "This is it. If we make the contest one that features Cedarhill scenes we can get that good old factor Civic Pride behind us."

"Perhaps Mr. Stevens would hang the pictures in the temporary exhibit room at the Museum," Gordon suggested.

Linda approved warmly. "That's a wonderful idea. Babs, you'll ask your father, won't you?"

Babs shrugged. "Oh, I suppose so, but I doubt if he'll fall for it. A lot of amateur prints." It was Babs now who seemed to be at cross purposes with the others.

"I'll ask him," Linda surprised herself by saying. "And, Peter, maybe you'd better have two or three money prizes, one in each group. Couldn't you hold a dance or a party or something to raise the money? The prizes wouldn't need to be more than five dollars apiece, just token prizes, and the rest could go for equipment for the Photography Club."

For the first time Babs's eyes lighted, but her look was all for Gordon. "And here's our star attraction!" she cried. "We will have a party, and Gordon Kenyon will play!"

She was wonderfully vital and attractive when she came alive like that, Linda thought. When the sulky look went out of her eyes and the sullenness left her mouth, she was really a knockout. Not even Gordon would be able to resist a girl who looked like that.

He did not try. "I'll be glad to play," he said gravely and Linda found herself liking him for not being big-shot, or hedging because he was really somebody and had payed for great metropolitan audiences.

Then he did something surprising. "Dance?" he asked quietly, touching Linda's arm.

For a little while she'd forgotten where they were and she was almost surprised to hear the music starting a new number. She slipped into Gordon's arms without looking up at him and somehow they were out on the floor.

This was dancing, she thought dreamily. This was really dancing, a rhythm that made you one with your partner so that your movements flowed smoothly to-gether as though you had always danced this way and always would. But she knew she had never danced like this before. She had never had a partner like this before.

He didn't talk, he didn't hum, he didn't hold her too closely, or too loosely. The music wove a pattern and they followed it as evenly and lightly as though they had followed it together a thousand times before. It was an old tune, *I'm Falling in Love with Someone*.

She moved to it happily, and again she had the strange feeling that she had had before with Gordon, that old hurts were being healed; that she could stop being angry and resentful, stop fighting. And yet there was a faint touch of sadness underlying the peace, as if she knew inevitably that the hurts would come again.

When the music stopped and Gordon led her back to Peter, who had been dancing with Babs, she felt a little dazed, as if she couldn't quite make sense about anything. She didn't have to try. Peter was so busy making out-loud plans for carrying out the new project that no one paid the slightest attention to her. Babs promptly annexed Gordon again and she was planning now, too. But her ideas followed the line of a party to raise money for equipment and prizes.

"Of course it can't be just a school affair," she said, "though we can probably get the use of the gym to hold it in. And we've got to make it something unusual, not just the same old dance, or a lot of kid games. It's got to appeal to older people too. Of course Gordon's playing will help pull them in, but we ought to work out something novel besides."

"Okay," Peter said, "you work it out. I'll get busy on the publicity right away. How about setting the end of the contest for six weeks away? If we don't leave 'em too much time there'll be more concentrated excitement over this."

Linda and Gordon took no further active part in the planning. They merely listened and now and then Linda found herself watching Gordon. But his attention was mostly for Babs, though there was no telling exactly what he thought of her. He looked as remote as ever, interested, but a little amused, a visitor who was enjoying himself pleasantly, not at all in a superior way, but as if he could never really belong to what was happening about him.

16 Turtles

At dinner that night Babs, for a change, was full of talk about coming events, plans for the contest and the party. But she made no mention of the possibility of using the Museum for the display of photographs, and Linda knew that her rash offer to talk to Martin about it had been left in her lap. She wished now, watching him, that she had not said she would ask such a favor of him. Somehow she could not imagine Martin Stevens becoming enthusiastic about an amateur show of this kind.

Mrs. Stevens was interested in Babs's party plans. "It would be nice to have the party climax the whole event and combine the showing of the pictures and the party at the same time," she suggested.

"But we have to get money for the prizes with the party," Babs objected. "So I suppose we'd have to hold it first."

"Not necessarily," Mrs. Stevens said. "After all, it's the glory of the awards that matters more than the small prizes. The judges could present blue ribbons for the winning pictures at the party. Then the prizes could be mailed by check later. That would be simple enough."

"It sounds possible," Babs said. "But the thing that worries me is how to make this affair something different, something we've never done in this town before."

"An idea occurs to me—" Mrs. Stevens's eyes met her husband's across the table and there was a twinkle in them. "Of course it wouldn't be something this town had never seen before, but it might be something this generation hasn't tried. Once when I was in school we had a lot of fun with—"

Martin's look brightened surprisingly. "I know! A box social!"

His wife smiled. "It might appeal to the present generation too. And the older ones would enjoy the nostalgic touch."

"What's a box social?" Roddy asked. "What do you do?"

"You could hold the affair in the daytime instead of at night," Mrs. Stevens went on, "so the grade school contestants could come too. Roddy, it's an old-fashioned sort of luncheon party where the girls all make up special lunches and pack them as attractively as they can. Then there's a sort of master of ceremonies who auctions off each box to the highest bidder. It can be lots of fun, if you have a good m.c. And of course each boy tries to buy the box belonging to the girl he likes best. Sometimes the bidding gets very exciting, and of course the boy who buys a lunch box gets to eat with the girl who packed it. Then you could follow with a dance in the afternoon."

Babs started to sniff the idea aside, possibly because it had come from Linda's mother, possibly because she felt it too unsophisticated for her tastes, but Linda broke in before she could voice her objections.

"That does sound like fun. I'll bet Peter will think so too. I'll call him up after dinner and ask him. And I like the idea of combining the prize-giving and the party as a climax for the whole contest. We could sell fifty cent tickets and then raise more money through the box lunch auction. Mother, I think it's a wonderful idea."

"Huh!" Roddy said in disgust. "I wouldn't spend *my* money on any old girl's lunch box."

"I suspect," Martin said dryly, "that the smaller fry had better bring their own lunches. And if you don't want to be too hard on the older boys' spending money, you'd better limit the raising of bids to pennies and nickels. As I recall, that sort of thing can run into real money if you're not careful."

There was a remembering look in his wife's eyes.

"Five dollars you paid for my box, Martin. And what five dollars would buy in those days!"

"The competition was keen," Martin reminded her. "And it was worth every cent. I can still remember that homemade potato salad and the chocolate cake."

"Though of course you've forgotten the girl!" his wife teased.

It was strange, Linda thought, listening to them, to imagine your own mother being your age and popular enough to have several boys bidding for her box. Probably there wouldn't be anyone to bid for her daughter's. Not that she'd care, not in Cedarhill. And at least all this remembering had thawed Martin into a mellow mood. He would be less apt to give her a stiff refusal when she made her request. She wouldn't ask him now while all the others were around. Too many interruptions were possible. She'd wait until he went into the living room to read after dinner.

But after dinner he did not go into the living room as she'd expected. Instead, he retreated immediately to his upstairs study, closing the door behind him. In spite of her good intentions, Linda sighed with relief. She could ask him tomorrow just as well. There was no urgent need to broach the matter tonight. An inner voice said, "You're just trying to postpone the evil day." This was the time to talk to him. Now, while he was remembering that party when he'd bid for Mother's box. But she turned a deaf ear to the voice and phoned Peter instead.

The new suggestion went over big with him. He thought the box social idea was terrific and asked Linda if she had tackled Mr. Stevens about the use of the Museum for the display.

"Maybe that wasn't such a good idea," Linda said weakly. "Maybe the exhibit ought to be held where we give the party."

"You mean in the gym at school? That would be terrible. Can you see a picture exhibit of any kind being hung around those walls? Besides, it couldn't stay up because of games. And we want these hung in a place where they can stay put for a couple of weeks and give people a chance to see them. If the contest goes over the way I hope, we'll stir up some real interest in photography in this town and then it will be easier to do the thing next year. Linda, if you don't want to ask Mr. Stevens, get Babs to do it. Or I'll do it, if you'd rather not take a chance on Babs."

"Oh, I'll do it," Linda promised, stiffening her spine for the ordeal.

When Peter hung up she walked resolutely up the stairs, Roughy at her heels again. He followed her around these days every minute she was home, as if she furnished a bodyguard against the fearful powers of the Khan. But the two animals had been avoiding each other since the big battle, and though they were scarcely on friendly terms, there'd been no further trouble.

Outside the door of Martin's study Linda hesitated uneasily. It was going to be a lot more difficult to make the request than she had anticipated this afternoon when she'd offered her services so recklessly. How could she ask a favor of a man to whom she had scarcely been civil since she had come to live in his house? How could she now pretend a friendship she felt no more than she ever had? Well—this wasn't something she was asking for herself. It was for the good of the whole town, really, if Peter's arguments were to be believed.

She rapped on the door quickly before she could change her mind again.

"Come in!" Martin called and she thought he sounded impatient.

"If—if I'm interrupting—" she began hesitantly as she opened the door, and then broke off because obviously she was interrupting.

He glanced toward the door and then, to her surprise, his impatience seemed to fade when he saw who it was. "Hello, Linda. Come on in. Anything I can do for you?"

"Well—ah—maybe," she said and swallowed a few times. This wasn't going to be easy at all.

He seemed to sense her embarrassment, for after a moment of waiting for her to go on, he turned his attention back to the desk before him, and left it up to her whether she would come in or go away.

Curiosity got the better of her this time. She came into the room and closed the door behind her, shutting Roughy out. Then she walked over to stand beside his desk, where she could watch the objects he was working with. Several turtle shells of different sizes lay strewn about the desk and Martin Stevens was working with a soft gob of something that he was apparently molding between his fingers.

"Wax," he said, balancing it on his palm for her to see. "Or rather, a mixture of waxes we had around the Museum. I'm trying to turn out a reasonable looking turtle for the diorama we're planning. I thought a turtle would be easy to do, but now I'm not so sure. The process of mounting a real turtle is pretty difficult. Besides, you can get a more clear-cut and lifelike model with wax than by using real tissue. Of course we can use the natural shell and we have plenty of those. So what we have to do is model the head, feet and tail. Tails and feet aren't hard, but the head isn't going so well."

Linda dropped into a chair beside the desk where she could examine the small wax objects Martin was experimenting with. She picked up a tiny webbed "foot" and looked at it. It might get by, but she suspected that she could make a better foot than that herself.

"We'll paint them later on," Martin said, "and the coloring will make them look more natural. But I'm afraid I'll never turn into an old master when it comes to sculpturing."

"Isn't a turtle's nose more pointed than that?" Linda asked. "It seems to me——"

Martin regarded the model thoughtfully. "Maybe. I've sent for a book that will give me adequate photographs of various species of turtle, but it hasn't come yet. I——I suppose I've been too impatient to get to work."

Linda glanced at him in surprise. Such a confession was more human than she'd expected.

He grinned sheepishly. "A highly unscientific approach, I'll admit."

"Wait a minute!" Linda said. "I've got an idea."

She hurried out of the room without explaining and started downstairs. This was pretty silly, going to so much trouble over a project she had so little interest in. But of course she did want to get Martin into a really good mood. How like him, though, not to have paid any attention to his son's pets.

Roddy was in the hall below and he looked up at her with an odd expression on his face. She noted briefly that Roughy was with him and that Roddy had a hand on the little dog's collar. But she had not worried about Roddy's turning into a tormentor since the showdown she had had with him, and she was too intent on her purpose to think much about it now.

"Roddy, could we borrow your turtles for a little while?" she asked. "Your father's trying to model a turtle's head out of wax and I think a real model would help."

Roddy took his hand off the Roughneck's collar and the little dog bounded away as if he had been restrained against his will.

"I'll get 'em," Roddy said, and disappeared toward the basement.

Linda waited and he was back in a few minutes with a pan in his hands. But he had no intention of trusting his pets to her care. He held the box away when she reached for it.

"I'm coming too," he said. "I want to watch."

They went back to Martin's study together. Roddy put the pan on the floor, selected two of the smaller turtles and brought them to his father.

"Fine!" Martin said. "Put them down there on the blotter and we'll see what they look like."

The turtles promptly retreated into their shells, but after a moment the livelier of the two put his nose out cautiously, blinked in his peculiar reptilian way, then put out his feet and began to push himself across the field of green blotter. After a moment the second one came to life too and Linda watched the little creatures with interest.

"Could I try?" she asked, reaching for a lump of wax. "I took a ceramics class once in school and I used to model a bit in clay."

"By all means!" Martin said heartily. "I'm willing to enlist anybody who looks like a willing victim."

Nothing would do but Roddy must try too and the piece of wax he chose was quickly gray and grubby looking. Linda worked her piece into the general size and shape Martin wanted. This turtle would be bigger than the live models, but the little ones, turning their noses, gave a much better idea than any picture.

It was quickly evident that of the three pairs of hands working with chunks of wax, Linda's fingers were the most skillful. It was a carving job too, she found, and borrowed a knife of Martin's to make the turtle head more lifelike.

"It's more complicated than you'd think," Linda said. "What's the diorama going to be like? Did you conquer the papier-mâché?"

Martin nodded. "I think so. I can get it the right consistency now. I'd like to use a sort of pond scene, with two or three turtles on the banks. I've got together some pieces of bark and branches that will look like tree stumps. If it's an autumn scene, we won't need any green leaves."

"How will you make the pond?"

"I got a small mirror at the dime store, but I haven't figured out what to do with it yet. It looks too much like a mirror. I tried painting it, but then it stopped looking like water."

"Maybe a clear piece of glass would do better," Linda suggested. "If you put it over some earthy-looking stuff—oh, I don't know, but you could experiment."

"What about helping me to experiment?" Martin asked.

Linda had finished carving a quite realistic looking eye for her turtle before she answered. She had meant not to be drawn into any of Martin's dull museum work and here she was at it in spite of herself. But of course this was for a purpose. This was to lull him into a friendly state so that he would say "yes" to the request she meant to make. Perhaps this was as good a time as any to make it.

"We were wondering," she said, not answering his

question, "about this photography contest we're going to hold. I mean—if the pictures were any good and if they were mounted nicely in uniform size, do you suppose—" It was queer how hard it was to ask anything of Martin Stevens. She stopped and swallowed.

"Do I suppose what?" Martin asked.

"Well, you have a room for temporary exhibits at the Museum, and we wondered—I mean Peter felt we couldn't show the photographs in the gym where we'll probably hold the party, and yet they'll be of real interest to the town and if they could be shown—"

This time she broke off because Martin was shaking his head regretfully.

"Perhaps it could have been managed if the date wasn't as close as six weeks away. But we schedule our art exhibits quite a while ahead of time and there's an outside collection of paintings coming in for the month of December. Our publicity's already going out about it and there isn't much we could do about that."

Linda's first impulse was to toss down her carving tool and the piece of wax that now looked very much like a turtle's head. She might have known that Martin would not accommodate his precious Museum to any amateur project. But she knew the gesture would look like childish pique, so she suppressed it and went on working doggedly at the turtle's second eye. As soon as she decently could she'd get out of Martin Stevens's study and she'd never ask another favor of him.

"I can see that it wouldn't do at all," she said stiffly. "We shouldn't have had such a foolish idea."

Martin gave up his own not-too-successful effort to turn wax into a turtle and sat for a long moment staring thoughtfully at the blotter. Already, Linda thought, he had forgotten her request and was absorbed in his own problems concerning the diorama. To her surprise it was Roddy who made the next contribution, suddenly backing her up.

"Aw, Dad," he protested, "couldn't you junk an old painting exhibit for once? This is important. Gosh! I'll bet a lot of people would even come to the Museum that never came at all before."

Martin looked at his son, the same thoughtful expression on his face.

"I think you have a point there," he admitted. "But while we can't, as you say, junk the exhibit, which in its own modest way is also important to the town, that doesn't mean I've dismissed the plan as entirely impractical."

Linda glanced up quickly while he went on in the same sober, considering tone.

"I was wondering if the basement meeting room would do. There'd be plenty of space around the walls for all the photographs you wanted to hang, and the present pictures could be put away for as long as you wanted the exhibit to remain. Which, of course, would depend on the interest shown in it locally."

Linda experienced a warm rush of what almost resembled liking for Martin Stevens. Perhaps she hadn't been fair. Perhaps there was a grain of the human being in him, after all, and he wasn't all cold fish. But before she could accept the proposal with delight, he had more to say.

"I don't know that it would work out—perhaps the room isn't big enough. But if you and Peter and Babs decide it would do, you could hold the party there too, right where the pictures are on display."

The party in that long room where Gordon had played, Linda thought. She could see it perfectly in her imagination with the chairs cleared out, except for some around the wall and—

"There's a small stage," Martin went on, as if he had to sell her the idea, "and our piano is a good one."

"I know that!" Linda said and gave him a smile that was for once completely natural.

He smiled back and just for a moment she wondered why she had ever thought his expression cold and remote. When he thawed like this he was practically human.

"If the Kenyon boy is going to play," he said, "our piano will probably please him."

"Since he's already tried it," Linda broke in, laughing a little. "Would it be possible to dance there?"

"Why not?" Martin said. "And if you follow through

on this box lunch business the stage will be fine for the m.c."

Roddy jumped up suddenly. "I got some business to attend to," he announced. "Lemme know when you're through with the turtles," and off he went without further explanation.

"Of course," Martin said calmly, "now that I've made all these generous offers, you'll be bound to repay me with the help I need in making turtles for the diorama."

"I thought there'd be a catch," Linda said, but she said it cheerfully, not minding now. He really had been generous and the least she could contribute in return was a little simple work that was also fun.

For an hour they worked together quietly, not talking much, yet with the old antagonism at rest between them. Linda found herself remembering the trick she had tried on Roddy, the trick which hadn't been too successful. "Get somebody to do something for you," Bob Hollis had said. Well, she'd got Martin Stevens to do something for her, and as a result he seemed to like her a little better, for the moment at least.

Later that night, after she had gone to bed, and while Babs was still puttering before the mirror with her nighttime beauty ritual, another slant on the situation struck Linda so suddenly that she turned her face against her pillow and shook with silent laughter.

Who had persuaded whom to do something? Hadn't she spent most of the evening working for Martin Stevens? Hadn't she glowed with pride over his mild praise when three extremely live looking imitation turtles had marched in a row across the green blotter, so that you had to look twice to see which were the real ones and which the make-believe? And before she left, Martin had extracted a promise that she'd see the diorama through to the end and perhaps help in some of the other problems which would arise in its construction.

Her father's psychology seemed to be working better on his own daughter than it had worked with Roddy. Or with Martin Stevens, for that matter. All he wanted was another pair of hands, another imagination to put to work on one of his projects. She knew well enough that she wasn't a human being as far as he was concerned, not any more than his own children were.

"What's so funny?" Babs asked, slathering cream on her face and rubbing it into imaginary wrinkles.

"Funny?" asked Linda innocently.

"You were practically shaking the bed," Babs said. "So I presume you were either laughing or sobbing, and I must say you don't seem to be the weak emotional type."

Linda flopped over on the bed so she could watch the other girl speculatively. What about pulling her into this stunt too?

"I'm over my hilarious mirth," Linda said. "I guess it wasn't very funny, really. Mostly I'm sorry for your father."

"Sorry for Father?" Babs echoed in surprise. "I can't imagine anyone less in need of being pitied."

Linda turned her attention to the ceiling and kept her voice casual. "He has his heart set on that diorama thing, but he's going to come a cropper with it."

"Why? Dad never comes a cropper with anything."

"The foreground's easy enough and even the animals can be worked up by amateurs if they're simple ones like turtles," Linda went on, as if Babs hadn't spoken. "But what he's going to do for a background I wouldn't be knowing. It'll take someone who's really good for that. Good with a paintbrush, I mean."

Babs said nothing at all, busying herself with cleansing tissue as she wiped off her shiny face.

"Oh, well," Linda said, "I expect he can get the art teacher from school, or somebody around town. But I know he's worried about it."

"Your subtlety overcomes me," Babs remarked, turning off the light and crawling into bed. "But in case you're interested, I'm not biting. G'night."

"Umph!" said Linda in disgust. As far as psychiatry went, she'd make a good patient and that was about all. But it was perfectly silly that Babs, with her talent, shouldn't turn her hand to helping her father with that diorama.

17 Double Date

The Shutter-Snappers had spent a busy day. A spell of cold weather had swept down upon Cedarhill, but Saturday had been bright with the necessary sunshine that would give good lights and shadows to photographs, and club members had turned out in a body.

They'd met in the lobby of the post office and had fanned out from there. There was no snow as yet, but ski pants and jackets, knitted caps and mittens were the rule for the girls, while the boys wore plaid lumberjack coats and wool trousers.

"You would start us picture taking at this time of the year!" Babs complained to Peter.

"You've got a point there, little one," he told her. "Next year we'll get going in spring. But thanks to your swell posters we've got a good start this time."

The post office, as well as other public buildings and several stores, had been willing enough to give prominent place to posters advertising the contest for home town pictures, and Babs, protesting every inch of the way, had been bullied by Peter into contributing three of them herself.

They were good too, Linda had thought. Especially the one they'd put up in the post office—a bold modern effect that nevertheless did justice to the town square and the old vine-covered courthouse, and, of course, to a couple of Shutter-Snappers, posed by Peter and Linda aiming their cameras at the scene from different angles. But though Babs had produced the posters, no amount of hinting or wheedling had persuaded her to interest herself in working on a background for her father's diorama. In spite of Linda's own determination to have no sly psychological tricks played on her, she had found herself so genuinely interested in the project, that regardless of her feeling toward Martin Stevens, she had gone to the Museum several times during week ends to putter around and try her hand at anything she could. Lacking a satisfactory background, the project was not going too well. But though she'd suggested Babs as an artist, Martin had been unwilling to ask anything of his own daughter, and Babs's disinterest remained complete.

At the post office the Shutter-Snappers had divided into teams of four or five and gone off in various directions through the town. Peter and Linda were the only owners of reflex cameras with a more complicated combination of shutter stops. Gordon had a folding camera of a good make, but most of the cameras which turned up were the ordinary box type. Linda had felt a little guilty about bringing her father's light meter, since it gave her something of an advantage, but Peter had made a little speech about equipment before they'd started out.

Expensive equipment was fine to have, he pointed out. And of course it was the ambition of every amateur to own all the adjuncts to good picture taking. The best blowups could undoubtedly be made from pictures taken by cameras with lenses so good that the sharpest detail could be caught even in a small print. Nevertheless, they were all pretty much in the same boat when it came to picking subject matter, except perhaps for Linda who had had a bit more experience than the rest of them. And an expensive camera could be just as guilty of catching an inartistic, lifeless shot as one that had cost a fraction of the price.

Buoyed up by Peter's pep talk, they'd gone their various ways to tramp through Cedarhill, looking for shots most typical of that particular home town.

Babs had brought no camera at all, despite Roddy's last minute offer to lend her the box camera Linda had given him. She had announced calmly that she had no interest in jiggling shutters and was going to help Gordon Kenyon select the shots he meant to take. Her artistic leanings, she explained modestly, would be of inestimable value to him. Gordon had accepted her offer cheerfully, but with his usual remote air of the amused observer who hovered on the outskirts, and Linda had a piqued moment of hoping all their shots would be terrible. Babs was going to learn that it took more than she realized to turn out really good photographs.

Into highways and particularly into byways, they'd gone, searching out country lanes, old houses, views of the bridges across the river that bisected the town. Linda had even tried a shot of the much-scorned Museum and Peter had cocked an amused eye at her. So, he seemed to be saying, she was getting to the place where vines took on character interest after all.

Though Babs and Gordon and Peter and Linda tramped the town together, Linda found little satisfaction in the outing. Somehow she had hoped that she and Gordon might drift off together in a few moments of the pleasant companionship they had enjoyed on two previous occasions. But Babs was beside him most of the time, and Linda could not be sure whether it was her arrangement or Gordon's. Certainly she was at her laughing, glowing best today, her lipstick as bright as the red jacket and knitted cap she wore, warmth and vivacity whipping an almost startling beauty into her face to replace the old sullenness.

Even Peter's attention was caught. "Pretty, isn't she —that gal from across the street?" he said to Linda when Babs climbed a stone wall to pose as a model this time, instead of resting her cheek against Gordon's arm while she looked into his camera finder.

"She's stunning," Linda admitted, but there was no enthusiasm in her tone. A girl who could be stunning when she wanted to be, and surly when no one who counted to her was around, wore a beauty that was hardly more than skin deep. Just how much, she wondered, was Gordon deceived by the surface? Certainly he watched Babs with a quiet interest that missed little that she did.

As the afternoon grew late, the whole crowd met again as they'd agreed in the park on the edge of town, where they could roast wieners and toast marshmallows and pour steaming hot chocolate out of thermos bottles picked up at nearby homes late in the day.

They gathered around the fire in the picnic grate and ate and sang and ate again. Tired feet seemed to be the rule and it was decided that picture snapping was a more strenuous sport than they'd thought. But when the food had disappeared and the party was breaking up, Peter was still reluctant to go home.

"There's a good picture at the Strand tonight," he suggested, looking at Linda and Babs. "What do you say we go? How about it, Gordon? Double date?"

"Second the motion, Mister President," Gordon said.

Babs was willing enough. "Fine! Anything to get the weight off my feet. What do you say, Linda?"

She seemed to have no choice in the matter. Everyone took it for granted that Babs would go with Gordon and Linda with Peter, and it was settled with a mere nod from her.

Only Peter seemed to note her lack of enthusiasm. "What's the matter, Linda? All this small town activity too much for you?"

She shook her head brightly. "It will be fun," she assured the others. She wasn't going to follow Babs's example and turn sullen when things didn't go her way. Besides, the last admission she would ever make was that a small town could be too much for her.

"It will give you a chance to see what a Saturday night town looks like," Gordon said, smiling at her over Babs's head. "That will be something worth taking back to New York."

Back to New York? The words seemed to echo through her hollowly. Somehow lately she had thought less and less of how she was going to get back to New York. Not that the longing wasn't sharp in her at intervals, but the prospect of making it come true seemed to fade a little more every day. More and more Cedarhill was pulling her into its own small circle of life, and more and more the violent effort it would take to break that closing-in circle seemed more than she could make.

She was beginning to belong to Cedarhill, not

willingly, but in spite of herself, more than Gordon
Kenyon would ever belong to it. It was easy enough for
him to talk about "going back to New York." Eventu-
ally that was what he was sure to do and the fact was
something hurtful to think about. She didn't want to
like Gordon so much. She didn't want to get hurt. But
in spite of herself her emotions seemed to be moving
down a road that had no satisfactory solution at the
end. Well, she wouldn't look ahead, not an inch. She'd
take each day as it came and live through the good and
bad hours it brought her.

This, she thought ruefully, was what Liz had warned
her would happen some day. Only Liz's warnings had
been gay, as if having it happen would be something
exciting and happy and wonderful. Watching Babs
calmly annex Gordon, made it considerably less than
happy. It would be her luck to go and fall for a boy
who hardly knew she was alive. There was no escaping
the fact that he appealed to her more than any other
boy she'd ever known. He would be someone worth
going around with, worth being "interested in" as Liz
meant the phrase. But it looked more than ever as if
there were not the slightest possibility that Gordon
would ever be interested in Linda Hollis.

The four went home to change and clean up for the
evening and then met again at the Stevens house and
walked downtown. The promise of a Saturday night
town had come true. Parking space around the square
and up the side streets was filled as it never was on a
weekday night. Shops were open for Saturday night
business, their windows brightly lighted. A good-
natured, laughing, talkative crowd jostled elbows on the
sidewalks and movement was slow.

Gordon, walking ahead with Babs, turned back to
the other two. "Just like Broadway, isn't it, Linda?" he
asked.

That was hard to see. There were no tall buildings
and the total sum of Cedarhill's bright lights would
have been a candle's worth on Broadway. There was
the small town stamp of the old-fashioned square with
its sleepy, vine-covered courthouse to further remove

the similarity. No, this certainly wasn't like Broadway, and she shook her head reproachfully at Gordon.

But he wouldn't accept her rejection of his idea. "Close your eyes a minute," he suggested. "Just listen to it. Get the feel of what I mean."

Because it was Gordon making the request she actually went through the motions. She held onto Peter's arm and went along for a moment with her eyes closed, listening. Funny, it did sound almost the same. The same clatter and buzz of voices. Then she half opened her eyes, allowing a sifting of the scene about her to come through. And suddenly it was as if she had been transported all those miles away and set down again at 42nd and Broadway.

She opened her eyes wide and flashed a look of understanding at Gordon. "I do see what you mean."

"It's people that make it the same," Gordon said. "That crowd streaming down Broadway comes from all over the country, and underneath they're you and me and our neighbors in Illinois and Texas and Oklahoma. There're just more of them, and the lights are brighter."

Babs sniffed openly. "Right now this looks to me like Cedarhill and points immediately adjacent."

"Don't mind her," Peter said. "She's the insensitive type."

Gordon laughed and turned back to the girl beside him, but somehow Linda felt faintly comforted. It was to her that Gordon had turned for understanding of his fantasy. He hadn't expected Babs to see what he meant. Probably he couldn't help it that she had quietly assumed proprietorship over him today. Not without being rude. It was even possible that if he had been left to make his own choice, he might have chosen to go to the show with Linda instead. A contrary voice inside her whispered that a boy who was strongly bent on one girl's company, wouldn't allow himself to be so easily thrown with someone else. But she didn't want to listen to the voice, or believe in it. It was just that Gordon wasn't the pushing, forceful type.

He didn't push or force things at the movie either. The two girls sat together, with Gordon next to Babs and Peter next to Linda. It developed that the picture was one Linda had seen in New York months before, but she didn't confess the fact, not wanting to spoil the others' fun. Parts of it were dull to see twice and she was just as glad when the lights went on for the brief intermission between shows and they filed out again into the cool evening.

Away from the lights of the square, Cedarhill's streets stretched quiet and dim. An occasional snatch of radio music poured out an open window. In fact, a good part of the town seemed to be listening to the same program and the same tunes accompanied them on their way from block to block. Babs began to hum a melody and Peter and Gordon joined in. But Linda did not sing. For her this was no enchanted evening, she thought, deep in melancholy induced by starlight and lamplight and music.

She was almost surprised to find him there, when Peter dropped out of the singing and slipped his arm chummily through hers.

"I don't go much for this romantic enchanted stuff," he said, "but it's been swell, Linda. How about doing it again next Saturday night? Just the two of us."

She was surprised and a little embarrassed. Peter was nice. She didn't want to hurt his feelings, but the last thing in the world she wanted was to go out next Saturday with him alone. She walked on in silence, not able to find words to answer him at once. Ahead, Babs clung intimately to Gordon's arm as they walked along. She was such an exciting person, Linda thought. How could she blame Gordon for having his interest caught, for judging only the surface.

Peter turned to look into her face for a moment. He did not repeat his invitation, nor ask why she hadn't answered.

"Babs tries too hard," he said gently. "Or else she doesn't try at all. Poor kid. She gets all mixed up inside."

"Poor kid!" Linda echoed, letting her resentment sound in the words. "I don't know how you figure when she just reaches out and takes anything she wants. She looks out for Babs all right. She doesn't even pay for what she gets, but nothing ever hurts her."

"That's what you think," Peter said. Then he chuckled. "Listen to me turning child psychologist! Now what Babs ought to do is take lessons from you."

"From me?"

"Sure. When a fellow asks her for a date, she ought to just ignore him. Play hard to get."

"Oh, Peter!" Linda said. "I'm sorry. I didn't mean —"

Peter patted her arm soothingly. "I get it. You were so eager to accept that you just forgot what I was saying right in the middle of the invitation."

Linda gave in suddenly. "You're all wrong. I do accept. It was nice of you, Peter, and I'd love to go. I know we'll have fun."

She felt better after that. Peter was a swell person and she liked him. She wouldn't hurt his feelings for anything. Besides, Gordon Kenyon was the moon, and it didn't do human beings any good to go reaching for the moon.

But all the way home, while she listened to Peter's banter, she wondered why it was that human beings had such a fatal weakness for wanting the moon.

18 Day of Surprises

It was only a few days later that Linda and Babs, coming home late from school after a Shutter-Snappers meeting, found Roddy on the way downstairs with a pile of empty cardboard boxes in his arms. The moment he saw them he called excitedly over his shoulder.

"Hey, they're coming! Watch out—they're coming!"

From the floor above Mrs. Stevens called back: "Don't let them come up yet, Roddy. Keep them downstairs for a few minutes more."

Roddy blocked the stairway importantly with himself and the boxes, his eyes dancing. "You can't go up," he announced firmly. "It's a surprise."

Babs exchanged looks with Linda and shrugged. "Probably a new set of green bath towels, or a rug for our dear little room. I can hardly wait."

"Oh, you!" Roddy said. He dumped the boxes over the railing, letting them crash to the floor of the hall, and sat down on the stairs, addressing himself to Linda. "What would you like best of all if you could have one wish? What would you like the very best of all?"

Linda smiled at his eagerness. Roddy had certainly changed in the last few weeks. Her mother must have been quietly taming the savage.

"I'm not sure," she told him. "There seem to be so many things I want."

"Guess one," Roddy ordered. "Just one."

Babs leaned on the rail to look down at the debris of boxes scattered in the hall. "Unless I'm mistaken, that sad looking hatbox is the property of Mrs. Burr. She won't like having it banged around."

168

"Burr's gone," Roddy announced triumphantly. "She's gone for good. Linda, guess something you'd like best."

Realization flashed through Linda. If Mrs. Burr had left—"A room of my own," she said to Roddy.

The grin that broke over his face answered her. "Can they come up yet?" he called again to Mrs. Stevens.

Linda's mother came into the hall, looking a little mussed and dusty. A straggle of hair was coming down over her forehead, and there was a smudge on her chin, but she looked as happy as Roddy.

"Come up, girls," she invited. "I hope you'll like the surprise Roddy and I have planned for you."

Linda flew upstairs, past her mother to Mrs. Burr's room and paused in the doorway. It wasn't the best, or the largest room in the house, but in that moment it looked palatial to Linda. It had been scrubbed and cleaned and polished. Linda's possessions had been moved out of Babs's room, along with the extra furniture and set about to good advantage. Neat, tailored draperies of homespun hung at the windows and there was a bedspread to match. On the small table by the bed stood the lamp Linda had used in her own room back in New York, and somehow it gave this new room the stamp of home. For a special welcoming touch there was a vase of yellow chrysanthemums on the dressing table, with a card attached that read: "To Linda with love."

Happiness and satisfaction welled up inside her. She hadn't fully realized how much she had missed her own room until this moment.

"Mother!" she cried and flung her arms about her in a squeeze that held all the gratitude that was so hard to put adequately into words.

In the middle of the hug something made her look over her mother's shoulder at Babs. The other girl was lounging in the doorway, her eyes a little hard and the usual scornful twist lifting her mouth. When she caught Linda's gaze upon her, she turned abruptly and started back downstairs.

Roddy, who had been wriggling and grinning with

delight over being in on the surprise, turned his grin into a scowl. "What's eating her?"

Linda gave her mother an extra pat and went quickly after Babs. Somehow, in this moment of pleasure over once more having a room of her own, it hurt to have Babs sarcastic and indifferent. Why couldn't she, just once, be happy for someone else's happiness?

"Glad to be rid of me?" she called after her from the top of the stairs.

"Sure am!" Babs snapped without turning.

Mrs. Stevens heard the exchange and came into the hall. "Will you come back here a minute, Babs?"

"What for?" Babs's tone was surly, but Mrs. Stevens ignored it.

"The surprise isn't all for Linda, you know. I hope you'll like your share too."

The other girl's expression was guarded, but she turned and came slowly back upstairs. The others let her step to the door of her room first and then crowded behind her. In Babs's room dotted swiss curtains hung at the windows and the faded bedspread was gone, replaced by a frilly one that matched the curtains. Mrs. Stevens had tried to please the individual taste of each girl. The furniture had been rearranged so that the room was no longer crowded, and a new piece had been added—a comfortable armchair, chintz covered, with a little footstool to match. And again there was the welcoming vase of chrysanthemums with a card attached. The message was plain, even across the room: "To Babs with love," in Mrs. Stevens's handwriting.

Babs looked stonily around, with not the slightest evidence of pleasure on her face.

Mrs. Stevens said gently to Linda and Roddy, "Come along, you two. I need your help."

But anger with Babs was replacing Linda's pleasure over what her mother had done. She had never in her life known anyone so rude and ungrateful as Babs Stevens. She didn't deserve to have anyone bother with her, or try to do anything for her. Linda started to say something sharp and critical, but at that moment the other girl glanced at her quickly and then away. In the brief look Linda saw that Babs's eyes were brimming with tears that she was trying furiously not to shed.

Linda turned back to the door as if she hadn't seen. "You know something?" she said. "Glad as I am to have my own room again, it's going to seem funny not to have you to talk to sometimes at night. How's about having me come over and visit you sometimes?"

Babs said, "If you want to," in a choked voice and Linda slipped quietly off to join her mother and Roddy.

"Now then," Mrs. Stevens announced in a brisk voice, "we've still got work to do. Roddy's been in on the surprise and he's helped me a lot, but we still have a closet to clean out, and trash to dispose of. Of course I've been sewing for weeks—spreads and curtains and a slipcover for that old chair I found in the attic."

"You knew all along Mrs. Burr was leaving?" Linda asked.

"Of course. But we asked her to help with the surprise by not saying anything. We really can't afford a housekeeper, Linda. And with as many helpers as there ought to be in this family, the work won't be too much. I want you to see the way Roddy's begun to help by fixing up his own room."

She pushed open the door of the room next to Linda's to reveal astonishingly shipshape order. Roddy grinned and bounced around almost the way the Rouchneck did when he was praised for something. If he'd had a tail, Linda was sure he'd have wagged it.

When he went downstairs to dispose of the boxes he'd flung over the railing, her mother dropped into the "visitor's chair" in Linda's room.

"We'll have to dig up something comfortable for you later on, instead of these two straight chairs," she said. "But I thought since you were getting a whole new room, Babs ought to have the other chair."

"Of course," Linda said. "And she likes what you've done. I know she does. It's just that she doesn't know how to stop being prickly and unpleasant."

"I know." Her mother got up and went across to close the door to the hall quietly. Then she dropped down on the chair again. "Privacy! It's wonderful. I haven't been able to talk to my own daughter in days, it seems. Linda, I need your help on more than the housework. You've made such a good start with Roddy that I've been able to go ahead a step or two farther with him, but—"

"I made a start with Roddy!" Linda echoed in astonishment. "I thought we were enemies in a temporary truce."

Her mother shook her head. "He thinks you're wonderful. Couldn't you tell just now how happy he was over your surprise?"

"But I—I mean all I did was scold him and threaten to break that precious giraffe, and—"

"No, honey. You made him get the feeling of what a terrible thing he'd done to you. But you didn't go on acting as if he were really bad. When you gave him that camera, I think you won him for life."

"I didn't think he cared anything about it."

"He does though. No, Roddy isn't our problem. Babs is. She's older and it's harder for her to soften and change. Roddy doesn't remember much about his own mother, so he doesn't resent me. Babs does. In Babs's eyes I'm the fairy-tale stepmother and she isn't going to trust me. But you can reach her, Linda. I know you can."

"How? I've tried to make friends with her, goodness knows. But she's all cement wall covered with brambles. You can't get hold of her without getting scratched. I've been clawed so often I'm tired of trying."

"The brambles are there to hide the break in the wall," her mother said gently. "I'm sure it's there, but I don't know how to find it. Until we do find it we can't make this a really happy home. Try, Linda. Please try."

Linda got up restlessly and walked to the window where she could look down upon the patchy rear lawn and the flower beds that had begun to take on a clean, fresh look since their arrival. She didn't know how to answer her mother. After all, why should she try to reach Babs? She didn't like the other girl very well. Besides, she doubted very much that there was anything besides strong cement underneath those brambles.

It was true that she'd been moved to tears just now, but Linda was sure that when she saw the other girl again, Babs would be as hard and ungracious as ever.

Her mother came to stand beside Linda and put an arm about her shoulder. "I can't tell you how happy I am that things are going nicely now between you and Martin. I mean the way you're helping him with the diorama and behaving in a friendly way toward him. It means that our adjustment problems in this new life are beginning to clear up. All except the one concerning Babs."

Linda stiffened her shoulders beneath her mother's arm. There was no use trying to explain that the problem of real adjustment with Martin Stevens could never be cleared up. She didn't like him any better than she ever had. She had softened toward him a little when he had offered the basement room for the party and photograph exhibit. But even in that gesture she knew he was merely doing something for the good of the Museum. Certainly he wasn't regarding her in any comradely fashion, as if she were a real human being. To him she was just another cog to be used whenever he could. He probably didn't even know she had feelings. No wonder he'd done such a hopeless job of being a father. He was much more interested in those wax turtles than in his own son and daughter.

Her mother must have sensed her withdrawal, for her arm dropped away from Linda's shoulders. But before she could say anything more, an interruption came in the form of sudden furious activity down in the back yard.

Across the grass raced the Roughneck, barking shrilly, and after him came Roddy Stevens yelling and chasing the little dog about the yard. Linda took one look and raced for the stairs. So Roddy had been tamed, had he? Roddy was a new character who wouldn't do cruel things any more? Like fun he was!

She tore out the kitchen door and into the yard, but by the time she reached the scene the chase had ended and she was in time to see Roddy carry the struggling, barking Roughneck through the basement door. Her first impulse was to shout at him to put the dog down, but curiosity stopped her. She wanted to know what he was up to. If she stopped him now he'd never tell her, and if she wanted to save Roughy from torment she had better know what was going on.

She went swiftly toward the house, slipped behind bushes that hid one of the basement windows, and dropped to her knees in the dirt to peer through the glass. Roddy had the lights on, so it was easy to see inside. The scene was a surprising one. Instead of teasing Roughy, the boy was trying to quiet him. And Roughy was not in the least afraid or resentful. Apparently the chase in the yard had been a game that Roughy now wanted to continue and that Roddy meant to end because he had another purpose in view.

As she watched, Roddy reached for a dish of dog food and held it temptingly under Roughy's nose. Willingly enough, the dog switched his attention from play to the prospect of eating, but Roddy did not set the dish down before him at once. Instead, he held it out to Roughy, coaxing him, but backing slowly away across the basement. And then Linda noted something else.

Over near the foot of the stairs, regally indifferent to Roddy and the dog, the Khan was having his own supper. He ate with small, dainty bites, neatly and precisely. Not until Roddy and the dog were close at hand, did the big cat look up from his dish. Then, to Linda's surprise, he returned to eating without concern. Roddy set the dog's dish down a few feet from the cat's and Roughy followed it eagerly. He was not quite so indifferent as the Khan about the proximity of his recent enemy, but after a moment's hesitation he went to work on the food, with only a glance now and then in the cat's direction.

Linda watched for a few minutes more and then got quietly up from her hiding place behind the bushes. Well! How long had this been going on, she wondered? Certainly it wasn't the first attempt Roddy had made in this direction or the animals would not have accepted the situation so calmly. He must have been working on his scheme secretly for quite a while. Her mother had been in on it too. Linda could recall several times when she had been about to feed Roughy and her mother had told her quickly that he'd been taken care of earlier. She'd supposed of course that her mother had fed him, but it must have been Roddy right along. She couldn't help but wonder why he had done it. Was there something more back of this than immediately met the eye?

She walked thoughtfully around to the front of the house so that Roddy wouldn't catch her out in back and know that she had been spying on him. Peter hailed her from across the street, pausing in his job of hedge trimming to wave the clippers at her. She sauntered over to watch him work, thinking about Roddy and Babs and the request her mother had made of her. Peter knew Babs better than anyone else.

She told him about Mrs. Burr's departure, about the new room, and about the way Babs had received the changes in her own room, first with sullenness and then tears.

"I was talking to Mother about her," Linda said. "I think she's a solid cement wall covered with brambles. I don't think there's any getting at her. But Mother thinks there are chinks in the cement. Maybe she's sort of a Secret Garden, like that book I read when I was a little girl. Maybe there's a gate somewhere under the tangle of vines."

Peter concentrated on his clipping for a few minutes, considering her words. "Are you looking for the key?" he asked.

Linda shrugged. "Not especially. She can stay a mystery, for all of me. She doesn't make much sense. One minute she's sharp and unpleasant and unkind, and the next she's doing you a favor you never expected."

"If you're consulting me as Dr. Crowell, the eminent psychiatrist, I'll give you my opinion. At fifteen dollars an hour, of course."

"Not even fifteen cents," Linda said. "But go ahead."

Peter dropped his bantering air. "I remember Babs's mother very well. She was an affectionate sort of person. Those kids were loved a lot. I mean kissed and petted and shown affection. After Mrs. Stevens died, it was—well, it was different."

Linda nodded. "I can imagine. With that cold fish of a father."

"Maybe he's not a cold fish. People are different. Take my own mother and father. Mom's always sort of slopping over. Anyway, that's what Dad calls it. She doesn't mind that he can't do the same thing because she knows how he feels inside. Maybe it's that way with Martin Stevens too. Maybe he just can't show Babs the kind of affection she needs. But if you want to find her Achilles' heel, I know what it is."

"Chinks in the cement, Achilles' heel—it's all one. I'm listening, Dr. Crowell."

He didn't smile. "She needs somebody to need her. We all want that, I guess, but most of us have it. Just get in trouble around Babs so that you need her help and watch what a softy she is."

Linda thought back, recalling the times when Babs had been helpful and kind. That time when Roughy had been clawed by the Khan, and when Roddy had got into Bob Hollis's things in the basement. But then as soon as everything was all right again, she was as unpleasant as ever.

"I'm afraid I don't want her for a friend enough to go around getting in trouble all the time, just so she can feel needed," Linda said. "That makes life too complicated."

"Right," Peter agreed. "But it's an approach. It's a way of getting through."

"Anyway it doesn't always work," Linda objected. "I tried to make her see how much she could help Martin if she'd paint a background for that diorama, and she got very hoity-toity and wouldn't lift a finger."

"Sure. She's suspicious and on the defensive. It's got to be the real thing, not something cooked up. Just the way you're on guard against Martin Stevens and won't let him be nice to you, even when he tries."

Linda's mouth dropped open in surprise. Then she whirled indignantly and started across the street.

"Don't go away mad," Peter called cheerfully.

She turned back for a second. "Amateur psychiatrists

can stir up an awful lot of trouble. You're meddling with things you don't know anything about!"

Peter turned his back on her and went clipping his way toward the rear of the house. Linda returned to the Stevenses and dropped into the swing on the porch. She pushed herself lazily back and forth with one toe, the other foot curled under her, and thought about Peter and the things he had said. She felt thoroughly annoyed with him. He was altogether too fresh and too much of a know-it-all. When Gordon Kenyon put out an opinion, he did it diplomatically and gently. He didn't slap and antagonize. And yet, somehow, Gordon's interest in people and in what was going on around him was always of the spectator variety. Peter had more of a tendency to get mixed up in life himself. Gordon stayed on the sidelines and watched. It made him more intriguing in a way, more tantalizing to know. If ever you could get him off the sidelines— She pushed the swing dreamily back and forth and stopped thinking about the problem of Babs Stevens.

19 Photographer's Model

It looked as if the photography contest was going to be a success. Pictures had begun to pour in, and not only were the Shutter-Snappers submitting their shots right and left, but a real interest had developed on the part of the town.

The newspaper was running pieces about interesting spots in and around Cedarhill in response to questions about places of local interest. Photographs were being submitted to a committee voted upon by the club, and put safely away till the day of the big party and opening exhibit.

Linda had experienced an unexpected sense of frustration over the whole thing. She had not intended to bother about entering a picture herself, but somehow, as she watched the photographs come in, the old fever began to stir in her. However, though she took shot after shot, she could not find exactly what she wanted.

None of her efforts satisfied her and she discarded them, one after another.

On this particular night she was working at the Museum, helping Martin assemble the diorama. The little scene had begun to take on lifelike proportions. Linda had managed to solve the problem of making the pool look like a pool by painting a sheet of glass on the underside with a brownish mixture of color that really gave the effect of looking through water into a muddy pool. Martin had been quite pleased.

Tonight they were fixing rocks and stumps, dried moss and the rest of their woodland collection, onto the gluey surface of the papier-mâché ground prepared to receive them. Linda had just posed one of her turtle creations on the bank of the muddy glass pond, and sat back to get the effect. Without warning inspiration struck her.

"I know!" she cried, jumping up from her place at the worktable. "I know what I'm going to use for a picture in the contest!"

Martin glanced up from his task of sprinkling earth on the prepared ground.

Linda pointed dramatically. "The diorama! That's my picture!"

"You mean just that alone—an imitation woodland scene?" Martin asked doubtfully.

"No. What I want is a scene here at the Museum. Here in this workroom. A flashlight picture taken while the diorama is still incomplete."

"Mmm. Sounds like a possibility," Martin said.

Linda ignored his lack of enthusiasm. She was sufficiently used to him now to know that he always thought about an idea for a long while before he decided whether to approve or disapprove. But she was a Hollis, and given to her father's quick enthusiasms. The moment the idea hit her, she knew it was what she had been looking for. The work done here at the Museum was a real part of Cedarhill. It represented the town too, and still more important, it had novelty. It was a scene no one else would present.

"I'll make it a flashlight picture," she went on. "You can be holding one of those turtles—just putting it into place and—"

Martin shook his head. "Sorry, but you'll have to get somebody else to pose. I prefer not to be in the picture myself."

She stared at him impatiently for a moment, wondering if she should plead with him, or argue. But she knew it wouldn't be any use. Probably he'd decided that it wouldn't be dignified for the director of the Museum to pose for anything so frivolous as a photograph in an amateur contest. Whatever his reason, he would stick to it with his usual unyielding tenacity.

"Anyway," she said, "I'm going home for my camera and some flash equipment. I'll be back right away."

Martin was obviously not too pleased with the turn of events. His interest lay in completing the diorama, and never mind about side issues. But he gave her a grave smile as she rushed off, and offered no spoken objections.

She hurried the few blocks toward home and went into the house like a whirlwind. There was a special shelf in the closet in her room that she kept for her camera and its attachments. Roddy heard her race upstairs and followed interestedly. Even Babs, who'd been washing her hair and had fluffed it out over her shoulders to dry, put her head out of her room to see what was going on.

"Fire anyplace?" she asked. "Don't tell me the Museum's burning down?"

Once or twice Linda had experienced the curious feeling that Babs was resentful of the help she was giving to Martin on the diorama. But now she paused in the doorway of her room and looked at Babs across the hall.

The other girl was wearing blue jeans and a plaid shirt. Her hair was nearly dry and it fell naturally into soft dark waves. Even when she wasn't dressed up, Babs looked lovely and Linda remembered her first impression—that the girl would make a wonderful model.

Linda pushed Roddy out of the way and crossed the hall. Another inspiration had struck her and she knew she had to carry it through.

"Babs, you've got to pose for me! I have the most wonderful idea for a picture to submit in the contest. But I've got to have somebody in it—it can't be just a still life. And you'd be wonderful just the way you are."

"What are you talking about?" Babs asked suspiciously.

"If you'll do this for me," Linda pleaded, "I'll leave you alone from now on. I need someone for this picture, and you'd be perfect."

"Doing what?" said Babs.

"Working on that diorama for your father. I want to take some flashlight shots of it in the making."

"Since I'm not working on it," Babs said, "it would be a fake."

Linda looked at her for a moment in speculative silence. "It wouldn't need to be a fake," she said thoughtfully. "It wouldn't hurt you to help on it when your father needs you so much."

Babs sniffed. "That's likely."

Linda thrust back an impulse to answer sharply. "I won't argue with you. And I won't coax. I'll just ask you, and you can answer me straight out. Babs, will you please come over to the Museum and pose for this picture?"

For a moment or two she wasn't sure what the other girl would do. Babs stood there in the doorway uncertainly, tugging at a corner of the towel flung over her shoulders. Then, abruptly, she pulled it off and tossed it onto the bed in her room.

"Okay, city girl. This will win you sixty-fifth place, but come along."

Roddy came with them, of course. He wasn't going to miss a show like this. All the way to the Museum Linda chattered about the diorama and photography, with Roddy interrupting now and then, and Babs walking along, remote and silent.

When Martin looked up from his work to see that Linda had brought his son and daughter back with her, his face lighted in greeting.

"More volunteers?" he asked.

"Nope," Linda shook her head. "One unwilling prisoner and one interested observer. Think we can do anything with 'em?"

Roddy spotted the diorama and went over to examine it. Babs draped herself on a chair with a great show of indifference. In one corner of the room stood the unsatisfactory background which Martin had finally decided would have to do for the diorama. Linda got it and set up the somewhat splotchy mass of green streaks that was supposed to represent woodland greenery behind the papier-mâché scene.

"Of course it isn't finished," she explained to Babs. "We have to get the foreground blended into the background before the thing's done, but it won't look so bad when it's completed, do you think?"

"I think it's horrible," Babs said flatly. "That background's going to ruin the whole thing. Who cooked that up?"

Linda sighed. "I did. We had to have something, but goodness knows I'm no scene painter. I thought perhaps we could get by with something impressionistic that would suggest what we want."

"If you squint your eyes it looks pretty good," Roddy offered.

Martin was watching them without comment, but Linda, glancing at him, caught a surprising twinkle in his eyes. He wasn't so dense; he knew perfectly well what she was up to.

"I tried my own hand at a scene," he said gravely, "but I decided Linda's was better. Roddy, bring over that canvas leaning against the wall there."

This was something Linda herself hadn't seen. Martin had actually tried to sketch in a scene and had begun painting it in one corner. His trees looked like props and his colors were wrong. But, looking at it, Babs came abruptly out of her lethargy.

"It's not good," she said judicially, "but it's better than that gunk Linda's painted." She picked up a pencil from the worktable and began sketching boldly over Martin's light lines.

There was a solemn, enveloping silence in the room. Linda held her breath, half afraid that the slightest sound might distract Babs from what she was doing and remind her that she couldn't afford to be friendly and pleasant. After a moment or two of working in complete absorption, Babs looked up and her eyes went from one to another of the three faces turned her way. Then she grinned at them cheerfully, though her words were as mocking as ever.

"Relax," she said. "Start breathing. The trap has sprung and the victim's caught. Why didn't you let me know you were in such a bad way?"

Linda and Martin exchanged glances over Babs's head. Then Linda began to set up her camera, with

Roddy's efforts hindering more than they aided her. Once Babs glanced their way and Linda grinned.

"Just keep working," she said. "I'll try some unposed shots and then do some arranged ones."

As she worked, Linda tried to remember her father's advice about flashlight pictures. His words came back to her sharply as she recalled so many of the points he had given her in discussions of his own pictures and those of beginners. Strangely, for the first time, it hurt less to remember his words, to work with his things. She felt closer to him than she had in a long time, and with less of a sense of loss.

Babs had found paints and was experimenting with color shades, in order to get the effect a diorama should have of blending into the background. She propped the flexible canvas she was working with behind the foreground material and curved it in semicircular fashion as it would stand when completed.

"If you put this big grubby looking rock on the far bank of your pond," she suggested, "it will hide the horizon line and I can continue with some pond and stream stuff in the background. What do you think?"

Martin considered the effect. "Sounds possible. If you do a good job with the painting, the illusion should be right."

"I'll do a good job," Babs said calmly and went back to work.

When Linda had completed her shots and packed up her camera equipment, she stayed uncertainly for a few moments watching Babs and Martin at work. She had never before seen father and daughter in such accord.

"Roddy," she said, waggling a beckoning finger at him, "how about helping me get this stuff back to the house? Maybe I can go over and get things started in Peter's darkroom."

Roddy was ready enough for action. Babs hardly looked up when they went out the door, but her father followed them into the hall. Roddy clattered ahead downstairs, but Martin stopped Linda with a hand on her arm.

"Thank you," he said gravely. "You've accomplished quite a lot tonight, Linda."

She was pleased with his praise. True, she knew she'd never be able to feel any real affection for Martin Stevens, but she had to admit that praise from him, praise that would never be given unless deserved, was worth having. She said good night in a more friendly manner than she'd ever used toward him and went downstairs behind Roddy, feeling a little proud and pleased with herself.

20 Quarrel

The box supper and opening of the contest exhibit were only two days off and the basement room at the Museum had been transformed. The folding chairs were lined around the room and all the paintings removed from the walls. The contest committee, assisted by a handful of volunteers, were busily engaged in hanging the exhibit pictures.

Linda was there, and of course Peter. Gordon had come with the rest, right after school, and gone to work with a will. Even Babs had turned up an hour later and was examining the exhibit a bit snootily.

It was Gordon who discovered the photograph Linda had taken of Babs working on the diorama. A long whistle drew the attention of the rest of the room.

"Say, this is really good!" Gordon said. He propped it against the back of a chair and stood off to look at it.

Linda turned, hammer in hand, from the picture she was tacking up and waited to hear more. She'd been fairly well pleased with the way the picture had turned out. It was the best of the lot she had taken, an unposed shot which had caught Babs placing the unfinished background around the diorama to try the effect. In Babs's absorption and interest, all the sulkiness had gone from her face and she made a lovely picture. The composition was good, Linda felt, and so were the storytelling qualities of the picture. Peter had been lavish in his praise, prophesying that she'd win first place hands down.

Oddly enough, Linda didn't particularly want that. Of course she'd like to live up to her father's name and show what Bob Hollis's daughter could do. But even more, she had been caught by Peter's spirited intention to make this an interesting annual event in Cedarhill. It would be better for future contests if a real home towner won first place this time. But to have Gordon discover the picture and praise it made her wonderfully proud.

Babs ambled across the room and stood at his elbow. "How could it miss—with a model like that?"

Gordon smiled his agreement. "The model's not bad, but the photography's better. Did you take this, Peter?"

Peter balanced himself on top of his ladder and looked around. "Wish I had. Linda took it. She's the only professional around here."

"I might have known." Gordon's eyes met Linda's across the room. "Nice going," he said, and went to work hanging the mounted picture.

Linda returned her attention to the stack of photographs on a chair beside her. The elation had gone out of her as quickly as it had risen. Of course Gordon had been attracted to the picture, since it showed Babs off to such good effect. His words, "I might have known," were no more than recognition of the fact that Linda should rightly possess talent for this sort of thing. She wished she didn't mind it that Babs was always at Gordon's elbow and he seemed always interested in her. They hadn't had any outright dates, but neither had Gordon made a date with Linda or any other girl.

There were times now and then when Linda decided resentfully that Gordon felt too good for Cedarhill. But in more generous moments she knew that wasn't true. He was often aloof and withdrawn. There had never again been a time like that one night when they had sat on the river bank and talked so honestly and frankly about themselves. But he was not being superior. She knew it wasn't that.

She kept her back turned upon the rest of the room, so that she wouldn't have to watch Babs playing up to him, teasing him, getting him to smile that slow grave smile that was somehow so winning. One by one she picked up photographs from the pile, working doggedly.

The committee, of which she was not a member, had sorted the submissions into their proper age groups and they were being hung in the same way, so that the judges could consider all of one category together.

Linda was working on the pictures submitted by grade school children and some of them were pretty bad. Nevertheless, the kids had gone to work with enthusiasm and in many cases imagination. Even when the photography was poor, there was often a story in the picture, and that counted for a lot. Now, however, lost in disturbed thoughts about Gordon, Linda had stopped looking at the subject of each picture as she hung it. She put them up automatically, her thoughts far away. For that reason she had not noted the picture in her hands until Peter called to her from across the room.

"What do you think of it, Linda?"

She came back with a start from a dreamy, long lost moment under the stars, and stared at the photograph in her hands. For an instant she could hardly believe her eyes. Then she held it off at arm's length to get a really good look.

There was just one person who could have taken this picture—Roddy Stevens. And for the junior group it was really very good. However, it was not the photography which interested her, so much as the astonishing subjects who had posed for the picture.

There was no mistaking the Roughneck, no mistaking Genghis Khan in all his royal beauty. The scene was near the back steps of the Stevens house and judging by the shadows the time was early morning. Roughy and the Khan were having breakfast. They were having breakfast, not in dishes distantly placed, but from one and the same dish! There was humor in the scene, too, because both animals were so completely in character.

Genghis Khan was eating in his usual dainty manner, a bit of food caught between disdainful teeth, with no attention wasted on the dog beside him. Roughy's nose was over the dish, but with one ear cocked in the Khan's direction and his eyes watching the cat warily.

Nevertheless, there were the two, the erstwhile bitter
enemies, breakfasting from the same dish.

Linda took the photo across the room and held it out
to Babs. "Will you look at what your young brother has
done. And I don't mean just the fact that it's a good
picture."

"Well, what do you know?" Babs said. "I had an
idea he was up to something, but I didn't know what it
was."

"It's a doggone good picture, too," Peter put in.
"What's more, he did every bit of work on it himself
over in my darkroom. He had to try the enlarging four
or five times before he could get it as good as that, but
he stayed right with it. I think photography's got a
convert there."

"Pat yourself on the back, Linda," Gordon said
quietly. "You did it, you know."

She flashed him a look of surprise.

"Of course you did," he insisted. "Babs told me
about what happened that time he broke into your
dad's pictures."

Linda shook her head and took the picture back to
place it on the wall, but her eyes were shining. Of
course she hadn't wrought the change in Roddy, not by
herself. It had been her mother too, and the pleasanter
atmosphere of the house, a little friendliness and interest. Bit by bit Roddy's antagonistic attitude had evap-
orated, without her fully realizing what had happened.
Probably it hadn't gone very deep anyway; it was just a
defense against a world that he'd thought didn't want
him.

Then, just as she was about to tack the photograph
in place, an impulse seized her. Smiling to herself,
Linda tucked the picture under her arm and hurried
upstairs to Martin's office. He and Miss Foster were
admiring the finished diorama in its place on a corner
table. Next week the special glass case that would pro-
tect it would arrive and it would take an honored
position among the nature exhibits downstairs on the
main floor. Babs had done the good job she'd promised
on the background and the result was a very natural
woodland scene, blending skillfully into the foreground

where lazy turtles basked on logs and mud banks in sunshine that would be furnished by an electric spotlight. This was the first time Linda had seen the whole thing assembled.

She held Roddy's picture behind her and went into the office. Miss Foster smiled a greeting, but Martin, absorbed, did not look around.

"It's awfully good," Linda said. "Babs has a lot of talent. Do you think she'll help with some more scenes now?"

Martin sighed. "She doesn't seem interested. I broached the subject, but she wouldn't be pinned down. I agree that she has talent, but she doesn't seem to care about art school, or doing anything constructive about it. Guess I just don't understand you kids these days. When I was young, I was bound I'd get the education I wanted and nothing was going to stop me. Show me the youngster who feels that way now."

"I don't believe that," Linda objected. But even as she spoke the words she wondered if she could prove them. Wasn't she herself a drifter too, very much like Babs? No one direction pulled her strongly. Mostly her one fighting impulse had been connected with turning backwards to the old life in New York. But next year she'd be through high school. Even if she returned to New York, it wouldn't be to the old life. And what else was there? It seemed to her that Gordon was like that too. He had a wonderful gift in his music, but he seemed ready to drift and accept whatever came his way, whatever was handed him. Only Peter was different. Peter would go places. He'd be something. But before she could form an answer to the words she'd resented, Miss Foster spoke her own opinion.

"Perhaps we forget when we get older, Martin. There were plenty of uncertain ones with no direction in our day too. It takes some people longer than others to grow up and find out what they want to settle for."

Martin shook his head again. "I can only remember that I wasn't like that and it disturbs me to find that my own children don't seem to have the get-up-and-go that I had."

"There's one member of your family who has it,"

Linda said, thrusting the picture forward. "Look what Roddy's done."

It was Miss Foster who exclaimed in delight and took the picture out of her hands to prop it against some books on Martin's desk. Linda, afraid that Martin didn't understand, began to explain hurriedly.

"He took the picture himself, and with Peter acting as adviser, he enlarged it, printed it and did the mounting."

"But before he could take it," Martin mused, "he had to get that cat and dog on speaking terms."

"That's what I mean!" Linda cried. "That took determination and patience and a lot of what you call get-up-and-go."

Martin's slow smile was somehow warming. He looked so pleased and hopeful, though even now there was no outward exuberance about him, as there would have been with Bob Hollis. He was simply quietly proud, and for the first time Linda did not feel critical of the fact. For him that was the right way.

"Thank you, Linda, for bringing this up here to show me," he said. "We'll have to work out some sort of surprise reward for Roddy, what do you say? Maybe you can help me on that."

She nodded happily and took the picture back downstairs.

That night, sitting in her own room at the desk she had improvised by refinishing an old table she'd found in the attic, Linda wrote to Liz, giving her friend an account of the things which had happened in Cedarhill lately, putting down on paper a few of her worries as well. Liz was still her best friend and they exchanged letters regularly.

She wrote first about the disturbing thing that had just happened between herself and Babs:

> Babs and I got home late this afternoon after getting the exhibit hung. Roddy was out on the porch with some of that wild life collection of his. Roughy was sitting a few feet away watching interestedly, but not getting into anything. I guess he's learned.

While I was trying to think of just the right thing to show Roddy how I felt about the picture and what he'd done in getting Roughy and Genghis Khan to be friends, Babs as usual blurted everything out. She said something about our having a budding photographic genius in the family and she said it in that cutting tone she uses when she wants to hurt. Roddy turned scarlet and started picking up his animals.

I was so mad at Babs I got absolutely wild. I gave her everything I'd been storing up ever since I came here. I told her that all she was good for was tramping on people's feelings and spoiling everyone else's fun. She was so busy being better than anybody else and sorry for herself because she had to associate with us that she never got a glimpse of how crummy she looked to the rest of us. I said that after she'd done such a good job on that diorama, the least she could do was offer to help out with another one when she saw how much her father wanted her to. But no—she'd been too busy being superior to Cedarhill and everything in it. Then I wound up by telling her she wasn't good enough for Cedarhill, not one bit good enough. And that she didn't deserve a father like Martin Stevens, or a brother like Roddy. Liz, I was so *mad!*

She just stood there staring at me with her face white and her eyes snapping as if in a minute or two she'd collect herself and bite my head off. But I didn't care. I wasn't through and I went right on. I told her Peter had her number all right when he said that the only time she was ever nice to anybody was when they were in a jam. But I added some to what Peter said. I told her I supposed that was as good a way as any to help her feel superior, at someone else's expense. Maybe I'd have thought up a couple more points, but right then she whirled around and went in the house. I'm sure you could hear the door bang four blocks away.

Roddy just sat there on his heels gaping at us both, while one of his snakes wriggled over to the edge of the porch and got away. Roughy put his nose between his paws and tucked in his tail the way he does when anybody scolds him and I had to pick him up and hug him so he wouldn't think I was angry with him. I told Roddy one of his snakes had escaped, but he didn't seem to care. The funny thing was he stood right up to me to defend his sister.

"You hadn't ought to have talked to her like that," he said. "She's okay. She just likes to shoot off her mouth. She don't mean half what she says."

I was shaking from "shooting off" my own mouth and I guess the grin I gave Roddy was shaky too.

"Anyway I'm proud of having a brother like you," I told him. And then I went on and said I liked his picture and thought it was wonderful the way he got those two animals to be almost friends. He gave me a sheepish sort of look and after a couple of minutes he climbed over the porch rail and jumped down into the garden to look for his snake. I couldn't go on yelling praises after him, so I gave up and went into the house to wash up for dinner. I was so disappointed over the way things had gone that I felt practically sick. Somehow I've got awfully fond of that little boy.

The door to Babs's room was closed and she didn't come down to dinner. I told Mother what I'd done and she said it was too bad, but it couldn't be helped now, and in a way Babs had it coming to her for belittling Roddy's picture. At dinner Martin made it up to Roddy by saying all the right things (sometimes I almost like that man), and Roddy cared a whole lot more about what his father thought than the rest of us anyway. Mother took a tray up to Babs's room after dinner, but she wouldn't open her door to get it and didn't come out all evening. When I came upstairs just now I tapped on her door and told her I was sorry I'd lost my temper, but she didn't answer. This is a kettle of fish. And I've done it all with my own little temper. I'm disgusted with Babs, but I'm disgusted with me too, Liz!

Linda made the last exclamation mark big and black by inking it in twice. Then she sat for a while with her pen poised over the paper, thinking about Babs. And about other things. Things she somehow found it difficult to write, even to Liz.

Day after tomorrow was Saturday, the day of the box supper. Tickets had sold like anything and the younger crowd was turning out in full force. They'd decided to run two parties. One in the afternoon for the youngsters, and the big affair, box supper and dance following, in the evening. There was to be no pairing off ahead of time in couples. You came as you pleased and you didn't settle for your evening partner until the supper boxes had been auctioned off.

In theory the bidding would be strictly on the merits of each box and no one would know whose box he was bidding for. But her mother had warned that it seldom turned out that way. You could never persuade the girls to keep the secret of their own boxes. And the boys usually kept close watch so they could bid for the boxes of the girls they wanted to be with for the evening.

All along Linda had assured herself that what happened at the affair didn't matter as far as she was concerned. She wanted to see the photography contest a success, but she didn't care about the rest. She wasn't well enough known in town so that many boys would investigate to see which box was hers, and she couldn't expect the bidding popular girls who had lived in Cedarhill all their lives would get.

It was quite likely, she explained in a brave paragraph in her letter to Liz, that no one would bid for her box at all. She had to be prepared for that and not mind if it happened. That was one of the penalties connected with this change. Of course there was Peter.

She paused in her writing to think about that. She had had a couple of movie dates with him which had been anything but romantic. In a way it was like going out with a brother. Peter wasn't any different on a date than he was any other time. He liked to talk to her, liked her company. Probably he'd bid something on her box at the party if no one else did, but somehow she couldn't be excited about the prospect. Oh well, she would just have to take what the evening handed her.

She finished the letter and addressed an envelope to Liz. Then she pushed back from the desk and sat a while longer looking out the window, dreaming a little.

What part would Gordon play at the party? Would he bid for Babs's box when the time came, or wouldn't he bid at all? Somehow she couldn't imagine his taking a strong and determined stand about anything. Of course, if the way Babs had been hanging around him lately meant that he wanted her to hang around, then undoubtedly he'd bid for her box.

Anyway, there was no telling till the time came. Dreaming didn't get you anywhere. At least she wasn't going to throw herself at Gordon, no matter what happened.

Her mother came upstairs just then and went past the open door of her room. Linda heard her cross to Babs's door and tap on it softly to ask if she might come in. What Babs's answer was Linda couldn't hear, but after a moment her mother went into her room and closed the door behind her. Linda waited uneasily for her to come out. But when she left Babs, she went down the hall to her own room and Linda could not know what had happened.

She felt a little jealous. In the old life her mother had always told her about everything. But evidently her own daughter was not to hear the result of her talk with Babs.

Then, after a moment, she shrugged the unpleasant thoughts aside. It would make things worse with Babs if her mother came right to Linda after a talk with her. It was more sensible this way.

21 Rival Boxes

It was late afternoon of the momentous Saturday. Linda had the kitchen to herself as she worked on the project of her supper box. She'd have liked to do it earlier, but Babs had taken over the kitchen at three o'clock and closed the swinging door, so Linda had stayed out.

Yesterday Babs had come out of her retreat, but she was cool and subdued, and spoke only in monosyllables to Linda when Linda spoke to her. The rest of the time Babs ignored her, and when it was possible avoided being in the same room with her. Apparently she had no intention of forgiving, or of making friends. Linda had no idea of what her box looked like because Babs had come out of the kitchen carrying it under a mound of brown paper, and had taken it right upstairs.

Thanks to Mrs. Stevens, the refrigerator was stocked with an imaginative assortment of good eats, though she'd left it to each girl to create her own supper box without suggestions from her. Linda had found herself considering ingredients in the light of what Gordon Kenyon might like, just in case he might be interested enough to find out which box was hers. Peter would be easy to please. He'd go for thick slices of bread slathered with butter and anything in between that spelled FOOD. Mrs. Stevens had baked both cake and pie, and judging by the wedges missing, Babs had helped herself liberally to both kinds of dessert. Linda decided to do the same. But when it came to sandwiches it would be more fun to fix up something delectable and sophisticated that an exceptional boy would appreciate.

Breast of chicken, for one thing. Combined with a savory dressing. You could do interesting things with cucumber and watercress too. She worked with one eye warily on the clock. The affair was scheduled to start at six and she had to bathe and dress before then. Both she and the box had to look as pretty as possible, and that required time for each.

Her mother had gone over to the Museum to help out with the youngsters' affair in the afternoon and was due back any minute. Linda wanted to have her box finished to show her by the time she arrived.

Even more important than the contents of the box was the outside, since that was the show window that would sell it to some masculine bidder. Though what use all this trouble was, she didn't know, since Gordon would probably bid on Babs's box anyway. Undoubtedly Peter would bid no matter how the box looked. So why, why couldn't it be Peter she wanted to please, instead of Gordon?

Nevertheless, she went right on laboring to make her box as attractive as possible. She'd spent half an hour yesterday in the dime store downtown letting her imagination run riot as she bought paper wrappings, lace doilies and ribbon. Her box had to be as artistic as she could make it, since Babs, with her talent, would create something really knockout, and she wanted to beat Babs at her own game, whether anyone bid or not.

Linda had found a large-sized shoe box to hold her sandwiches and had lined it neatly with wax paper. For a color scheme she'd decided on blue and white with a touch of silver. She'd covered the box deftly on the outside with blue and white striped paper, and now she packed the sandwiches and dessert into it neatly. It was full to the brim. In fact she was afraid everything was going to get slightly squashed when she put the cover on. She tried it out gingerly, hoping for the best.

Next came the final decorations. From the white paper doilies she cut scallops of lace and pasted them around the rim of the box just below the edge of the cover. The effect was decorative and unusual. Then she tied the whole with lapping strands of blue and silver ribbon, knotting the two colors in a many looped bow on top.

The front door banged open just as she stood back to admire the finished effect, and Roddy dashed into the house yelling at the top of his lungs.

"I gotta blue ribbon!" he shouted. "I won first prize with my picture!"

Linda ran into the hall and caught him up in a hug that swung him clear off the ground. Her mother, moving at a somewhat slower pace, was not far behind him and her eyes were shining.

"Isn't it fine to have a son like Roddy?" she cried. "Martin and I are practically bursting, we're so proud."

Roddy wriggled out of Linda's grip, but not resentfully. It was just, she suspected, that, being unused to it, he was self-conscious about demonstrative affection. Roughy heard the uproar and came running in from the back of the house to add his own barks of excitement and approval. Roddy pulled the little dog's feet from under him and tumbled him on his back. The Roughneck took the play delightedly, helping Roddy get rid of some of his surplus exuberance.

"Where is Babs?" Mrs. Hollis asked. "She'll have to hear the news too."

"She's upstairs getting dressed for the party," Linda said. "And unless she's deaf she's probably heard it already."

There was a moment's silence, while they all looked inquiringly up the stairway, but Babs's door stayed closed, in spite of the sound and fury which had been going on in the hall below.

Babs, apparently, meant to show no interest. For a moment Roddy looked disappointed. Then he said, "Aw, she don't care about kid stuff like this."

"Well, we care," Linda told him. "And it's not kid stuff. But I've got to dash, Roddy, if I'm going to be ready in time. Look, you two, how about coming out to see my supper box?"

They followed her into the kitchen and her mother uttered a cry of pleasure. "Linda, it's beautiful! It's one of the prettiest boxes I've ever seen. You'll have half the boys in town bidding for it."

Roddy was silent and Linda regarded him anxiously. After all, the box should have masculine, not feminine appeal. "Don't you like it, Roddy?"

He twisted up his mouth, considering the matter. "I guess it's all right. It sure is pretty."

"Then what's wrong with it?" Linda demanded.

There was a time when Roddy would have blurted out his criticism vindictively, but this new Roddy was anxious to please.

He grinned at her. "Aw, it's all right. I was just thinking it doesn't look like it would hold much to eat."

Linda sighed her relief. "It holds plenty. Don't worry about that."

She started upstairs with the box and Roddy called after her. "Say! That picture you took of Babs looks swell in the exhibit. I hope you win first prize too."

Linda leaned on the rail to smile down at him. "Thanks, Roddy, but it would never do for one family to walk off with more than one prize. Besides, there are some daylight pictures entered that are very good."

She hurried upstairs just in time to meet Babs coming out of the bathroom. Linda spoke casually, as if nothing had gone wrong between them.

"You've got a head start, but I'll try to catch up. Want to wait for me so we can walk over together?"

"I'd sooner go by myself," Babs said curtly and went into her own room.

Linda sighed. Acting like that wouldn't help. After all, she had apologized for her outburst. But if Babs was going to slap at her every time she tried to be nice, she might as well give up. Two could play the game of being snooty and unforgiving.

Getting dressed for the party was not the leisurely affair she had hoped it would be. Back in New York when she went out she'd always hurried through her preparations as quickly as she could, coming out at the last minute looking what her father had called "neat but not gaudy." Somehow today she'd wanted a long time to get ready. She'd wanted a lengthy soak in the tub with her mother's sweetly scented bath salts. That morning she'd put her hair up in pin curls and she'd wanted to experiment with a new part and a more feminine hair-do.

But now she had to rush with her bath and run a quick comb through her hair, letting the soft curls tumble as they would. The dress she'd brought from New York and had had no occasion to wear in Cedarhill before, was white, with a full flaring skirt, tiny scallops around the neckline and little cap sleeves. The only touch of color was a braided blue leather belt with a silver buckle. Blue shoes with ankle straps echoed the belt color and made her feel quite dashing and festive. She picked up her gay supper box and whirled before her closet door mirror to get the full effect.

She and the supper box matched beautifully, which had been her plan. Even Liz would approve of her tonight. She looked less boyish with make-up on and with her hair softened from its usual severe state.

Before she opened her door to leave, she looked slowly around the small room she had grown to love— at the neat bedspread, the familiar lamp on the bed-table, the desk she had worked so hard to refinish. When she saw this room again much later tonight she would know things that were hidden from her now. She would know whose box Gordon Kenyon had bid for. She would know whether the party had been wonderful fun or a bitter disappointment. Would she come home to this room tonight joyfully? Or would she come here to a haven to ease something hurtful? Would it be painful later to remember this moment of anticipation before she went out to the test of the party?

Feeling a little solemn, she opened the door and stepped into the hall. Babs stood at the foot of the stairs, Babs in yellow taffeta that set off her dark beauty to perfection. Linda experienced a panicky moment in which she wanted to run back to her room and not go to the party at all. How could any boy even think of a choice when there was a girl around who looked like Babs Stevens? Then she straightened her shoulders and went slowly downstairs. After all, she had to be herself; she didn't really want to be an imitation of someone else.

Babs looked up as she came downstairs, but what

she thought of this transformed Linda did not show in so much as a flicker of her eyes. As far as Babs was concerned, Linda might just as well have been wearing dungarees and an old shirt.

Lest Linda think she had relented and waited for her after all, she explained quickly. "Peter's taking us over. Your mother asked me to wait. I suppose she wants her big-happy-family to go together."

"Where's your supper box?" Linda asked, more curious than she liked to admit.

Babs's gaze rested briefly on the blue and white perfection of Linda's box. Then she looked carelessly away.

"It's gone on ahead. Dad left early to see how things were going and he took it for me."

"Don't you want anybody to know it's yours?" Linda asked, puzzled.

"Don't worry—I'll take care of that," Babs said coolly.

Then Mrs. Stevens came downstairs to join them. She looked lovely, Linda thought, in her navy blue. The supper box she'd prepared early in the day had been tied in plain white tissue and decorated with an old-fashioned nosegay fringed with lace paper.

She smiled at them proudly. "Stand up straight, both of you, and let's see how you look. Turn around, Babs. Fine. I think we've conquered that sag on the left side of your dress. You look beautiful. Now then, Linda."

Linda turned slowly, wishing she didn't have to share this familiar last minute check-up with Babs.

Her mother nodded her satisfaction as Linda made the last turn. "Perfect! Both of you. I'm going to be very proud of my daughters tonight."

Babs sniffed and turned away, but Mrs. Stevens was busy calling directions to Roddy about going down the street to neighbors for dinner, and ignored her rudeness.

The honk of a horn outside summoned them and they hurried into their coats. Peter got out of the car to watch as the three came down the steps and when he saw them he tore his hair in mock despair.

"How is a man to know which of you sirens to bid

for?" he groaned. "Do you think I'm rich enough to buy you all? Mmm—neat boxes there. Where's yours, Babs?"

Babs repeated her superior sniff and climbed into the back seat when Peter opened the door.

"Okay, my proud beauty," he said, "if you scorn riding in front with me, maybe I can persuade Linda."

Linda got willingly into the front seat, trying to counteract Babs's irritating mood with her own cheerful acceptance of any arrangements offered. Mrs. Stevens sat in back beside Babs and they drove off to the Museum.

There was a group of boys out in front when they drew up and Peter nodded wisely.

"Spies have been posted," he said. "It's my guess the box owners will be no surprise to the bidders."

Babs left them at the door and ran upstairs while Linda and her mother hurried their boxes into the hands of the supper committee. A long table on the platform had been heaped with supper boxes and it looked as gay as Christmas time. A division had been made so that teen-agers' boxes were at one end, grownups' at the other. That would prevent anyone from bidding in the wrong group unless he wanted to. Linda glanced quickly over the array, wondering which one belonged to Babs. Somehow she didn't mind how many stunningly wrapped and decorated boxes there were, just so long as her own was prettier than the one Babs had brought.

Some whistles from the boys and a burst of applause made her turn toward the door. Babs was making a dramatic entrance with her own contribution. She had gone to none of the artistic pains Linda had expected her to. Instead, she had done something much more canny. Hers was not even a box, but a big straw basket, obviously overflowing with good things to eat. A huge red satin bow on the handle was the one decoration, but you could tell from the outburst which had greeted Babs's appearance, that it was the contents that rated with male appetites. Linda's spirits sank as she saw Babs's basket take its place on the table. Certainly it dwarfed everything else in sight.

She tried to shrug her mood aside. After all, this wasn't a life or death matter. It was only for fun. Besides, Gordon wasn't even in sight yet. Perhaps he wouldn't come at all, and then what happened wouldn't matter. She might as well relax.

Quite a crowd had turned out. Predominantly the group was young, mostly from high school. But there was a smattering of the town's professional and businessmen and their wives, and a few teachers from school. Even at the moderate fifty-cents-a-ticket admission price, the Shutter-Snappers were doing all right. There'd be some equipment now for the darkroom at school.

Linda roamed about alone, looking at the pictures in the photograph exhibit which she'd not been able to examine properly while hanging her share. Roddy was right. Her own picture of Babs working on the diorama looked very well mounted and hung. It was an interesting shot, but she was enough her father's daughter to recognize its technical flaws. The shadows were too dense in the lower lefthand corner and spoiled the balance of the whole. She was perfectly willing to admit that other pictures in the exhibit were better than hers, and she didn't mind.

There was one she liked especially. Its background was a small white church out on the edge of town. The shot had been taken on Sunday morning when the congregation was coming out the door. Emphasis was on a group of three, father, mother and small daughter. There was a homey American touch to the picture which she liked. Whoever had taken it had a good deal of perception.

The sound of a chord struck on the piano brought her away from the pictures and she turned to look toward the end of the room. Mr. Sam Dodge, who owned the town's largest dry goods store, had taken his place on the platform as master of ceremonies. Peter had assured her earlier that he was Cedarhill's best m.c., and he'd been elated over snaring him for this event tonight.

But Linda wasted no more than a glance on Mr. Dodge. She shifted her position till she could see the piano below the stage. Gordon Kenyon had come. He'd taken his place on the piano bench and it was he who had played the quieting chord.

The box supper was under way.

22 Box Supper

The program began with music by Gordon Kenyon. The buzzing of the crowd hushed as everyone looked for seats. With two or three others Linda found her way to the steps on one side of the stage and perched herself there, across the room from the piano, but close enough so that she could watch the player, as well as listen to the music. Once she looked around for Babs and saw her at the far end of the room. Her eyes were closed as she listened and her face looked sad, instead of sullen, so that for an instant Linda experienced a stab of pity.

Babs was so much her own enemy. But she'd never see that, never let anyone help her to change. Always she carried a chip on her shoulder, always she was ready to slap at the hand reached out to touch her. But just for this moment her defenses were down and she looked the lonely, unhappy girl she was.

Gordon's first number was a lovely Beethoven sonata and the applause when he finished was appreciative. For an encore he played a medley of popular tunes in an arrangement of his own, Cole Porter, Irving Berlin, and then a tune that made Linda glance toward the piano, to find Gordon smiling gravely in her direction. It was the request she had made of him that time he'd played for her here in this very room, *Oh, What a Beautiful Morning!*

She smiled back at him and then turned away almost shyly. He had chosen that piece to please her. He had wanted to please her. The knowledge made her feel suddenly happy and a little choky at the same time.

Then the music was finished and Mr. Dodge took over the show again. He was short, cheerful, and plump, with a quick wit and a friendly air that made you like him at once.

"We're all getting hungrier by the minute," he said, "and there's a pretty tantalizing array of culinary talent displayed on this table. But before we can get to the big business of the evening, which is to find out who eats which supper, there's the matter of the awards to the photographic winners in the high school and adult groups."

He gave the Shutter-Snappers a nice boost and then read the names of the winners in the grade school category, as they had been decided that afternoon. Linda felt a surprising surge of personal pride when Roddy's name was read. Next Mr. Dodge announced with proper dramatic pauses the names of the blue ribbon winners in the older groups. "Sunday Morning, American Style" won the high school award, and Linda discovered that it had been submitted by Peter Crowell. She felt a little guilty over having been so absorbed in her own affairs that she hadn't even asked to see Peter's entries. She tried to make up for the omission now by catching his eye to smile her pleasure at him. But he was watching the ceremony of having the blue ribbon pinned to a corner of his picture and didn't look her way.

She was pleased to have her "Diorama" receive honorable mention, but now anxiety had begun to rise in her in nervous waves. When the awarding of prizes drew to a close she knew the auctioning of the supper boxes would be next. She began to wish her mother had never suggested this scheme, wish that she herself had not taken it up so blithely.

As the minutes ticked along to the crucial event, she realized how much it mattered to her, in spite of all her warnings to herself. If no one bid, she'd be humiliated. She'd want to hide. But if the wrong people bid, it would be nearly as bad. She didn't dare look Gordon's way now. Not for anything would she let him see how much this moment meant to her. Besides, he'd come so late, he probably wouldn't know one box from another.

Mr. Dodge had made the last award and was waving his short arms for silence. The applause died away and all eyes turned toward the stage.

"We've devised a little scheme here," he explained, rattling a box of bingo numbers at them. "Naturally the lady whose box is bid on first, or at least early, stands an advantage, since there are more bidders in the market in the beginning. To keep everything fair we've given each supper creation on this table a number. The numbers are matched by those in this box. I'm going to ask Miss Hallie Foster of the Museum to step up here each time and draw a number to determine the order in which the boxes will be auctioned off."

There was no escape now, Linda thought. This was worse than being in a school play and waiting in the wings for the inevitable moment when you'd step out before the footlights, sure that you'd forget your lines.

Now the auctioning began, with Mr. Dodge extolling the virtues of each box, and pleading with the bidders. One by one the boxes were knocked down to the highest bidder and each winner accepted this box and carried it to where the girl who had packed it waited. In some cases there was little competition, but it was no slight upon the owner of the box. Some of the boys and girls who went together steadily had the matter settled practically ahead of time. And husbands, of course, bid on their wives' boxes. There was a bit of fun when the town's bachelors jumped in, however, and began mixing things up.

Each time Miss Foster stepped up to draw a number she looked shy and flustered, but underneath that uncertain air, Linda suspected she was having the time of her life. Now she put in her hand, stirred the numbers around and drew one out, announcing "Number 9."

Mr. Dodge glanced over the table, located the number and pulled Linda's box out of the pile. Linda stared at the floor and held her breath. Her heart was thumping so heavily she was afraid the people around could hear it. She knew her face was burning and she wished she had chosen a less conspicuous place to sit than here on the steps. Not that she was alone there, but she felt practically as though she herself were on exhibit, instead of the box.

Mr. Dodge really went to town on the box's artistic merits. Anyone who could create so noble an exterior for a mere supper box, he told them eloquently, would of course have done amazing and delectable things to the contents. In fact, he assured the audience, his own mouth was watering and he wasn't sure but what he'd bid on this one himself.

But when he held it up before the room, there was a vast and engulfing silence.

Why had she ever entered a box? Linda thought miserably. No matter how pretty it was, the fact remained that she wasn't known in Cedarhill. She wasn't like these boys and girls who'd grown up together. She was a stranger whom the others had not yet accepted.

Martin Stevens bid fifty cents and she wanted to sink through the floor. Undoubtedly her mother had told him it was hers and prompted the bid. It would be a double disgrace if her family had to bid on her box. If it went to Martin for that sum she was sure she'd never be able to raise her head in Cedarhill again.

Then Peter's voice called a ringing "Seventy-five," and Martin raised it to a dollar. Peter topped the bid promptly with a cautious "Dollar ten," and Mr. Dodge began a humorous plea to them not to be such cheap skates. The Shutter-Snappers' treasurer, a boy Linda had hardly noticed, suddenly bid a dollar and a quarter and Mr. Dodge went into ecstasies of pleading.

There had not been a word from Gordon and Linda knew the grim truth. If he'd troubled to find out about the boxes, he was waiting to bid on Babs's box. Linda Hollis had never stood a chance with him and she never would. All she wanted now was for the ordeal to be over. If it couldn't be Gordon, she didn't care who won.

Martin, having started the ball rolling, dropped out of the bidding and Peter said "A dollar thirty" determinedly. The other boy showed no signs of raising the bid and Mr. Dodge went into the last phase.

"A dollar and thirty cents I'm bid!" he protested. "A measly dollar thirty for a dream of a box like this.

Ladies and gentlemen, haven't you the imagination to visualize the appetizing contents of this little treasure?" But no one raised the bid and he lifted his gavel in defeat. "Going—"

"Five dollars," said a quiet voice from the neighborhood of the piano, and Linda looked up to see Gordon Kenyon smiling at the auctioneer. Mr. Dodge regarded him in stunned silence for a moment and then rose to the occasion. Not a box so far had gone up to five dollars.

Nevertheless, in spite of her surprise and pleasure, Linda felt a little uncomfortable. Gordon had made himself conspicuous and different again, as he had that time in the current events discussion.

For some reason she glanced toward Peter and found him fairly wigwagging a message to her and she knew perfectly well what he meant. He was asking for some signal, just a smile, that would say "go ahead." If she responded he'd be foolish enough to overbid that five dollars. She looked at him for a moment, her face expressionless, and then turned away.

This time there was no opposition to the "going-going-gone!" of the auctioneer and Gordon went up to get his box amid a smattering of applause. Linda sensed that the clapping was not as enthusiastic as it had been for other bidders. Everyone knew and liked Peter. Gordon was the outsider and he'd been a bit spectacular. Cedarhill could not give its entire approval to his last minute entry.

Not that she cared what Cedarhill felt, Linda thought, as Gordon came over to drop the box into her lap and seat himself on the step below her. Now the situation had been made clear, even to Babs. Gordon had made his own preference public. She glanced in Babs's direction and for an instant the eyes of the two girls met. But Babs's stare was stony. It betrayed nothing of her feelings. She wore a superior little smile on her lips as if she were above such childish amusement as this.

Later when Babs's basket came up the bidding was heated. Peter was back in the lead again and it went to him finally for three dollars. If Babs was pleased, she did not show it, and Linda suspected that she would give Peter an unpleasant evening for having bid first on another box.

As a matter of fact, when it came to the actual gathering for supper, most of the couples did not eat in isolated pairs, but grouped themselves as usual with their friends and family. Peter and Babs, Martin and Joyce, and Linda and Gordon drifted together naturally enough. Gordon told Linda her box was too pretty to break into and Peter agreed and suggested they all eat out of Babs's basket, which contained enough for an army anyway. Babs ignored the banter, as if she felt herself quite above it.

Not until the three volunteer pieces from the school orchestra tuned up for dancing, did Linda have any feeling that she and Gordon were alone. As the younger crowd broke for the floor when the music started, Gordon drew Linda out for the first dance. Oddly, she was ill at ease with him, uncomfortably shy. If only she could talk to him cleverly about some interesting subject it would be fine. But after she had murmured awkwardly that she'd enjoyed his music, and he'd replied that he'd enjoyed her supper box, she seemed stricken dumb.

If Gordon noticed, he seemed not to mind. He was silent himself, concentrating on dancing. And as before at the school dance, Linda found herself matched to an ideal partner.

For the second dance Peter suggested a trade of partners, and Linda was glad to find that he felt no rancor over the way the bidding had gone. But of course Peter would never be annoyed about anything like that. He was too big a person, too nice. And with him Linda could feel natural again.

"You were crazy to go bidding on my box like that," she told him. "You had a look in your eye as if you meant to keep right on."

"With encouragement I would have," Peter said cheerfully. "But I could see I'd lost the lady to the fascinating Easterner, so I decided to stay within what was left of my allowance this month."

"I'm glad you showed that much sense," Linda said.

"Peter, your church picture is wonderful. I'm terribly proud of you. Why didn't you tell me that was your entry? I'd already picked it as the best and I'm glad the judges agreed with me."

"You've been sleepwalking for days," Peter said. "I haven't been able to attract your attention long enough to tell you. What's been eating you lately?"

They bumped into another couple, due to Peter's usual habit of forgetting to watch where they were going, and by the time they'd disentangled themselves, and the boys had exchanged cheerful insults, Linda had an answer for him. Perhaps it wasn't the entire answer, but it would do to sidetrack him.

"Trouble with Babs," she explained. "I pinned her ears back a couple of days ago and she hasn't forgiven me. I guess I lost my temper and what I said must have hurt."

"So that's why she's gone sour on the world," Peter said. "She's practically in a mood to curdle cream. It's like I told you—she's our number one problem child!"

Linda shrugged. "She's not my problem child. I've washed my hands of trying to be friends with her. It's a good thing I have my own room and can get away from her. I'd like to see you solve this one, Dr. Crowell."

He grinned at her, but offered no further suggestions. When the dance ended and they joined the others, Gordon touched her elbow, drawing her aside.

"Linda, I'd like to talk to you. Do you think we could get away for a while?"

She wanted to do anything Gordon asked her to, even though she wasn't sure her mother approved of her breaking away from the party after no more than a couple of dances. But whatever they might think, neither Martin nor her mother offered any objections, and Gordon led the way out to his grandmother's car.

Again, the moment they were alone, she felt constrained and stiff and wordless. The easy feeling she'd had with Peter gave way again to awkward self-consciousness. She was pleased because Gordon wanted her to himself, but she couldn't be natural about it.

"Let's go back to the place by the river where we talked that other time," he suggested. "Think you'll be warm enough in your coat? It's not awfully cold outside tonight."

"I'll be warm," she said. Somehow she was sure that she'd have been able to give the same answer if there had been a roaring blizzard outside. She so wanted to do and be whatever Gordon wanted.

He put the car in gear and Linda leaned back against the seat with a sigh of satisfaction, relaxing for the first time that evening.

23 New Roots

There was a full moon shining above the river, so that they hardly needed the flashlight Gordon brought from the car to point their way through the underbrush near the bank. He found a big flat rock and spread the car robe over it for them to sit on.

The night was cool, but not raw, and there was no wind stirring. Silence lay serenely upon Cedarhill, with only the soft lapping of the water at their feet and the occasional kerchunk of a frog to break the utter stillness. Linda drew the collar of her coat up about her ears and pulled up her knees so she could rest her chin on them. She felt peaceful now, no longer uneasy and self-conscious. And as soon as she forgot herself, she found she could talk.

"It's funny," she said, "the way the quiet bothered me in the beginning. I'm getting so used to it now that I like it. I don't miss the taxi horns any more."

Gordon slipped her cool hand into his own warm one. "I'm glad you're fitting into Cedarhill, Linda. I thought you would. Only you've done it a lot quicker than I expected."

That was partly due to the fact that he was here, she felt, but she couldn't tell him so. From now on, she suspected, she was going to love Cedarhill, because of Gordon Kenyon. But she couldn't tell him that either.

"I've never gone around much with girls," he went on, almost as if he were thinking out loud. "Oh, I've gone to the usual dances and private school affairs because my mother wanted me to, but mostly I liked the company of my music best. There weren't any girls I liked very well. Until now."

Linda's heart did a quick thud under her ribs and she held her breath, not knowing quite what was coming next, but wanting him to go on.

"There are things about you I think are swell. I like the way you took that uprooting and started to fit yourself into Cedarhill as soon as you got over your first resentment about the change."

"Oh, but I didn't!" Linda protested. "I fought it like anything. In lots of ways I haven't been nice at all."

He gave her hand a squeeze. "Maybe you didn't like it, but you pitched in anyway. Helping Mr. Stevens with that diorama. Working in the Photography Club. Helping Roddy to get interested in something that would keep him out of mischief and start him off on the right track."

"How do you know all those things?" Linda asked.

"What do you think I do with my time—sitting in the wings watching? The fellow who watches and listens, sees and hears. You've been too busy getting into the middle of things to really know what was going on. You haven't stayed safe and uninvolved the way I have, but I admire you a lot more than I do me."

She wouldn't let him point a critical finger at himself. "But it's different with you. I mean you have your music. You couldn't ever belong to a town like this."

"You don't think so?"

She waited, not answering. He was getting at something, but she couldn't tell what just yet.

"What are you going to do after graduation next June?" he asked.

"I don't know. State College, I suppose. It's close enough."

"Then what?"

She listened for a few moments to the silvery lapping of the river along the rocks below them. "I don't know. I just don't know."

"You ought to try for something connected with photography, Linda."

"Maybe I will. Lately I've got back my interest in it,

thanks to Peter and his doings. Gordon, what are you going to do?"

He was silent for so long that she was half afraid he didn't mean to answer. Then he said quietly, "That's what I wanted to tell you about. I'm going away next week. Back to New York for good."

She pulled her hand away quickly and thrust it deep into the pocket of her coat. She'd always known that he would have to go back, that New York was where he belonged. But she had not wanted to face the truth, because of the way it would hurt. This was the first time anything as sweet as this had happened to her, and now, even as it was just beginning, it had to end.

"The divorce has been settled," he went on in a voice that was a little hard. "So I'm going back to live with my mother. I'm going on with my music."

"But that's what you want to do, isn't it?" Linda asked in a small voice. "It's what you have to do."

"Yes," he said, "it's what I have to do." He turned to her suddenly, not touching her, but studying her face in the moonlight. "I wonder if you'll understand? I mean about how I've felt this way about you, but still not asked for dates, never even taken you out to a movie, the way Peter has."

"No." She felt a little numb. "I don't understand."

"It didn't seem fair to ask you to go out with me. Maybe—maybe even get you a little interested in me. I mean if you could be interested."

"I already was," she told him simply.

For a moment longer he sat there, not saying anything. Then he stood up, helped her to her feet.

"We'd better go back," he said, and she felt her cheeks grow warm in the darkness. She shouldn't have told him how she felt as frankly as she had.

For a moment she stood above him there on the rock, and then he swung her down to the ground, tipped up her chin and kissed her lightly, quickly before they turned back toward the car.

They went together, hand in hand, but Linda felt that her world was breaking up around her in the old painful way again. Oh, it wasn't fair to find someone like Gordon and then lose him in the very moment of finding him!

When they were back in the car, Gordon switched on the dashboard light and sat for a moment in silence, while Linda pulled her coat collar up about her throat, and huddled down in the seat, shivering more than was due to the cool of the night.

"Maybe I shouldn't have told you," Gordon said. "But somehow I wanted you to know before I went away. I wish I could say now that I knew we'd see each other again sometime. But I don't know that. I'm going one way and you're going another. But I'll always remember tonight, Linda."

"So will I," she said faintly.

He started the car and they went down the block. At the cross street Linda touched his arm. "Please—do you mind taking me straight home? I—I don't want to go back to the dance."

"Of course," he said.

There was no further conversation between them until the car stopped in front of the Stevens house. He covered her hand with his own for a moment.

"Will you write to me, Linda?"

She thought about that solemnly. With all her heart she wanted to say "yes." Letters from Gordon would be something to cling to, to help ease the loneliness. On the other hand, writing to him would keep all this alive that much longer. It would be better for them both if it was allowed to fade out as soon as possible. There was a time, even a few months ago, when she would have clung weakly to some tie with him. But she was a stronger person now than she had been then. Strong enough to do the hard, wise thing. Strength was one thing trouble gave you.

"It's better not to, Gordon," she told him gently.

He nodded, gave her hand a last squeeze and let her go. A moment later she was running up the steps, letting herself into the house.

Roddy had gone to bed. She could hear his quiet breathing through the open door of his room when she reached the top of the stairs. Her own room beckoned as a haven. She could rush in there, get out of her dress, fling herself down on the bed in the dark and cry the way she longed to cry. Life had gone so right for her tonight, and so wrong, all in the same instant.

But at the door of her room she paused, blinking back the tears that were burning to come. There was a better treatment than giving in to them and tearing herself to pieces emotionally—if she could do something, work at something with her hands, occupy her mind with something physical and solid. It was that old rule of her father's working again. You couldn't think of two things at once, he'd said.

She crossed the hall quickly, opened the door of Martin's study and went in. The light on his desk switched on to show the various parts of the new museum project they were working on, a scene of bird life Martin wanted for his next diorama. He wouldn't mind if she came in here and worked for a while. She was always welcome in his study now.

She sat down in the chair before his desk and spread a cloth over the lap of her white dress so that she wouldn't soil it, and examined the materials before her. Since this was to be a bird scene, they were using actual tree branches and twigs. But the leaves were dry brown and needed tinting to brighter autumn hues. It was a delicate, painstaking job, but after a bit of experimenting, they'd found it could be done, and the result was more realistic looking than the use of artificial leaves.

She mixed colors in the pan before her and went methodically to work. But you could think of two things at once, she discovered. Or perhaps it was that while her hands were busy, her mind turned to other matters. She could not absorb herself wholly in what she was doing. The thought of Gordon was there in her mind, sharply, painfully. But the work helped, nevertheless, and it held the tears back for a while longer.

She heard the others come home from the dance and hoped that no one would open the study door to see what she was doing. All she wanted was to be let alone. The desk lamp wouldn't be visible from the front of the house, so if her mother didn't look into her room, she wouldn't know she was here.

The usual sounds of people getting to bed went on for a while and she began to think she was safe. If she could just work here until she was so weary she could hardly keep her eyes open, then perhaps she could go to bed and fall asleep right away. The thing she dreaded was lying awake, thinking about Gordon, all the bittersweet thoughts that wanted to crowd in. She wanted to keep those at bay as long as she could.

Then a step sounded in the hall and someone turned the knob of the study door. Linda concentrated fiercely on the leaf she was tinting and did not look up. Perhaps whoever it was would go away and let her alone. But it was no use. The intruder came in and closed the door behind him. Linda looked up to see Martin Stevens watching her gravely from across the room.

She expected questions, expected that he'd remind her that it was late and urge her to get to bed. Instead, he came over to the desk and picked up a paintbrush.

"I'm not much good at this," he said, "but maybe you can use an extra hand."

She said "Okay," in a careful voice, so that no quiver came through. He went to work helping her quietly, without trying to make conversation, and somehow she did not mind having him there.

They worked together for another half hour and then Martin threw his brush down wearily. "Guess it's past my bedtime. How about making me some coffee before we turn in?"

She found that she could smile at him naturally as she put her paints away. They went downstairs through the darkened house softly like conspirators and turned on lights in the kitchen. Oddly enough, moving around, making coffee, raiding the icebox and setting plates on the kitchen table for a midnight snack, she felt better than she had before. Besides, this was one more way of postponing the evil moment of going to bed.

As they sat down at the table, she wondered how much Martin knew. What had Gordon said when he'd gone back to the party without her? Had he told them all he was going away?

"Good coffee," Martin praised, setting down his cup.

"Don't know how I can have a crack to fill after all the food tonight, but it seems I have."

"Me too," Linda admitted. She'd been too excited at the party to eat much, and now, in spite of the misery waiting to crowd in on her, she could apparently eat.

On his second cup of coffee, Martin looked at Linda. "What about that surprise we're going to plan for Roddy?"

This was a safe enough subject and Linda plunged into it willingly. "I think he'd like a darkroom in his own basement more than anything else. A partition could be put up without too much trouble—there's plenty of room."

"Good idea." Martin looked pleased. "We'll plan it together, maybe with Peter's help. And, Linda, I've been thinking of something else. I wonder if you'd care to lend those photographs of your father's for one of our regular upstairs exhibits at the Museum? Say some time in February."

She agreed eagerly, feeling a little choked up because he wanted to do something as nice as that.

"It's good having you here, Linda," he went on gently. "I haven't been much of a success as a father and I know it. You and your mother are helping Roddy and Babs more than you know."

"Not Babs," Linda said.

Suddenly she felt she couldn't stay down here for another moment. The held-back tears were coming for sure now and she knew she didn't dare stay lest she disgrace herself. She pushed back from the table, smiling at him tremulously, but unable to say a word. She ran out of the kitchen and upstairs to the safe harbor of her own room.

But as she opened the door she saw it was no longer a safe harbor. The bed lamp was on and the pajama'd figure of Babs Stevens lay sprawled across the bed.

For just an instant Linda was furiously angry. To have Babs invade her privacy at a time like this was more than she could take. She had had all she could stand of Babs Stevens and she didn't mean to take one more thing from her now.

Babs pulled herself up against a pillow and stared at

her defiantly. "Go ahead! Tell me what you think of me. I guess I've got it coming."

Linda felt the anger die away, leaving her limp and emotionless. "I don't want to tell you anything. I'd just like to be by myself, please."

"Gordon's going away, isn't he?" Babs asked.

"I don't want to talk to you." Linda unzipped a side fastener and pulled her dress over her head. When she came out from under its folds, Babs was still there.

"I know what you think," Babs said. "You believe all that stuff Peter told you about how the only time I'm ever nice is when somebody's in trouble. So you think I'm here because I'm sorry about you and Gordon."

Linda went on undressing, getting into her pajamas. "I'm not thinking about you at all. I don't care anything about you."

"That makes sense," Babs went on calmly. "Can't see why you should. Trouble is, I've been thinking about me, as well as about you and Gordon. I'm not here because I'm sorry for you. I'm here because I'm sorry for me."

"You're always being sorry for you," Linda told her. "That's nothing new." She picked up her hairbrush and began violently to brush the curls out of her hair.

Babs leaned on one elbow to watch her. "Don't do that. You look nice that way. It's a shame to spoil it."

Linda whirled about. "Are you going to get out of this room?"

"Nope," Babs said. "Not till I've said my say. So you might as well relax and listen. Anyway you're so mad at me now you won't do any weeping about Gordon. You want to know something? I've hated you from the minute you arrived in this town."

"That's not news. What else?"

"What you don't know is the reason. I've hated you because you have everything I don't have. People like you right away. You know how to make friends. Right under my nose you walked off with my boy friend."

"Walked off with your—what on earth are you talking about?"

Babs nodded. "Peter. I've considered him my property since I was old enough to be interested in boys. But I guess he was kind of sick of the way I acted and he liked you right away. I don't blame him. But I was envious of you and that didn't make me like you any better."

"I don't want Peter," Linda said sharply.

"That's because you've got Gordon in your eyes just now. Stardust and stuff. You'll get over it. Gordon's all right, but he's going to be tied to his music for years. Maybe forever. And besides, he isn't what Peter Crowell is for one minute."

"I thought you liked Gordon pretty well yourself?"

"I wanted to pay you off for taking Peter. That's what I meant by all that stuff about fair play. But I couldn't even manage that because Gordon liked you too. He was nice to me because he couldn't get rid of me without a good shove, and he's not tough enough to shove anybody. That goldfish bowl technique's no better than an ostrich putting his head in the sand."

Linda dropped down on a chair abruptly. "Goldfish bowl technique?"

"Didn't he tell you about that? What his grandmother said when he was a little boy and all the rest?"

Linda closed her eyes, thinking about that lovely moment under the stars when Gordon had let down his guard and opened up for the first time. She thought it had been just to her. The knowledge that he'd told Babs too made her feel a little sick.

"Anything more?" she demanded.

"A lot more. You told me off the other day and I hated you more than ever. Because the things you said were mostly true, and true things that are ugly hurt a lot."

Linda waited in silence. Suddenly Babs flopped over on her stomach and hid her face in the pillow.

"Your mother was sweet to me and I was as nasty to her as I could be. And tonight Peter gave me a lecture. I'm in wrong with just about everybody. I—I guess there isn't a lot more after all. I guess I've done all the damage I can."

This time it was Babs who was crying. Linda sat down on the bed and began to pat her shoulder awkwardly. She half expected the other girl to pull away from her touch as she'd always drawn angrily away from every other friendly overture, but Babs lay where she was, crying into the crook of her arm.

"G-G-Gordon tries to be a goldfish," she wailed. "And I t-t-try to be a toughy, and in the beginning all you wanted was not to get involved. Peter's the only one who's r-r-right. He jumps into life and gets busy living it."

Linda put an arm across Babs's shoulders. "You've put that well. Anybody who can see things straight like that is going to be all right. Besides, you're not a toughy really. You're an old softy and I like you that way."

A little to her surprise she was beginning to find that she did. Babs's prickliness grew out of a fear of being hurt more than anything else. All she needed was to learn to trust people and stop hurting herself.

"I've been jealous of the way Roddy and Dad like you too," Babs went on in a choked voice. "That's why I was nasty about Roddy's picture. I guess the only person who ever really liked me and understood me was my mother."

"Now you're talking nonsense," Linda told her promptly. "You've just got the bad habit of handing anybody who tries to be nice to you a handful of burrs. Goodness knows everybody'd be crazy about you if you'd just act pretty."

"Not Peter." Babs sighed. "You don't know how lucky you are."

Lucky, Linda thought. Lucky, when she'd just discovered how Gordon felt about her and lost him in the same breath?

"Gimme a handkerchief," Babs said, sniffling. Linda handed her one and she sat up on the edge of the bed and blew her nose. "Of course you're lucky. You've had two boys in your life who've liked you. I've never even had one. I mean not one I liked at the same time. Don't you see—that gives you a sort of confidence I haven't got."

"Maybe," Linda said. She hadn't thought about it in just that way. "But there are plenty of boys in this town who'd like you if you'd let 'em."

"You really think so?" Babs asked so earnestly that Linda began to laugh. For a moment Babs stared at her as if she were going to get angry again. Then she joined in a little hysterically. It felt good to laugh again. Tragedy, Linda was discovering, couldn't ever be really damaging, if you could just keep on finding something to laugh about.

"Oh, goodness! I almost forgot," Babs cried, jumping up suddenly and scooting back to her own room. She returned in a moment with a folded piece of brown paper in her hand. "It's a note from Peter. I—I think he knows how it is with you and Gordon. Look, we'd better trade pillows—I've got yours all wet. Here's mine in exchange."

She switched the pillows and hurried out the door. A moment later she stuck her head back in. "Good night, sis," she said softly.

"Good night yourself, sis!" Linda called after her, feeling gulpy again.

Then she took Peter's note over to the bed lamp to read it. Judging by the grease spots, the paper had once wrapped a sandwich, but Peter had circled the spots with legs like spiders and fitted his words in between.

Dear Linda:

How's about a date for Saturday? You might as well get used to being my best girl now as later, because I'm a determined character and I get what I go after. You don't have to like the idea right away. But you will as soon as I've had time to make it clear to you that I'm a very remarkable guy.

I'm kidding a little, Linda. But that new roller skating jernt is opening up out on the highway next Saturday, and it might be fun to go. Sorry I only got to tramp on your feet through one dance tonight.

Regretfully,
Peter.

She read it through twice, smiling a little. Then she tucked it under her pillow and turned out the light. In the darkness some of her unhappiness about Gordon came back, but Peter's note under her pillow helped. He didn't have to do much in the way of showing her what a swell person he was. She already knew. He'd wanted to make her laugh in this note tonight, but he'd wanted to put out a hand for her to grasp too.

She'd go with him roller skating Saturday. But she'd get him to make it a double date this time and find someone for Babs. And before they started out, she, Linda, was going to give Babs such a course on how to be likable that Babs would turn out to be the most fascinating gal in town.

Having settled that, she sighed and fell to listening to the soft sounds of the night. A nice town, Cedarhill. It had something. Even without Gordon Kenyon, it had something. Must be she was putting down new roots.

Other SIGNET Titles You Will Enjoy

☐ **THE GRADUATE by Charles Webb.** The highly praised first novel about the misadventures of a brilliant young post-graduate who revolts against his solid-gold future. An Embassy Picture starring Anne Bancroft and Dustin Hoffman. (#Q4731—95¢)

☐ **CHOCOLATE DAYS, POPSICLE WEEKS by Edward Hannibal.** A story about today, about making it, about disaffection and anguish. Here is a modern love story told from the inside and told with an honesty that is sometimes beguiling, sometimes shattering but never doubted. "Sensitive . . . fresh . . . Mr. Hannibal works close to the bone—and he works very well."—**New York Times Book Review** (#Y4650—$1.25)

☐ **A LOVING WIFE by Violet Weingarten.** By the author of Mrs. Beneker, this is the poignant story of a middle-aged housewife whose world is turned upside-down as she decides whether to be a loving wife—or a loving mistress. Soon to be a Columbia Picture starring Joanne Woodward. (#Q4449—95¢)

☐ **THE BRIDE by Alex Austin.** The startling novel of a young wife who is suddenly thrust into a sophisticated career and finds herself outgrowing her husband's world —and his love. (#Q4293—95¢)

THE NEW AMERICAN LIBRARY, INC.,
P.O. Box 999, Bergenfield, New Jersey 07621

Please send me the SIGNET BOOKS I have checked above. I am enclosing $_____(check or money order—no currency or C.O.D.'s). Please include the list price plus 15¢ a copy to cover handling and mailing costs. (Prices and numbers are subject to change without notice.)

Name_____

Address_____

City_____State_____Zip Code_____
Allow at least 3 weeks for delivery